Café Wars

Based on true events

DAVID LEE CORLEY

"War is the continuation of politics by other means."

Carl Van Clausewitz

PROLOGUE

On May 8, 1945 - VE Day - there was an outpouring of pride and relief. Germany had finally surrendered and Europe was once again free from the fascist menace. The war in Europe was over, while the war in the Pacific continued but that war too would soon wind down and everyone knew it.

Europeans and American servicemen were packed into the streets and squares of every city for one enormous block party. There was an abundance of champagne and pats on the back. Bands played on every corner, the people sang patriotic songs and revelers danced in circles with their arms interlocked. The police did what they could to keep things under control until they themselves were overcome by the merriment or too drunk to care. Politicians with generals at their side pontificated to cheering crowds. There was a military parade down the Champs-Élysées in Paris where onlookers packed twenty deep along the boulevard waving French flags.

It was the end of a war and the beginning of another…

Setif was a French Algerian market town west of the country's second largest city - Constantine in northern Algeria. There was a drought and famine in the region. Colonial militia leaders had been spinning conspiracy theories as to its cause. It was foolish propaganda but most of the colonists were farmers with little education, and were superstitious. The colonial militias gained in numbers and were determined to protect their fellow colonists.

The Algerians outnumbered the French colonists nearly four to one in the region. Nationalism had been growing as the war in Europe drew to an end. The Algerians were hopeful that the French would release their country in exchange for the loyalty they had shown during the war when France was overrun by Germany and the Free French government found its new home in Algiers.

The French had other ideas and had been shoring up their military position as troops and resources from the war in Europe became available. France's politicians were determined to reestablish the French colonies in North Africa and Southeast Asia. The French government would need the revenue from the colonies to rebuild France which had suffered greatly during German occupation.

Algerian protesters began to gather early in the morning and their numbers grew to four thousand by mid-day. Their placards and chants demanded independence. There were some that were willing to settle for an independent Algeria closely associated with France. The rebel leaders realized that once they had won their county's independence they would still need the French engineers to operate the power stations, waterworks and railroads. Algerians would need access to French universities if the officials that led their country were ever to learn to survive on their own. But independence and self-determination were non-negotiables for the Algerians.

Colonial militia leaders watched as the Algerian crowds grew in strength. To quell the protest, the militia began removing the protestors' banners and Algerian national flags. The militiamen used the butts of their rifles and long batons if met with resistance.

The protestors became more violent, setting fires, breaking windows and overturning the farmers' trucks and town buses. Both sides had had enough and their frustration reached boiling point. The protestors formed barricades in the streets. The militia saw this as a threat, like a tick digging in.

The militia formed a line in front of the barricades and demanded the protestors disperse. They didn't. The militia opened fire killing two protestors and injuring several more. The town exploded in violence. The Algerian nationalists killed one hundred and two colonists over the next two days. The militias backed by French soldiers killed over six thousand Algerians. Women were raped and corpses were mutilated on both sides of the conflict.

In the end, the French restored order. Trials were promised but never held. Things were left to simmer then cool. They didn't…

ONE

March 2, 1954

The hills of eastern Algeria were covered with wheat and semolina fields blowing gently in a hot wind. An Algerian teenager wrapped a wire around a grenade attaching it to a telephone pole. He and his friend had stolen a crate of grenades from the back of a French Army supply truck while the driver took a piss. When the young Algerian was finished he arranged the grenade's ring so that it stuck out just like the other six grenade rings on telephone poles on the edge of a road. At the far end of the line of telephone poles was his friend armed with a rifle keeping watch for French ground and air patrols.

The young Algerian readied himself and checked to ensure that his pistol was firmly tucked into the waistband of his pants. He placed his forefinger in the first grenade ring. He called out a warning to his friend, pulled the first grenade ring and took off running down the line of telephone poles. The spoon on the first grenade sprung open starting its timer. As he passed each telephone pole he reached out and grabbed the grenade ring. His friend cheered him on.

The first grenade exploded, shearing off the base of the telephone pole. It crashed to the ground, tearing loose the telephone line from the preceding pole. The young Algerian continued to run and pulled the pin on the last grenade. That was when he heard the crack of a rifle and saw his friend's head explode like an overripe cantaloupe.

The young Algerian hit the ground creating a cloud of dust and pulled the pistol from his waistband. The telephone poles behind him continued to explode and crash to the ground. His attention was fixed on the horizon. There was a French Army sniper out there somewhere and if he didn't find him quickly, he would suffer the same fate as his friend. He wished he had his friend's rifle instead of his pistol but the rifle was too far away to reach without exposing himself further to the sniper. The pistol would have to do. He was a good shot with the pistol. His uncle had served in the Foreign Legion and had taught him to shoot. He was hopeful until the last telephone pole exploded and crashed down on top of him crushing his body like roadkill. His days of blowing up telephone poles were over.

A man rose from a nearby hilltop and walked down to ensure the two saboteurs were indeed dead. They were. He carried his rifle - a relic from World War I. He was not a French soldier. He was a pied-noir – a foreign settler from Europe - that lived on a farm that had been in his family over seventy years. Hearing a slight tapping sound in his phone's receiver while talking to his brother in Italy, he had decided to investigate. Sabotage was common in the outlands.

Like most pied-noir, he hated the native Algerians and thought of them as inferior and dirty. He knew they wanted to kill him and his kind. And for what? Trying to scrape a living from the land? He had no sympathy for the two Muslim boys that he had just killed. Technically, one of the boys had killed himself by blowing up the telephone pole but the man would claim the boy's death as one of his kills when he recounted the events to his family and friends. He would leave their bodies for the crows.

Café Wars

He was not worried about French justice. There was an understanding between the French and the pied-noir who settled in their colonies. The French police and army could not patrol everywhere. Algeria was the largest country in all of Africa with almost one million square miles. The pied-noir and their militias were allowed to protect their communities and farms, even if it meant killing the occasional troublemaker… or two. The French would look the other way.

He was angry about the telephone poles. It would take weeks to get the telephone company to repair the damage. The technicians were very busy these days repairing downed lines. He slung his rifle over his shoulder and walked back to his farm. He had been born in Algeria. He had raised his family here. He would die here. It was his home and he loved it like breath itself.

I will do better next time, thought Lieutenant Colonel Marcel Bigeard as he walked through the highlands of North Vietnam. Bruno, as he was called by his friends, was one of eleven thousand seven hundred prisoners that had fought for the French Army at Dien Bien Phu. After fifty-four days of bombardment from Viet Minh artillery and countless human wave attacks, the French ran out of ammunition. There was some question as to whether they had officially surrendered or simply stopped fighting. Bruno knew that he had not surrendered. He had been knocked unconscious during a final breakout attempt by the men under his command. He was lucky. He had a hard head.

The Viet Minh leaders were ill-prepared for the French capitulation. They had never taken so many prisoners in the entire eight year war. The French had run out of food and water in addition to ammunition and the Viet Minh were expected to feed them. They barely had enough rice to feed their own troops let alone their prisoners. They had no choice but to move the prisoners north to the Viet Minh bases near the Chinese border. It was over three hundred and seventy miles through thick forests and mountainous terrain. More than half of the prisoners would die of disease, dehydration and starvation during the march. It was a disgrace against humanity. It was war.

Bruno understood war. He accepted it. His throat was parched. He had not drunk any water in three days and it hadn't rained, even though it was monsoon season. A cruel joke from mother nature. It was hot during the day while they marched and freezing cold at night when they tried to sleep. It never occurred to Bruno that he wouldn't survive. It wasn't that he was afraid of death. He was the bravest man he knew. He was sure he would die in battle, not on a Sunday afternoon stroll through the mountains. At least he thought it was Sunday. He had lost track.

At the beginning of the march he had helped those that fell, or collapsed, to get back on their feet and continue. The Viet Minh killed anyone who was too weak to continue. They saw it as humane. Better the bayonet than to suffer until they finally died of dehydration or starvation. After a week, as hundreds, then thousands, died, Bruno began to believe they were correct. He let his men fall and rest in the clouds of dust until they were released from their agony by their capturers' bayonets, or simply died.

Café Wars

The bayonet was not for him. He was a paratrooper and a commander at that. It was important that he show himself as a good example to his men. It was his duty to live to fight another day.

He thought about escaping during the night. The Viet Minh were not very vigilant about watching their prisoners. Where could their prisoners go if they escaped? They wouldn't last long in the mountains by themselves. Their best hope of survival was the very place the Viet Minh were taking them - the prison camps in the north. They had been told there would be food, water, and even some basic medical supplies at the end of the march. Besides, the Viet Minh and the French were already sitting at the square tables in Geneva negotiating a ceasefire. The French soldiers would probably be released after a few months of captivity. *How sad* thought Bruno. *The Viet Minh are our best bet.* And so he marched with the other survivors… one foot in front of the other…

It was dark and muggy like most nights in the highlands of Vietnam. Tom Coyle stood at the edge of an airfield and watched as the Daisy Mae, a C-119 Boxcar Cargo Plane, approached. Both of her engines were smoking badly and she was losing altitude fast. Her landing gear was up, meaning she would land on her belly without wheels.

The aircraft hit the runway with a shower of sparks that lit up the night. Both of the engine props bent under. She bounced into the air and slammed back down again. Her wing fuel tanks ruptured and sparks turned to flames.

One of her tail booms ripped off the back of the wing. The Daisy Mae spun around clockwise as she continued to slide and veered to the left of the runway. Her left wing dug into the wet ground and flipped the entire fuselage into the air. She cartwheeled three times and disintegrated into pieces, throwing off her engines, wings and remaining tail boom. The cargo hold and cockpit stayed together and tumbled to a stop on the left edge of the airfield.

Coyle ran toward the burning hulk. He dodged the burning parts and pieces of sheet metal scattered across the ground. He reached the rear of the hold where one of the rear doors had broken off.

He climbed inside and moved toward the cockpit. Both door hinges were broken and the cockpit door was ajar. He pulled open the broken door and tossed it to one side. He hesitated, afraid of what he would find inside. He entered the cockpit.

It was a tangle of twisted sheet metal with hanging control panels and wires sparking. The entire front of the cockpit had collapsed. The Daisy Mae's pilots, James "McGoon" McGovern and Wallace Buford were still in their seats. Buford was dead, his neck broken. McGoon groaned, his head bled from pieces of the windshield that had shattered and cut him during the crash. Coyle moved to his side and looked down. A large gash in McGoon's chest was bleeding badly. McGoon looked up, "Coyle?"

"Hey, buddy. Nice landing," said Coyle.

"Yeah. One for the history books," said McGoon, weakly. "How's Buford?"

"He's seen better days, McGoon."

"Dead?"

"Yeah."

"Oh, that's a shame. He was a good man."

Coyle looked down at the front control panel sitting on top of the two pilots' legs. "McGoon, can you feel your legs?"

"Not really."

"It's okay. I'm gonna get you outta here."

"Nah. It's too late."

"What do you mean?"

"I'm dead, Coyle."

"What are you talking about?"

"Will you do me a favor?"

"Of course. Whatever you need, McGoon."

"Take care of my girls, will ya?"

"You know I will."

"Promise me."

"I promise, McGoon. I swear. I'll do it."

"Good enough. You'd better go."

"I ain't leaving without you, McGoon."

"Yeah ya are. They're coming."

"Whose coming?"

"Them," said McGoon motioning with his head toward the tail of the aircraft.

Coyle turned and saw three Viet Minh soldiers with their submachineguns leveled. They opened fire, spraying Coyle and McGoon with bullets.

Coyle woke in a cold sweat and gasped for breath. Brigitte Friang laid by his side, shaking him awake from his nightmare. "It's okay, Coyle. It's not real. It's just a bad dream," said Brigitte speaking English.

Coyle had not yet learned enough French to communicate effectively. He calmed and said, "It's those damned pills they gave me for the pain."

"You need to be patient and do as the doctors say. You still have a good-sized hole in your shoulder. I think you need the pills."

"I'd rather live with the pain than the nightmares."

"Do you want me to get you some water?"

"Yeah. Water would be good."

Brigitte got up from their bed and exited the bedroom. Coyle lay back down and stared at the ceiling. The hotel room had a coffered ceiling with wood-carved panels painted to match the plaster. It was more luxurious than Coyle was accustomed to and made him feel out of place. Brigitte reentered with a glass of water. Coyle drained it in three gulps. "Thanks. What time is it?"

"A little after two. I'm sorry I woke you."

"It's okay, darling. I've grown used to it."

"I've got to go back to McGoon's bungalow," said Coyle. "I've got to find the girls. I think it's the only way these nightmares will stop."

"The girls?"

"Nyuget and Chau."

"McGoon's whores?"

"Housemates. McGoon's housemates."

"It's the same in French if you pay them."

"Fine. McGoon's whores."

"Are you sure you're up to it?" said Brigitte.

"Yeah. I'll be all right."

"Okay. We can fly back to Hanoi after the signing."

"No. We both know you need to stay here in Geneva. Your magazine expects complete coverage and that means interviews with everyone and their dog once the peace agreement has been signed. The politicians will want their minute in the spotlight. Easy pickings for a pro like you."

"It's really just a lot of posturing if the South Vietnamese and the U.S. don't sign. Besides, your health is more important than my job."

"I appreciate the sentiment, but I'll be fine. Besides, someone needs to pack up your apartment in Hanoi."

"You're not going to pack up the apartment."

"No. I won't actually pack anything but I can supervise and make sure everything makes it back to Paris."

"You'd do that for me?"

"...for us. Yes."

"Are you sure?"

"I'll be fine."

Brigitte lay back down beside him and brushed the hair off his forehead. "I can't believe it's actually ending after eight years," she said.

"Worried a war correspondent like yourself will have nothing to write about?" said Coyle.

"There will always be something to write about. The world is not a peaceful place. There will always be a war somewhere."

"I suppose you're right... and gainfully employed. Which is good. One of us should have a job that pays the bills." He smiled. "I could get used to being a kept man."

Brigitte hit him, careful to avoid his wounded shoulder. He moaned in mock pain. He closed his eyes and pretended to go to sleep. It was the only way to get her to fall asleep and she needed her rest. He was far from sleep and would stay up remembering what had happened and considering what might be next.

Coyle slept on the plane flying back to Hanoi until his nightmares overtook his slumber. He would wake not knowing where he was at. It would take a few moments of confusion before he realized that he was safe. Riding in the back of a plane rather than in the pilot's seat was unfamiliar to him and made his butt sore.

His shoulder was another story. During the fall of Dien Bien Phu, Coyle and Brigitte had attempted to escape the French garrison through the outlining forest around the airstrip. Brigitte accidently tripped a booby-trap and Coyle pushed her out of the way to keep her from being skewered by several sharpened stakes. In the process he was skewered himself and they were captured by a Viet Minh patrol. Soon after, they were released so that Coyle could deliver a message to the Americans from General Giap, the Viet Minh commander and architect of the offensive that defeated the French. The wound festered and eventually became septic. It almost killed him. The doctors were forced to cut away a large amount of infected flesh around the wound and healing had been a slow process. He had not be able to fly since the incident and was getting antsy.

Coyle loved to fly. He was good at it. One of the best, some said. It seemed natural to him like he was born to sit in a cockpit. He had flown in four wars. In the beginning, he had flown combat aircraft. Now he only flew cargo and transported troops in the C-119 Boxcars. He had lost his taste for combat and killing. There was no glory in it as he had thought when he was a young man and first joined the Army. He knew now that war only created misery and sorrow. He had seen enough pain and death to fill a lifetime and wanted no more of it.

These last six months, Coyle had been flying for the French Army as a subcontractor through Civil Air Transport (CAT). CAT was an aviation services company founded by the American General Claire

Lee Chennault. The company would eventually be purchased by the CIA and become known as Air America. CAT paid well and did not require Coyle to fly combat missions as part of his contract.

He had tried to go back to the United States and fly commercial airlines but it just wasn't a good fit. He couldn't stand the whining passengers complaining that the aircraft cabin was too cold or too hot. *It's an aircraft for Christ's sake,* he thought. *You'd think it was a luxury cruise liner.*

He was looking forward to spending time with Brigitte in Paris. He would pick up a job flying cargo that gave him weekends off. She would spend her time writing articles for the magazine and working on her book about her adventures as a war correspondent flying with the French paratroopers. There would be long dinners with her friends where he would feel lost, because everyone was talking in French, but he didn't care, because Brigitte was laughing and smiling. That's all he really wanted… to make her happy. It would be a good life.

Brigitte had a cute apartment in the old Jewish quarter called 'Le Marais.' It was an easy walk to Notre Dame, the Seine River and the Louvre. He liked the sidewalk cafes, the pastry shops and little bookstores, with their floor to ceiling shelves stuffed with dusty editions of Hemingway's 'A Moveable Feast.' The underground metro made getting around easy and Paris was one of the world's best walking cities. There was so much to see and do everywhere. Best of all, he liked waking up next to Brigitte. She was not an easy woman but he loved her and would do anything to protect her – as he had proven several times in Vietnam.

The airline waitresses served cocktails and the evening meal. The steak he ordered was far from hot. He didn't say a thing. Life was good. Why push it?

Ho Chi Minh was not happy. His army had won at Dien Bien Phu, and the French were demoralized. Both sides had paid a heavy price. Both sides had lost their best soldiers. The French were still dangerous. They had only used 10% of their total fighting force. Ho had used 50% of his, together with most of the munitions for his artillery. His army was out of position, stuck in the highlands, shepherding French prisoners, and the monsoons were taking their toll on his lines of communication, making troop transport all but impossible. It would take months to reposition his soldiers and replenish his supplies. It would be six months before his army was ready to fight another major offensive. And while he prepared, the French would recruit more South Vietnamese into their fighting force and train them to kill his brothers and sisters.

His representatives had the momentum at the negotiating table in Geneva. The French politicians wanted out of Vietnam but that could change like the wind if the French generals were able to secure a military victory or the Americans decided to enter the war. He had the Chinese and the Russians on his side but they were growing weary of the eight year war and were threatening to cut off aid if he did not make a deal with the French. The Russians had suggested that Ho accept the current deal and wait until the French left, before continuing the struggle. Ho questioned whether the Russians or the Chinese would be willing to continue the war once the peace was won.

The deal on the table was a bitter pill to swallow. It divided Vietnam in two – the North and the South. There would be a ceasefire and an exchange of prisoners. The French would withdraw and leave both Vietnams. The two Vietnams would be independent. Elections would be held within two years and Vietnam would once again be united… maybe.

The South Vietnamese government was not agreeing to the deal but the French had decided to go ahead without them. America had offered to step in and guarantee South Vietnam's survival. The Americans did not like the deal either. They didn't trust the North to have free and fair elections. They were blinded by their ideology and hated the communists. It was true. Ho Chi Minh was a communist but he was a nationalist first. He loved his country and its people. He had spent his life fighting for their freedom. To Ho, communism was a means to an end. A method to fairly redistribute the land that the French had taken and to give his people a chance at happiness. It was about the people, not ideology. If he thought capitalism could feed his people he would gladly accept it. But he had seen the greed of the French. They had stolen the wealth of Vietnam and given little back to the people. He had seen capitalism at work. It offered little hope. Ho would remain a communist until the end and the Americans could pound sand if they didn't like it.

Ho and his people would accept the deal that was offered. They would be patient and wait until the French had left just as the Russians had suggested.

But it wasn't over. Not until Vietnam was once again unified. He knew there were more battles to be fought and more blood to be shed.

Brigitte sat with the other journalists to witness the signing of the agreement between the Viet Minh and the French. It was a sad day for her. She loved her country and up until that day, Vietnam was part of France. The tide of anti-imperialism had been swinging against the European powers since before World War II. The colonies wanted their independence and they saw that their European masters were weak from fighting a World War that bled them dry. It was now or never. The time to strike. And strike they did.

Vietnam was the first of France's colonies to win its independence through revolution. Others would surely follow. Morocco and Tunisia had already refused to join the French Union. Cambodia and Laos were newly independent countries and were already considering shedding the protection of their former master.

Algeria was the most troubling. Algeria was not considered a colony but part of metropolitan France. Algiers, the capital of Algeria, had been the city the Free France government used as a capital while Paris was occupied by the Germans. The ties were strong, or so the French thought.

Brigitte thought about the benefits France had brought to her colonies: commerce, railroads, hospitals, universities and, of course, government with its codex of laws. Before France, most of the colonies had gone through civil wars and changed their heads of state multiple times. It was difficult for a nation and its people to progress when one never knew what the policy and laws would be in the future. France had brought stability and modernization to its colonies. There was little question the people had benefited and progressed under their colonial masters. But their desire for self-determination outweighed the benefits and now they wanted their freedom. They were willing to fight for it, and France had proven she was willing to fight to keep her empire intact… even if she didn't always win.

The South Vietnamese leaders were noticeably absent from the signing, Brigitte scribbled in her notes. Their fate had been decided by the Viet Minh, French, Chinese and Russians. Their country was divided without their consent. They would acquiesce for the moment and adhere to the terms of the agreement without actually signing it. They did not believe that the North Vietnamese would keep their word. But the French were leaving, with or without their approval. Better to be rid of them and be free to fight the coming war as they saw fit. Only the Americans stood by their side and declined to sign the agreement. But would America stand by the south when they were betrayed by the north? Would America's help be enough to fend off the communists?

Brigitte attempted to be objective when she wrote her articles but she was a patriot. She was after all… French. She had joined the French resistance during the German occupation of France. She had been captured and tortured to reveal the names of her co-conspirators. She wanted to be brave and resist the Gestapo, but their methods were effective. When the

Gestapo finally released her, she spent the rest of the war in a German prison camp wondering if the information she had revealed had caused the deaths or imprisonment of her comrades. It was a heavy burden to bear.

The French magazine *Politiques Internationales* that employed Brigitte had already informed her that she had been replaced by a younger reporter in Hanoi and she was to return to France. They had no intention of letting their star war correspondent remain in Vietnam as France's influence withered away. That job was assigned to a new reporter that still needed to prove their worth. Fresh meat for the journalism grinder.

Brigitte had become a well-known celebrity for her reporting during the siege of Dien Bien Phu. Her parachuting into the valley in the opening battle of the campaign had enthralled her readers, as she knew it would. Brigitte wanted to be famous and wasn't afraid to admit it. She wanted people to read her writing and if it took jumping from an airplane to accomplish her goal, then so be it. She had been awarded her parachutist brevet which she wore proudly on her tailored jumpsuit. Dien Bien Phu was her fifth jump with the French paratroopers, but not her last.

The magazine would put her out for interviews and photo ops like a prized pony. She had already had an appearance on the American television show "What's my line?" as a challenger. She didn't mind as long as there was still time to write. Once her book was finished she would need all the publicity she could get.

Café Wars

Tonight there would be a grand party at the French embassy to celebrate the signing of the agreement. She had purchased a new evening gown that revealed just enough skin to catch the eye and yet covered just enough to be treated serious. She had feigned disappointment that Coyle would not be there to see it. In reality, she was relieved. She had kept quiet about her relationship with Coyle. It wasn't a secret, but she didn't want her relationship with the American pilot to distract from her own accomplishments. She was not the type of woman that would stand behind her man. She would stand with him, or sometimes in front of him, whether he liked it or not. After all, he knew what he was getting into when he first started courting her. She figured her moxie was part of the reason he was attracted to her. She was a woman to be reckoned with. A challenge to be met.

Brigitte waded through the crowd when the signing ceremony was finally concluded. She spotted Brigadier Generals Jean Gilles and Jacque Massu in a group of officers near the doorway. As she approached, Gilles saw her, smiled and gave her a hug. "Brigitte, you look lovely."

"Thank you, General Gilles. I see you have polished your eye for the occasion," said Brigitte.

"Indeed I did. Would you care to see it?" Gilles enjoyed popping out his glass eye whenever possible, especially when young ladies were present.

"No thank you, General. I have seen it quite enough. Best save the surprise for the un-indoctrinated."

"Brigitte and I jumped into Dien Bien Phu together," said Gilles turning to the others in the group. "Do you remember, Brigitte?"

"One does not forget such an experience," said Brigitte. "He puts his eye in his pocket when he jumps."

"One does not want to go searching for a misplaced eyeball when under fire," said Gilles.

"Good policy," said Brigitte.

"Brigitte, have you met Brigadier General Massu?"

"Yes. We met in Saigon in '52 I believe. How are you, General?"

"Quite well, considering... Not exactly an auspicious day, is it?" said Massu shaking her hand. "This is what one can expect when your hands are tied by the politicians in Paris."

"I'm sure I would find many that would agree with you, General," said Brigitte. "Have you heard any scuttlebutt on when the Viet Minh might release their French prisoners?"

"Worried about Bruno?" said Gilles.

"Bruno and the others. I would feel better if I knew they were receiving their Red Cross packages."

"Doubtful," said Major Paul Aussaresses.

"Mademoiselle Friang, this is Major Paul Aussaresses," said Massu. "If anyone would know, he would. He is in charge of my intelligence unit."

"Your reputation proceeds you, Mademoiselle Friang," said Aussaresses shaking her hand.

"And yours, Major," said Brigitte, slightly weary. She had heard stories of the Massu's major and his studies of the art of interrogation.

"I do not believe it will be long before our prisoners are released. The Viet Minh don't have the food and medical supplies to care for them. That being said, I'm also sure there will be some last minute conditions attached to their release," said Aussaresses.

"And will we comply?" said Brigitte.

"I would imagine," said Massu. "Paris wants to wash its hands of the entire affair as soon as possible. Nobody is in the mood to quibble."

"So, where to next?" said Brigitte.

"Algeria I would imagine," said Gilles.

"You think the situation is that serious?" said Brigitte.

"Yes. They have seen the Vietnamese insurrection succeed. Now they will want their own," said Gilles.

"Algeria is not Vietnam. I doubt the politicians will give it up so easily," said Massu. "France's honor is at stake. We have lost enough face for a time. We will fight to win it back and perhaps our hands will finally be untied."

TWO

Ahmed Ben Bella sat in an Algerian café finishing his tea. He knew he was being watched. Someone was always watching him and occasionally trying to kill him. He had already survived multiple gunshot wounds and a bomb blast intended to end his life while hiding out in Egypt. He was a hard man to kill.

He was tall and considered good looking by most women. He had returned to Algeria under an assumed name with a forged passport like a goat entering a wolf's lair. But he was no goat. He had fought for the French in World War II and won several medals for his bravery, including the Croix de Guerre and the Medaille Militaire, which Charles de Gaulle had awarded to him personally. The French Army had trained him well. Now, they and the pieds-noir militias, hunted him. He was a troublemaker, and they wanted him dead.

Messali Hadj and Bella were the founders of Organisation Speciale (OS), the paramilitary wing of the Mouvement National Algérien (MNA) - a political organization lobbying for Algeria's Independence and secretly preparing to take up arms against the French as soon as the time was right. With the signing of the

Geneva Accords that freed Vietnam from French rule, that time was approaching. Algerians were energized by the French defeat at Dien Bien Phu and saw the light at the end of a long dark tunnel – their own bid for Independence. Bella was in Algeria to build on that momentum. It was a big risk, but he was used to big risks.

He would need to shake whomever was tailing him before he met with the leaders of the other underground organizations later that evening. They would meet in secret knowing full well that anyone of them could have been turned by the police or worse… the militia. If any of them had been turned by the enemy it would mean jail for the rest of them and most likely torture that would end with their disappearance. Bella was familiar with torture and knew to hold out as long as possible, then become a fountain of both true and false information so his opponents could not tell the difference and would discount whatever he said. Naturally, he would prefer to remain free and avoid any unpleasantness but he was not afraid. Few things frightened Bella. Many were frightened by Bella. He was a veteran assassin when required and he too knew effective methods of torture.

He paid his bill and rose from the table. He would need to expose the person tailing him. It wouldn't be hard. He walked across a square, entered a side street, and turned down an alley between two tall buildings.

The man following Bella was a member of Le Main Rouge (The Red Hand), a secret terrorist organization run by the French counter-intelligence service. It was the Red Hand that in 1952 had gunned down Ferhat Hached, an early leader of the Tunisian

Independence movement, and had blown up a civilian freighter smuggling arms into Algeria. His assignment today was not to kill but simply to follow Bella. The leaders of Le Main Rouge knew that Bella was not a man to be trifled with and that when the time came to kill him they would need to send their best.

The man rounded the corner and entered the alley. It was deserted. It was as if Bella had vanished. The man knew that was impossible. Not enough time had passed for Bella to reach the opposite end of the alley. Bella was there someplace in the alley hiding. The man walked further into the alley checking doorways and stairwells leading to the basements of buildings. Halfway down the alley he heard a noise from above. He looked up and saw Bella on a fire escape landing. Bella released the ladder directly above the man. The heavy iron ladder fell and the leg of the ladder speared the man in the head killing him instantly. It looked like an accident and that was the way Bella liked to dispose of his enemies. Accidents generated fewer questions.

Bella entered the futbol stadium through the maintenance tunnel exit. It was dark. Larbi Ben M'Hidi, commonly known as Si Larbi, stood in the shadows holding a submachinegun at the far entrance of the tunnel. Bella stopped, lit a cigarette and studied Si Larbi at a distance to determine if he was a threat. One could not be sure who was friend or foe these days even if you were both on the same side. Disagreements between the leaders of the underground organizations often led to bloodshed. Si Larbi was only thirty years old and had already made a name for himself as a brave fighter in the underground movement. Bella could not be sure of Si Larbi's intent, but proceeded anyway.

Si Larbi studied Bella as he approached like a prize fighter sizing up his opponent. There was recognition in the young man's eyes. He knew Bella's reputation and had seen his face in an Egyptian magazine. "You're late," said Si Larbi speaking in Arabic, the common language of North Africa.

"It could not be helped," said Bella.

"You have a tail?" said Si Larbi looking back down the tunnel.

"Had," said Bella.

Si Larbi nodded his approval and led the way into the stadium. "You brought a gun," said Bella.

"Do guns make you nervous?"

"No but we said no guns," said Bella. "I keep my word."

"I always carry a gun. It makes me feel better. Like my mother's tit when I was a child."

"If you are caught with a gun the French will hang you."

"Best not get caught then," said Si Larbi with a smile.

Bella and Si Larbi climbed up the stadium stairs and joined a group of seven men. "You're late," said Messali Hadj the co-founder of the OS.

"He had a tail," said Si Larbi.

"So did we all but we are not late," said Messali.

"A thousand apologies," said Bella.

Messali and Bella had not spoken in almost a year. They had been friends when they started the OS together and had watched each other's backs during secret military operations against the pied-noir, the

European settlers that had been given preference to the best farm lands by the French and full French citizenship. This infuriated the Algerians. As the time for the real war of Independence drew near, the two men had become estranged and the OS had split into two factions. The two leaders had different ideas on how to achieve Independence.

Messali did not believe an all-out war with the French was necessary or prudent. It was too risky and would cost the lives of thousands of Algerians. He preferred to influence public policy through insurgency, as they had been doing. Why change course when you are winning? was his thought. The French politicians were already feeling the pressure of anti-colonialists at home in Paris and throughout Europe. Even the Americans were putting pressure on the French to relinquish her colonies. A war could harden the positions of the French politicians against the Independence movement. The Algerians could lose the support they had fought so hard to gain over the years and lose their chance of self-determination for another decade.

Bella was tired of waiting for the French politicians to do the right thing and free Algeria. The Vietnamese had just won their Independence by openly fighting the French and defeating them with guerilla tactics. The Algerians could do the same. They had learned from the Vietnamese and knew which tactics worked against the French. Now was the time to publicly rebel and fight before the French public recovered from the shock of the French Army's defeat at Dien Bien Phu.

Introductions were made by Messali who everyone knew. Messali wasn't the leader of the group. There was no leader. That was the point of the meeting. These nine men were the leaders of the individual underground movements that had formed since the Setif massacre. They did not trust each other, and often suspected ulterior motives from any action taken. However they all shared the same goal of Algerian Independence and were prepared to die to accomplish it. "The time has come to strike at the heart of the French while they are weak and still preoccupied with their withdrawal from Indochina," said Si Larbi. "The people are ready and willing. The revolution should begin without delay."

"We must consolidate if we are to beat the French," said Bella. "We need to fold all of our movements into one organization."

"And who would lead?" said Messali.

"All of us," said Bella. "We form a council."

"A council?"

"Yes, a war council of sorts."

"A council is a lousy way to fight a war," said Messali. "All of us getting together every time a decision needs to be made? It will slow our movement down to a crawl."

"I agree but it is the only way to keep us from fighting with each other."

"It's not the only way. We could vote on a leader," said Messali.

"We could but it is unlikely we would all follow. Our political ideologies are too diverse. A council would be forced to accept and respect our different ideologies if it were ever to expect to get anything done."

"Like I said, a bad way to run a war," said Messali.

"We wouldn't need to meet on every decision together. We could elect leaders of the various operations. The council would only decide on overall strategy and major tactical decisions concerning the entire organization. We could each be in charge of a region of the country."

"And who would get Algiers?" said Si Larbi.

"We would decide that… as a council."

"You have a name for this new organization?" said Si Larbi.

"I was thinking the 'National Liberation Front' or 'FLN' for short," said Bella.

"You've given this a great deal of thought, my friend," said Messali, suspect. "And what of the OS?"

"We form a new military branch and fold the OS and the other military wings into the new branch."

"We are to become your lap dog then?" said Messali.

Bella bit his tongue and kept his temper in check as he said, "My only desire is to beat the French before they can regroup. Consolidation is the best way to accomplish that goal. The French people are fed up and have no stomach for war. That will change over time. We must strike now while we have the opportunity. We can decide on which path the country will follow once that mission has been accomplished and Algeria is free. After all we are all brothers in the faith."

Nobody disagreed that night. But only six of the nine would go on to form the FLN. Messali was not one of them. He would fight his own battles his own way with his own followers. Animosity and jealousy would fester like a rotting wound. It would mean trouble for Bella and the FLN.

Café Wars

Coyle had his arm in a sling as he rode in a trishaw through Hanoi. It was mayhem. There were thousands of Vietnamese families carrying everything they thought of value on bicycles and in hand carts. Anything with wheels that could carry a heavy load was put to use. The mother and father took turns pulling the load while the other herded the children carrying backpacks and suitcases.

Their goal was simple – South. The French were leaving and the communists were coming. For anyone that had been even remotely associated with the French, life was over in the North. The Viet Minh had shown little tolerance for French collaborators and had a tendency to shoot first and ask questions later. Politicians, teachers and business owners were prime targets of retribution and were the first to leave.

The flow of refugees went both ways during the three hundred days of transfer that was permitted by both governments. It was obvious by the traffic heading south that was backed up for hundreds of miles which people were more concerned for their safety.

Over one million Vietnamese Catholics fled south when the CIA's planes dropped flyers that read "The Virgin Mary is going south." The politicians knew that a new war would be coming soon and the more people on their side when it happened, the better their chances of victory.

The French were less concerned. They believed their citizenship still protected them. They sat and watched the exodus from their favorite sidewalk cafés and coffee houses. Some were even considering staying behind once the communists arrived. The North Vietnamese would need the French to operate the power stations, water works and trains. The French had vast trade networks that could keep the wheels of commerce moving and generate tax revenue for the new government. French plantations provided the food to feed millions of Vietnamese and even excess that was exported. Many thought it might even be more lucrative to operate under the Vietnamese than the French. Vietnamese officials were much cheaper to bribe than French officials.

The French underestimated the hatred they had generated over the years of colonialism. At times the French had been cruel to the Vietnamese. They were quick to put down dissent with incarceration, and rebellion with violence. Compromise had been seen as weakness.

The Vietnamese were always considered second class citizens and for decades had been denied full citizenship in France's empire. The Vietnamese were paid very little and unions were not allowed under French colonial rule. The French entrepreneurs made their fortunes from Vietnamese misery and sweat.

Coyle watched abandoned buildings and houses being looted by mobs as the trishaw rolled past. Most were stripped of anything of value. A few were set on fire. The looters weren't angry – just desperate.

The trishaw driver had demanded one U.S. dollar to take Coyle into the colonial part of Hanoi. It was dangerous. He didn't want French francs which he saw as more useless than paper. Nobody knew what the Vietnamese currency would be once the communists took power. The American greenback and the British Pound Sterling were seen as safe and became the only acceptable currencies for several months in the North. Gold and silver jewelry were also acceptable, as was rice. The value of everything was measured by weight on questionable scales. Barter was the main system of commerce. Famine, and the disease that always follows it, spread fast.

The trishaw pulled up in front of McGoon's bungalow. Coyle climbed off the bench in front of the driver. He paid the man one U.S. dollar as promised. The driver seemed pleased and made motions with his hands signifying he would be willing to wait until the foreigner was ready to leave. Coyle made motions like he would be staying and that the driver shouldn't wait. The driver was disappointed, spat on the ground and pedaled off to find another fare.

Coyle waited for a long moment in front of the one-story house. The yellow paint had faded even more than he remembered it, and the surrounding vegetation had clearly been neglected. He wasn't sure why he was hesitating to go inside. He had rehearsed how he would tell the girls about McGoon's death, although he was sure they already knew. McGoon was a well-known character in Hanoi and word of his death would have traveled fast. He felt bad that he hadn't come before today. His justification was that he was in and out of the hospital most of the time as the doctors tended to the infection in his shoulder. But he knew that was just a lousy excuse.

The truth was that he didn't want to think about McGoon. Coyle was there when he died. It was one of the traumatic events of his life, and that was saying a lot for a guy that had fought in four wars. Now

McGoon was haunting his dreams. Mourning McGoon wasn't going to bring him back.

He had wired money to the girls through Western Union, so they had enough to eat and pay the rent, but he had left the message part of the wire blank. He didn't know what to say or how to say it in Vietnamese. He wasn't even sure the girls knew how to read.

He was filled with dread when he finally walked toward the front of the bungalow. The girls would probably have put up some sort of memorial or shrine of their fallen caretaker. There would be a photo of McGoon. He would just avoid looking at it, he thought. His feelings changed when he saw the front door ajar and the lock broken. His pace picked up almost to a run.

He pushed the front door open. It was dark inside. He wondered if the girls had paid the electric bill or even if they knew they needed to pay it to keep the ceiling fans and lights working. He moved to the shutters over the front windows and opened them to let some sunlight in. He was shocked by what he saw. Everything was gone; the furniture, the posters on the wall, even McGoon's custom-made tropical island bar. There were palm fronds and seeds on the tile floor as if they had blown in through the open front door. He called out the girls' names. There was no response. He moved to McGoon's bedroom figuring the girls probably slept together in the big bed while McGoon was away.

He pushed open the bedroom door. Everything was gone including McGoon's big bed and the dresser where he kept his gaudy Hawaiian shirts, neatly folded and placed in the drawers after the girls washed and ironed them. McGoon's closet had been emptied and the wooden jewelry box where he kept his father's pocket watch and the mountain lion tooth necklace that he had had since he was a kid was gone too. Vanished like it never existed. But it had and so had McGoon. Coyle was suddenly angry. It wasn't like he wanted any of McGoon's junk. He just felt like it should still be there like it meant that McGoon was still there. But it was all gone.

Coyle went into the girls' bedroom and into the guest room where he had stayed until he could find his own place when he first arrived in Hanoi and McGoon had taken him in like an abandoned puppy. Everything was gone. The icebox, the sink, the toilet in the bathroom, everything that had even the faintest of value was gone... and so were the girls.

Coyle was filled with emotion. It was Coyle's fault that McGoon and Buford had been killed. McGoon had insisted on flying low when Coyle parachuted into the French garrison to be with Brigitte. If McGoon had flown at a safe altitude he and Buford would have avoided the Viet Minh anti-aircraft guns and still be alive. He had failed to keep McGoon alive and now he had failed to take care of the girls. He punched the wall several times and almost broke his hand. He didn't feel the pain and even if he had he would have welcomed it. He deserved pain. He sat on the floor in the middle of the empty bungalow and wept like he never wept before.

Brigitte was busy staring at the half-typed page in her typewriter. *It's crap,* she thought. *Men died. I owe them more than this piece of garbage.* She pulled the paper from the typewriter and set it on top of a stack of finished typewritten papers. Then she pushed the entire stack over the edge of the desk and into the trashcan.

Her apartment was small, with only one bedroom, a bathroom with an actual bath, a kitchen with a breakfast nook, and the living room that led out onto a patio just big enough for the two chairs and small table. She was pleased when Coyle told her that everything he owned fit into one canvas duffel bag. She had been feeling a little guilty that the bottom of the bedroom's one closet was filled with shoe boxes. It was Paris after all.

Coyle could fit everything in two drawers in the dresser and had no need for closet space except to hang up his leather flight jacket. He could use the coat closet in the living room for that. When she was out on assignment with the paratroopers she only had one jumpsuit and one pair of jump boots. She lived like the men she jumped with, and they saw her as one of their own. But when she was home in Paris she was more relaxed and liked to dress up. Coyle would see a different side of her when he finally arrived and she thought he would like it.

She put a new piece of paper into the typewriter. The phone rang. Brigitte stared at the phone like it was a viper. *It could be Tom*, she thought. It rang again. *It could be Damien*, she thought. *Better to be safe than sorry.* She didn't answer it.

Linh, Brigitte's Vietnamese housekeeper, answered the extension in the bedroom. "Shit," said Brigitte.

Linh peeked out the bedroom doorway and made a writing gesture followed by a hand chop which meant it was Brigitte's editor. Brigitte sighed and picked up the phone. "Good morning, Damien," she said.

"How's the book coming along?"

"It's really taking shape," said Brigitte looking down at the typed papers in the trash bin.

"Great to hear. What page are you on?"

"Page? I am still outlining, Damien."

"Did you throw everything in the bin again?"

"Yeah. It's crap. It's like something a student would write to impress her teacher."

"It can't be that bad, Brigitte."

"Oh, but it is… was."

"Why don't you fish it out of the trash and let me look at it? You know I will give you an honest opinion."

"That's what I am afraid of, Damien. I don't think my ego could take your criticism right now and I just had all my kitchen knives sharpened."

"Okay. Fine. But promise me this is the last time you start over without letting me at least look at what you have written."

"I promise to do exactly what I want when I do it."

Damien laughed and said, "Yes you will."

"So why did you call? I know it wasn't to check up on my book."

"You're right about that. I have an assignment for you."

"An assignment? I don't do assignments, Damien. The deal was I write what I want."

"I know. I know. But Ines decided she was in love again and abandoned her desk to go after some Italian race car driver. I swear this time I am going to fire that woman when she gets back."

"No. You won't, Damien. She'll come back in tears and you'll forgive her like you always do. Hell of a way to run a magazine if you ask me."

"I wasn't asking you. But I do need your help… if you'll give it."

"What was she working on?"

"Algeria. Things are really heating up down there."

"Yeah. I've heard. What angle was she taking?"

"Honestly, I'm not sure. Her notes are all covered with hearts and racecars. You would be free to develop the story however you see fit."

"If I take it, I'll need a travel budget."

"Of course. Just no long weekends in Nice."

"That was one time, Damien. And I did end up writing a piece on it."

"Which I threw in the bin."

"I didn't say it was a good story."

"Look. If you'll take the assignment, I may be convinced to look the other way if you decide to bring Tom along on any of your journeys."

"I should be so lucky. He's back in Hanoi searching for whores."

"What? Really?"

"I'm kidding. Tom and I are fine… I think," said Brigitte taking a moment to consider. "All right. I'll do it. It may do my writer's block some good."

"Procrastination. That's the spirit!"

"Au revoir, Damien." Brigitte hung up the phone before he could respond.

Brigitte pulled the blank paper out of the typewriter and set it back on the stack of new paper. "Linh, I am going out," said Brigitte.

"You want I make dinner?" said Linh stepping from the bedroom.

"Not for me but you can help yourself to whatever I have that isn't moldy."

"The wine?"

"Except the wine. We both know what happened last time. We don't need a repeat of the barf-o-rama incident."

"Barf-o-rama?"

"Never mind. No wine."

Linh nodded that she understood. Brigitte picked up her purse and exited the apartment.

THREE

It was 3 a.m. and still dark when Yacef Saadi rose from the bed in his home above his business in eastern Algiers. This was not unusual for Saadi; he was a baker, and bakers always rose early. Before his morning tea, he would start the fires under his ceramic stoves. He would make the first batch of bread dough and let it rise for twenty minutes while he drank his tea and ate a bit of dried goat meat to give him strength.

His wife and children would wake later. His wife and oldest daughter would sell his baked goods to his neighbors that visited the bakery's shop. His two oldest boys would use their bicycles to deliver his bread to restaurants and tea houses. Saadi knew how to sell baked goods. It was easy. Just make sure your shop was up wind from your customers. The aroma would do the rest.

Saadi's bakery specialized in kersa, the Algerian flatbread cooked in a stove-top skillet. The raised circles on the bottom of the cast-iron skillet gave the bread its distinctive look and helped cook the center of the bread. He made the dough with sunflower oil, salt, semolina and water, then fried the bread in vegetable oil which gave it its nice flavor and made the outside crispy.

Saadi loved making bread. He also loved making bombs. He was very good at both.

It was 11 a.m. when his bakery sold the last batch of bread and he closed the shop. His day's work was half done. The other half would be done in the back of the bakery out of public view.

He removed his apron and hung it on a nail in the wall by the doorway separating the shop from the bakery.

He walked into the back of the bakery. There were seven young women lined up like a squad of soldiers. He looked at each closely and studied their faces and their eyes. They were all beautiful Algerian girls. He consulted with an older woman, a hairdresser and a young man, a tailor. He picked three of the girls - Marwa, Ludmila and Nihad. Marwa was the most attractive of the three and would be useful in obtaining intelligence from enemy soldiers. But Saadi knew that Ludmila was the real treasure. She could easily pass for European and had an intensity in her eyes.

Saadi thanked the others. The rejected girls left, some with tears in their eyes. They wanted to serve their country and their families would be disappointed that they were not selected.

With the other girls gone, the tailor went to work measuring the girls for the European style dresses he would make. Once the tailor was finished, the hairdresser cut Ludmila and Nihad's hair short to the shoulders as was the French style. She left Marwa's long curly black hair as it was. It added to her beauty. There would be a manicurist that would shape their finger and toe nails and apply the colorful polish that all the European women preferred. There would be a woman that taught each girl to apply makeup and a French teacher that taught them basic phrases they could use to buy a bus ticket or order a coffee in a cafe. Their tongues were not used to French, but the teacher kept at it until their accents were undetectable.

Each girl was taught how to load, aim and fire a pistol and how to properly dispose of the evidence once the deed was completed. They were also taught simple self-defense skills that including gouging at the eyes with their long fingernails, kicking the genitals and how to use their elbows to break the nose of someone holding them from behind. They were taught what to do if they were captured and the various ways of committing suicide when no weapon was present. It was hard work and took over two weeks before they were ready.

When the transformation was complete, Saadi performed a final inspection of his little army of spies. They were impressive. They may not have looked French, but they appeared upper class European and that was good enough for his purposes. The French military treated Europeans differently than the Algerians. They were not eyed with suspicion and could enter train stations and dine in restaurants without being searched. The police would not demand to see their identity papers or produce passes to travel from one end of the city to another. Being pretty didn't hurt either. Most of the French soldiers were young and would want to impress the young ladies. An enamored soldier might even do one of the young girls a favor when asked. *Yes,* thought Saadi. *These girls will do nicely.*

The final touch was a string of pearls bestowed on each of the girls by Saadi. A reward of sorts for all their hard work and loyalty to the cause. Few Algerian women could afford jewelry, let alone pearls. The pearls were the satin bow on a package that made them special… that made them each a present to be opened by the enemy. They looked so innocent and pure. They were not. They were deadly sirens.

François Mitterrand, France's Interior Minister, walked through the train station. The dull grey sky of Paris covered the glass canopy ceiling above, offering a well-diffused light for passengers. He stopped and looked up at the electronic board that posted the current schedule of trains and their platforms. He did not notice Brigitte move up beside him with a suitcase in hand. She set the suitcase down behind Mitterrand and looked up at the schedule as if oblivious that the minister was next to her. Mitterrand found the departure platform for his train and turned to move off. He stumbled over Brigitte's suitcase. "Oh, I am so sorry," said Brigitte. "I should be more careful."

"It's quite all right, Mademoiselle," said Mitterrand and then realized it was Brigitte. "Oh, merde."

"Minister Mitterrand, what are you doing here?" said Brigitte feigning surprise.

"You know what I am doing here, Brigitte. Otherwise, why the ambush?"

"Ambush? I don't know what you are inferring, Minister. I am on my way to see my aunt in Bayeux. She's not feeling well."

"Ah, well… your aunt. I hope she feels better. Now if you will excuse me? I am on holiday."

"Since I ran into you, I wonder if you wouldn't mind answering a few questions?"

"I would love to but I am late and I don't want to miss my train. You understand."

"Of course. I will walk with you."

"What about your train?"

"It doesn't leave for another hour."

"Fine."

"Would you mind?" said Brigitte motioning to her suitcase and pulling out a pencil and notebook from her purse.

Mitterrand grunted his displeasure and picked up her suitcase. They walked toward the platforms.

"Really, Brigitte. I don't understand why you insist on playing these charades."

"I don't know what you are talking about but if I did it would be because you instruct your secretary that you're always busy when I try to schedule an interview."

"Okay. I surrender. Ask your questions."

"Why are the Algerians, having fought for France in World War II, still denied French citizenship?"

"Algeria. Jesus. This is why I need a holiday. Your question is political. I am the Interior Minister. I merely execute the law. I do not write it."

"You are not a politician?"

"No. Not currently."

"And if you were?"

"I would say that it has long been France's policy not to tamper with the nationality of the natives in its colonies."

"If we do not offer them citizenship and the benefits that it brings with it, why should they be loyal and fight for France?"

"I don't believe the current government is concerned that the Algerians fight for France as long as they do not fight against it."

"So, they are fighting?"

"Of course they are fighting. The Algerians have seen the victory of the Vietnamese. Their leaders are opportunists."

"Do you believe France is facing another war for Independence?"

"No. The Algerians do not have the support of the Chinese. They have no army."

"They have the support of the Russians."

"Who told you that?

"You know I don't reveal my sources," said Brigitte. "It seems land reform is the biggest stone in the Algerian shoe. Would you agree?"

"I agree that the Algerians are upset at some of the laws concerning redistribution of land to the European colonists. But they are fairly compensated for their land."

"They may be compensated for the raw land but they are not compensated for any improvements on the land or any crops in the ground at the time of confiscation."

"I wouldn't know. I am not an assessor."

"There is no justice without knowledge, wouldn't you agree?"

"Yes. Of course. I will look into the matter."

"It's been going on for a hundred years. You've had plenty of time to look into the matter."

"Perhaps I misspoke. I will revisit the matter. But this is no excuse for violence and disorder in the streets. There are methods available to the Algerians that do not require protests and rioting. We are a nation of laws."

"But those laws are not equally applied to citizens and non-citizens."

"That may be true but the Algerians have been given a voice in Parliament. Their representatives are free to propose changes to the law and make their arguments."

"Those seats are mostly held by colonists that have settled in Algeria and a few tribal leaders. Hardly a fair representation of the will of the people."

"You asked your question. I gave you an answer."

"The party line answer?"

"The Interior Department's answer."

"What will France do if the protests continue to grow or worse – turn into more riots?"

"What we have always done… protect France and her interests."

"And is it in France's interest to put down any revolt?"

"There are protests and a few misinformed troublemakers that occasionally turn to violence. It's hardly a revolution."

"…Yet," said Brigitte and saw that Mitterrand was losing his patience with her. She already had several good quotes from the minister and decided to push him further in hopes of an outburst that could be turned into a headline. "I wonder if France's leaders have learned from the war we just lost that the time to address colonial grievances is before the revolution begins, not after?"

"You're trying to make a mountain out of mole hill, Brigitte. Find another way to sell your magazines,

Mademoiselle Friang," said Mitterrand putting down her suitcase and continuing on without her.

"Have a nice holiday, Minister," said Brigitte.

Mitterrand turned briefly and offered her the bras d'honneur as he walked away in a huff.

The shoeshine station near the gates at Algiers international airport was a coveted job. Travelers waiting for their planes saw it as the perfect time to get the Algerian dust wiped from their shoes before returning to Paris or other European cities. If they were leaving France they saw it as a good time to empty their pockets of francs so the tips were generous. Most of the men that worked the shoeshine station were in their forties and fifties. They had worked there for decades.

Zaki was Marwa's younger brother. He had just turned sixteen and had lost the baby fat that made him look boyish. He had an easy-going smile and was considered handsome by most of the girls in his neighborhood. He was a spy for the FLN and his position at the airport shoeshine station had been arranged. The FLN leaders wanted to know who was flying in and out of Algeria. The shoeshine station was also a good place to overhear conversations between government officials and diplomats traveling together.

Zaki used a nearby payphone to call a number he had memorized whenever he saw or heard something or someone worth noting. He usually made several calls each day. None of the other shoeshine workers questioned Zaki. They knew who he worked for and why he was constantly leaving his customers' half shined shoes to make his phone calls. Whenever he would leave, another shoeshiner would step in and finish the job he was working on. That was the deal. Nobody made trouble for Zaki. Nobody dared.

Zaki was working on a pair of wingtips worn by a Dutch wholesaler when he saw Sami Djaout picking up his ticket at the airline counter. Zaki had been given the photos and names of the top MNA operatives. Zaki had memorized them. He waited until Sami had left the counter and entered the passport control area for departure, before abandoning the wingtips and what promised to be a good tip from the Dutchman. The shoeshiner next to him slipped in and finished the wingtips.

Zaki crossed the ticketing area and approached the ticket agent that had sold Sami his ticket. Zaki shook the agent's hand leaving a folded up bill in the agent's palm, the way a customer bribes a maître d' for a good table at his favorited restaurant. The agent simply said, "Paris" and went back to helping the next customer in line. Zaki moved off to the payphone and made his call.

FOUR

Coyle stood in front of a Hanoi storefront and studied the writing on the glass door. From what he could tell it was both the establishment of the Bui Lam Dung Detective Agency and the VinDoc Translation Service specializing in French, English, American, Chinese, and Russian. The store's windows had been covered with boards to protect against looters, like a business owner digging in for the long haul. He wondered if the hotel concierge that had given him the recommendation was on commission. It didn't matter. This was as good a place to start as any, he thought. He entered.

An older woman wearing glasses sat behind a desk typing. He guessed by the stack of foreign dictionaries by her typewriter that she was translating a document. "Do you speak English," said Coyle.

"British or American?" said the woman without the normal Vietnamese accent.

"Is there a difference?"

"Oh yes. Very much. A truck in New York is a lorry in London."

"I suppose you're right about that. I'm American."

"I know. I can tell by your accent. How may I help you?"

"I'm looking for Mr. Dung."

The woman called out in Vietnamese toward a doorway covered with a curtain in the back of the office.

The largest Vietnamese Coyle had ever seen appeared in the doorway. He was tall and broad; his shoulders barely fitting through the narrow doorway. He was fat but Coyle could tell there was muscle hidden beneath the fat. It was deceiving; almost a facade. "I'm Mr. Dung. How may I help you?" he said in a heavy Vietnamese accent.

"My name's Tom Coyle. I'm looking for a private investigator."

Dung moved forward like a tank and shook Coyle's hand. Coyle had been right about the muscle; the man's hand was like a vise. "Please have a seat," said Dung motioning to a chair in front of an empty desk. "Coffee?"

"Sure," said Coyle sitting.

Dung put a tea kettle on an electric hot plate in the corner of the office. He scooped several tablespoons of coffee grinds into a metal cup with holes in the bottom. He poured condensed milk into the bottom of two clear glasses and set a small spoon on each of the saucers under the glasses. He set the metal cup with the coffee grinds over the mouth of one of the glasses. "How did you hurt your arm if I may ask?" said Dung.

"It's my shoulder. I was speared by a tree branch," said Coyle.

"That must have hurt."

"Yeah. You could say that."

"I don't mean to pry but curiosity goes with the job you understand."

"I get it."

"Besides, I like to know who I am working for. One cannot be too careful in my line of business these days. How does one get speared by a tree branch?"

"I was at Dien Bien Phu if that's what you are getting at."

"I thought it a possibility. But you are American. Not French."

"I'm a pilot. I fly cargo for the French."

"And troops at times?"

"Yes. I dropped troops when required."

"Such a waste. All those men… on both sides."

"Yeah… a waste."

"And the tree branch?"

"I was captured. I tried to escape."

"A booby-trap?"

"Yes."

"You are lucky you survived. Many did not."

"Yeah. Lucky."

When the water boiled, Dung poured it into the metal cup filling it to the brim. The hot water mixed with the grinds and dripped down into the glass. The hot coffee didn't mix with the condensed milk but sat on top. It would need to be stirred. When the first cup was filled he moved the metal cup over the top of the second glass and poured more water. Coffee was expensive. His guest would get the first pour and Dung would take the second. His wife sitting at the typewriter, Mrs. Lam, got nothing. "So how may I help you, Mr. Coyle?" said Dung sitting down across from Coyle.

"I'm looking for two girls. Women really," said Coyle.

"Americans?"

"No. Vietnamese," said Coyle handing Dung a photo of McGoon with a big cheesy smile standing on the bungalow's back patio between the two girls. Coyle remembered taking the photo with a Brownie camera that he had bought a few weeks after arriving in Vietnam. He had left the photo at Brigitte's apartment after showing it to her. He had planned on giving it to McGoon but never got around to it.

"Who is the man?"

"James McGovern. He was my friend. Everyone called him McGoon."

"Was?"

"He died at Dien Bien Phu. He was also an American pilot flying for the French."

"I see. I am sorry for your loss. Why do you want to find these two girls?"

"He was taking care of them."

"And they were taking care of him?"

"Yes. You could say that."

"Mr. Coyle, these types of arrangements happen often in Vietnam. When the arrangement has concluded for whatever reason, the girls usually go on to find another patron."

"That may be and if they did then that's okay. I just need to know that they are safe."

"You feel an obligation toward your dead friend?"

"Yes. Something like that."

"Do you know their names?"

"The one on the left is Chau and the one on the right is Nyuget," said Coyle pointing to each of the girls.

"And their family names?"

"I don't know."

"It will be difficult to find them without their family names."

"I know. I've got money."

"Of course you do. You're American."

"They lived with McGoon in a bungalow in the French quarter. Maybe his neighbors know their names."

"It's possible, but girls such as they are not usually sociable with the neighbors, especially if the neighbors are foreigners. Maybe a maid or another girl employed such as themselves, yes?"

"Yeah. That might work. I would have asked around but I don't speak Vietnamese."

"Not many foreigners do."

"Any idea how long it will take?"

"No. Not until I begin the investigation and see what I can discover. I will require a retainer."

"Of course. How much?"

"Five hundred American dollars."

"Five hundred? That seems like a lot."

"Working in Hanoi these days is risky. The closer we come to the communist takeover the more dangerous it will become."

"Yeah. I can see that. All right. I'll need to go to my bank and get the money."

"I will go with you… after we finish our coffee of course."

They stirred the condensed milk into their coffees and drank.

Brigitte walked through Jardins des Champs-Élysées that ran along the north side of the boulevard. It was the end of summer and fall was fast approaching. The leaves in the trees were bright yellow and would soon turn to orange, then brown before falling. She was happy to be in Paris. She had missed it while away on assignment in Indochina.

In her mind the world was full of fascinating places, but nothing beat Paris. In the distance sat the Arc de Triumph at the top of the boulevard and behind her was the Louvre; two of the world's greatest architectural wonders. The River Seine was to her left with its exquisite bridges and the cobblestone sidewalks that lined its banks. And then there were the parks. Paris was filled with parks lined with trees and plenty of trimmed grass for an afternoon nap. She loved it all. Her only regret was that Coyle could not be with her.

Brigitte had to admit to herself that she felt petty and jealous. Why was Coyle so hell-bent on finding those two girls? She questioned whether McGoon ever saw them as anything more than playthings. What kind of relationship could they have had with him more than sexual? They didn't speak English and he didn't speak Vietnamese. But Coyle was determined to find them and help them. He had even hired a private investigator. The situation in Hanoi was deteriorating quickly and she was worried what would happen to Coyle. She knew he could take care of himself under normal circumstances. God knows he had proven it in Dien Bien Phu. But what was happening in Hanoi was different than a war. It was panic and becoming chaotic. People did dangerous things when they felt insecure and threatened by an unstable future. They became desperate. She had seen it before in Paris when the German's invaded, and again in the prison camps when the Germans realized the Russians were coming.

He will have to leave Vietnam soon, she thought. I will demand it. No… not demand. Coyle wouldn't like that. He is his own man and must be convinced. I will just tell him. I almost lost him once. I don't want to risk that again. If he is going to be in my life, we must spend our time together. He should be here with me, where we are safe.

She considered that thought that for a moment… *What the hell was happening to me?* she thought. *I am a woman that jumps out of planes into a raging battle. Now listen to me… where we are safe?* She didn't like the feeling the thought had created. Love would not destroy Brigitte Friang.

As she walked through the park, Brigitte glanced over at a mother sitting on a bench fussing over the contents of a baby carriage. Next he'll want to have a baby together she thought. A baby? I am not a woman that stays at home and changes diapers… although a baby from the two of them would be adorable. A baby would cement their relationship and give them a common goal in life, something they lacked now. What would they name it? What if it was a girl?

She snapped out of it and looked at her wrist watch. She was late for her meeting. Enough daydreaming. There was work to be done. She picked up her pace.

Sami Djaout was relieved when he saw Brigitte Friang approaching the café where they had agreed to meet. He had arrived early to secure a table and she was running late. He thought she might have changed her mind. She had become a celebrity since Dien Bien Phu and her interviewing him was of great value to his missions. He had two objectives – first, to increase international awareness of the Algerian struggle for Independence and second, to raise funds from the large Algerian expatriate community in Paris for Messali Hadj's MNA organization. A story in Brigitte's magazine would help with both objectives.

He knew what Brigitte looked like from her photos in the magazine and in the newspapers that had announced her arrival back in Paris a few weeks earlier. She however did not know what he looked like. He stood and waved to her.

Brigitte saw the young man waving and nodded to him figuring that he was the MNA representative she had agreed to meet. The growing unease in Algeria was turning into a big story and promised to get bigger as protests grew in size and violence. Sami had offered to meet near her apartment, but she didn't like giving out her address. The MNA was considered one of the more peaceful Algerian Independence organizations, but there were some violent acts that had been suspected to have originated with the OS, the paramilitary wing of the MNA. It was better to meet in public where she knew she would be safe.

She understood that her notoriety made her a target for kidnapping and didn't want to take any undue risks. There that word was again… risks. Besides, she loved this café along the Champs-Élysées. It was a great place to people watch and she was one of the people that its customers liked to watch.

Café Wars

As she made her way through the narrow aisles of tables, Brigitte noticed a woman moving up quickly towards Sami. The woman was Marwa. Brigitte thought the woman must be an associate or perhaps another journalist that had seen her and was now trying to horn in on her interview.

Brigitte was close enough to get spattered with specks of blood when Marwa pulled out a revolver and fired three times into Sami's chest.

Brigitte's time working with the French military had taught her to hit the deck whenever she heard nearby gunfire. She landed hard on the cobblestone floor of the restaurant's patio. Patrons screamed and ran. *Get down,* she thought. *You're just an easy target when you run.* She considered yelling something to the fleeing crowd but then wondered if she also was the assassin's target.

She looked over at Sami as he collapsed to the ground knocking over his chair and grabbing the table cloth as he fell. The hot tea he had ordered came crashing down on top of him and burned his face. It was the least of his concerns. The three bullets in his chest were what focused his attention. He was bleeding badly and in shock. His eyes met Brigitte's. He looked confused. She wanted to help him but she was frozen in fear.

Marwa walked over and fired a coup de grace into Sami's temple, killing him. She looked over at Brigitte. Brigitte was looking straight at her. She knew Brigitte would be able to recognize her in a police lineup if it ever came to that. Marwa would have killed Brigitte but she had been given specific orders by Saadi to leave her unharmed. Marwa turned and ran off through the fleeing crowd. The Café Wars of Paris had begun.

Brigitte sat in a police station giving a description of the assassin to a police artist. "Her hair was long and black. It had tight curls."

"Did she have bangs or was all her hair the same length?" said the artist.

"Same length."

"What about the shape of her face?"

"It was long and shaped like an oval. Her eyebrows were thick but they had been plucked and shaped recently. There was a little bit of swelling."

"That's very good. I'm surprised you'd remember something like that."

"Yeah. So am I."

"What about her lips and nose?"

"Lips were full and her nose was long but not too thick. Delicate. She was very attractive."

A detective approached and said, "You mentioned you were there to interview him… the victim."

"Sami Djaout. Yes."

"Why were you interviewing him?"

"He represented the MNA."

"The terrorists?"

"I don't know if they are terrorists or not. That's one of the things we would have discussed, I suppose."

"Do you meet with terrorists often?"

"Like I said… not sure they are terrorists, but yeah I meet with potentially dangerous people all the time.

"And that doesn't scare you?"

"I'm cautious, but no, it doesn't scare me. When I interview someone they don't want to hurt me because I am going to tell their story. If anything they attempt to charm me, hoping I will portray them in a good light."

"So did he mention that anyone was trying to kill or do him harm?"

"No. We never actually talked, except on the phone. He was killed before the interview started."

"That's too bad."

"That he was killed?" said Brigitte.

"No. That he didn't say anything that would help us find his assassin. As far as Monsieur Djaout goes… good riddance."

Brigitte was exhausted by the time she returned to her apartment. Most days she would take the stairs up to the third floor, but today she was just too worn out, and elected to take the elevator. She hated the idea of being trapped in the contraption if the electricity went out, but today that just didn't seem important.

She pushed open the front door to her home and entered. Linh had already left for the day. It was late and Brigitte was hungry. She was too tired to make anything nutritious and the thought of going out again was completely unacceptable. She scrounged through kitchen cupboards and found an open box of tea biscuits. They were stale but she ate them anyway and washed them down with the last of a bottle of red table wine she had drunk the night before.

She thought about what had happened. She could not help but replay the assassination over and over in her mind. She wondered if she had missed something crucial that would help the police find the assassin that had killed Sami.

The woman had looked Algerian, maybe Moroccan. It didn't make a lot of sense. Most Algerians were for independence. Why would one Algerian gun down another Algerian and in Paris no less? She supposed she could have been working for Ultra – the militant pied-noir group - or the Red Hand. Brigitte played back the scene in her mind and she noticed something... when Sami was on the ground and he watched the assassin walking toward him, he had the look of recognition in his eyes. He knew the woman that killed him. That would explain the look of confusion when he looked over at Brigitte.

She had kept her head and was still alive. She would write her story in the morning. That was the great benefit in working for a magazine, no tight newspaper deadlines, plus her stories were allowed a higher number of words that a newspaper. She had space to explore a story in depth. Most good stories required space to report them correctly. But right now all she wanted was a bath and sleep.

She drew a hot bath. She unbutton her blouse and slipped it off. She looked at the specks of blood covering the front of the blouse. It was ruined. She would need to buy another. She tossed it in the trashcan. She looked in the mirror and saw the specks of blood on her face. Sami was all over her.

Most people would panic seeing another man's blood on their face, but not Brigitte. She knew death all too well. She had seen plenty of men torn up much worse than Sami. He was lucky, she thought. He died quickly and without much pain. She remembered the underground hospital in Dien Bien Phu where she worked for several weeks during the siege. The smell was the worst part of death. Most human do not smell pleasant in their final moments of life. She shivered from the memory.

She used soap and a washcloth to scrub off the dried blood. She didn't want Sami mixing in with the bath water. She hardly knew the man and it didn't seem appropriate.

She slipped into the hot tub and leaned back. She thought of Coyle. He would surely read about the murder in the western newspapers that were flown to the major cities in Vietnam bi-weekly. She knew her name would be at the forefront of every story about the assassination. He would be worried about her and call. The one thing she could always count on was Coyle's need to protect her, whether she liked it or not. She was ashamed to think that maybe Sami's death was not all bad… if it got Coyle to come home to her. She closed her eyes and thought of Coyle wrapping her in his arms and holding her close. It was a good thought after a bad day.

It was dusk. Bella sat on a berm overlooking the Mediterranean Sea. The lovers that had come to watch the sunset were gone. He was alone with his thoughts.

He had started a civil war between the underground factions that he knew was inevitable and he knew he was right for starting it. But that didn't make him feel any better. Bella had struck the first blow and knew that Messali would retaliate for the murder of his representative in Paris. That wasn't why

Bella felt bad. He had betrayed his mentor. A man he loved like his own father. The only thing he loved more was Algeria.

The decision to kill the MNA agent in Paris was simple. The more distasteful the FLN could make the war, the sooner it would end. Even though it had been ten years after the last rebellion, Parisians were accustom to violence in their streets. The difference was that they were the ones rebelling during the Nazi occupation and they were the ones shedding foreign blood. Now the Algerian rebels were rising up against them and taking the fight to the cafés and restaurants that Parisians so loved. There would be no peace until this was over. No relaxing coffee and a cigarette as the crowds strolled by the outdoor patios. It would not be a popular war if Bella had anything to do with it.

The violence Bella and the FLN were about to unleash on the French and the pied-noir would benefit both Algerian Independence organizations. The French would be faced with a dilemma – fight another guerilla war with the FLN as they had done with the Viet Minh or give into the Algerians' demands and grant them Independence. The MNA would benefit by looking more moderate. Given the choice between the FLN and the MNA, the MNA would be seen by the French as the lesser of two evils. The FLN would benefit by capturing most of the news headlines and would attract the Algerian youth and more radical elements to their movement. This was exactly what Bella needed. He wanted young recruits that he could train to fight his way and experienced veterans that had no qualms about doing what was necessary to win a war.

Messali was wrong. The underground organizations for Independence had to consolidate if they were going to beat the French as the Vietnamese had done. Bella knew that Messali's organization was small but it would grow as the rebellion grew. Bella could not afford to have Algerians choose between the two organizations. He needed every man he could get. The FLN would become stronger as the MNA diminished in power and influence. Messali's followers would abandon the MNA and join Bella's FLN once they realized that their struggle against both the French and the FLN was doomed.

Bella convinced himself that, even though they disagreed, Messali would be proud of what his student had become. More than just a fighter, Bella was now the leader of a movement that would hopefully lead to Independence. Bella also convinced himself that if given a chance he would kill the old man. It saddened him that he had grown to hate the French more that he loved Messali.

FIVE

It was early morning. Coyle was running his preflight check on the C-119 he was going to fly to Paris. He had not read the newspapers and knew nothing of the attack in Paris involving Brigitte.

His felt his shoulder had healed to the point he could fly again and he was anxious to get back in the pilot's seat. He had informed his former boss at CAT and he immediately gave Coyle the route to Paris to ferry troops home.

Coyle was one of the few pilots that could handle the big C-119 boxcars. After many heroic attempts to resupply the French troops at Dien Bien Phu, the French had more aircraft than pilots to fly them. The C-119 could carry three times as many passengers as the next biggest aircraft in the French fleet. Soldiers were anxious to leave Vietnam, plus France was falling behind in lowering its troop commitment levels according to their agreement with the North Vietnamese. The French did not want a restart of the conflict. Not now. Not when they were almost out.

It had been an international embarrassment for France, once the world's greatest military force under the leadership of Napoleon, to lose to a third world nation like Vietnam. The more time that passed the more the French government just wanted to forget the whole damned affair.

France was an American ally and Coyle didn't like seeing the French in such a weakened state, especially with the Cold War boiling up. But he was also conflicted about France's motives during the Indochina War. They were an imperialist government trying to hang on to their empire. Vietnam was a colony fighting for its freedom as America had once fought for its Independence from Britain. It was true that the Viet Minh were backed by the Russian and Chinese communists and therefore the enemy of America.

And then there was Brigitte. She was definitely French and as much as she tried to report the truth her French bias showed through her writing. Coyle had volunteered to fight for the French at Dien Bien Phu, but that was more to save Brigitte who was trapped within the garrison than to support the French cause. Coyle decided keeping his mouth shut was the wisest move. Whatever the Indochina War meant, it was over and everyone just wanted to get on with their lives.

Coyle heard a familiar sound in the distance; the low, deep voices of men singing 'Le Marche.' He turned to see a group of French paratroopers marching toward his aircraft. At their head, was Bruno. His uniform and the uniforms of the men under his command clung to what was left of their bodies which was mostly skin and bones. The muscles from years of training were gone and the skin on their faces sagged off their cheek bones. The average French soldier had lost over 50 pounds during the four months of captivity under the Viet Minh. They were the lucky ones. Many had starved to death.

Bruno stopped his men in front of the aircraft loading ramp and approached Coyle. "You made it, Monsieur Coyle," he said.

"And so did you, Colonel Bigeard… at least some of you," said Coyle.

"Yes. I went into Dien Bien Phu with over 800 paratroopers under my command. Now I have forty. Not much of a battalion, I fear."

"I was referring to the meat on your bones. You've lost a few kilos."

"Oh, yes. The Viet Minh did not understand the appetite of the French."

"I heard. I tried to imagine you eating rice every day."

"Rice every day? That would have been nice."

"Well at least you are on your way back home. French croissants and cheese should fatten you and your men back up in no time."

"Yes. Yes. I think you are right. How is Brigitte?"

"She's good. Back in Paris writing for Politiques Internationales."

"And you are here?"

"I had some things I needed to attend to before I joined her."

"Ah, then you will be living in Paris with Brigitte and I?"

"Yeah, I guess I will."

"Do not worry, Monsieur Coyle. I shall keep a good eye on Brigitte for you while you are gone."

"I am sure you will."

"With your permission, my men will board."

"Permission granted."

Bruno moved off to supervise the loading of his men and their gear. Coyle continued his preflight check, but his mind was elsewhere. He liked Bruno but he did not trust him when it came to Brigitte. And he wasn't sure he trusted Brigitte when it came to Bruno.

Brigitte sat at her kitchen table typing a story and drinking the last of a bottle of wine. She often drank while writing. Nothing too heavy. Wine helped her relax and lose her inhibitions about writing poorly. Respect from her readers was something Brigitte craved and that need often got in her way by creating a kind of writer's block. Two glasses of wine solved writer's block. Four or five glasses of wine and she was useless. It was a fine line that she tread. At the moment she was creeping toward the line. She finished the last paragraph when there was a knock at the door.

She placed the security chain that she had installed between the door jam and the door. It allowed her to see out without completely opening the door. After the assassination at the café, she felt security was not a bad idea. She opened the door and peered out through the gap.

Coyle and Bruno were standing in the hallway. She had no idea that either was coming. Without a word, she slammed the door shut so she could remove the chain.

Coyle and Bruno looked at each and shrugged. "I've been locked up in a prison for the last four months. It must be you," said Bruno.

"What did I do?" said Coyle.

"I have no idea. What did you do?"

Brigitte fumbled with the lock and opened the door. She hugged Bruno first which was not lost on Coyle. Coyle understood but could not help feeling jealous.

"You are free, my little Bruno," she said. "You are nothing but skin and bones."

"I may have lost a kilo or two," said Bruno.

She released Bruno and wrapped her arms around Coyle kissing him multiple times. "I had no idea you were coming. Why didn't you call?"

"I was gonna, but then I thought it could be a nice surprise," said Coyle.

"Come in. Come in." Brigitte ushered them into the apartment.

"We shall celebrate. A chicken or goose, I think," she said.

"Both sound good to me," said Coyle.

"And me," said Bruno.

"Do either of you know how to cook a chicken or a goose?" said Brigitte.

Both shrugged no. "Then we shall go out," said Brigitte. "I do not know how to cook anything not in a can."

"But you're French. I thought all French knew how to cook," said Coyle.

"You thought wrong," said Brigitte grabbing her coat and purse.

"Brigitte is a modern woman, Coyle," said Bruno. "I assure you she has other attributes you will appreciate far more than cooking."

"Listen to Bruno, Tom," said Brigitte pushing them out of the apartment and closing the door behind her.

The restaurant Brigitte had chosen was a bistro near her apartment. She had considered taking them to one of the more touristy restaurants near the Eiffel Tower or the Opera House but decided against it because of the noise and smoke. Tourists smoked like chimneys. Besides, the wine at the bistro was good and cheap. The food was simple. Coyle was a little disappointed that goose was not on the menu. He had never tasted goose and imagined that if anyone knew how to cook a goose if would be the French. He settled for the bistro's amuse-bouche - goose foie gras on a cracker and a complimentary glass of house wine.

Brigitte ordered an entire boeuf en croute with a side of Gratin dauphinoise for Bruno and refused to take no for an answer. The beef pie was normally served to two or three people and the gratin potatoes were cooked with almost a half of a kilo of cheese. She was determined to fatten him up as quickly as possible before he was shipped off to battle again.

Coyle, who ordered the beef bourguignon, was fairly certain the pie would kill Bruno before he finished it by bursting his shrunken stomach and suggested he chase it down with a bottle of red wine to help with the digestion.

Brigitte ordered a plate of escargot and the coq au vin for herself. French women were known for eating portions meant for squirrels. Brigitte was the exception but still managed to remain slender.

Brigitte was a celebrity, and good for business. The bistro owner came over to ensure she was happy once her meal had been served. She was. He stayed for a short visit and another complimentary glass of wine for each of them.

As the night wore on, so did the stories. "I can't believe we are all here," said Coyle. "That we survived that hell hole."

"Oh, Dien Bien Phu was not that bad. We had food and wine up until the end," said Brigitte.

"What followed was far worse," said Bruno.

"We all heard the stories. How did you and your men survive?" said Brigitte.

"Many didn't. Those that did had something worth living for."

"And what was that for you?" said Brigitte, hopeful.

"France, of course," said Bruno. "…and my men. There wasn't much I could do for them except to encourage them to hang on."

"Any idea where you are going next?" said Brigitte.

"I have been offered a position at École des Troupes Aéroportées – France's school for paratroopers."

"Then you would live here in Paris?" said Brigitte lighting up.

"Yes. You can keep an eye on me. Maybe find me a woman that can cook goose."

"Hard to imagine you as a teacher," said Coyle.

"I agree," said Bruno. "But I suppose it is important to pass on what I have learned over the years. It could save many lives and help France win the next war."

"The next war?" said Coyle.

"There will always be war. We are not a peaceful species."

"And where will be the next war?" said Brigitte.

"You tell me, Brigitte," said Bruno.

"Perhaps here in Paris."

"You think it's that bad?"

"It's not good. The Algerians want Independence and I believe they will go to great lengths to earn it."

"You were lucky you were not the target," said Bruno.

"Target? What are you talking about?" said Coyle, concerned.

"You need to learn enough French to read the newspapers, my friend," said Bruno.

"And you should learn to keep quiet when affairs do not concern you, Bruno," said Brigitte.

"What the hell is going on?" said Coyle.

Brigitte considered for a moment, then said, "Last week there was a man that I was supposed to interview at a café. He was gunned down by an Algerian assassin in front of me. At least I believe she was Algerian."

"She?"

"Yes. The assassin was a woman."

"Did the police catch her?"

"No."

"Then she could still be out there hunting for you."

"She did not want me. She was with the FLN. It was a message to a competing organization."

"A message?"

"Of sorts, yes."

"Why didn't you tell me?"

"I was going to – at the proper moment."

"And when was that?"

"Not here. Not now," said Brigitte growing angry. "Thank you for that, Bruno."

"Better not to let it fester," said Bruno.

"So, what are they doing about it?" said Coyle.

"The police are searching for the woman. I gave them a good description."

"The police are useless," said Bruno. "I'm sure the killer is back in Algeria by now."

"I meant your magazine. How are they going to protect you?" said Coyle.

"They are not. I am a war correspondent, Coyle. They know I have faced far worse than this and that I can handle myself. You should know the same." She got up from the table. "If you will excuse me, I am going to pee… by myself."

She stomped off to the toilet at the back of the bistro. "Now she's mad at you," said Bruno.

"You love to stir the pot, don't you?" said Coyle.

"It's a talent," said Bruno finishing the last of the beef pie.

Gamal Abdel Nasser, the de facto president of Egypt, was not happy when Bella entered his Cairo office and took a seat on his couch. Nasser had just foiled an assassination plot against himself by a member of the Muslim Brotherhood. The current Egyptian president, Mohamad Naghuib, was under suspicion of being one of the conspirators against Nasser and had been placed under house arrest. With the Egyptian generals backing him, Nasser had taken over as chief executive of Egypt until he could be rightfully elected president by the people. "We have a chance to show the world that we are a civilized people and you start a war with a fellow Arab," said Nasser getting right to the point.

Café Wars

"It was necessary," said Bella. "We need to consolidate our forces to defeat the French Army."

"You will never defeat the French Army. They are too rich and too powerful. They can replace their troops at a much faster rate than you can. The French Army is well trained and battle tested having fought an eight year war in Indochina. Given enough time they will crush you and your rebellion. Besides, you do not need to defeat the French militarily. You are fighting a political battle and your little civil war is not helping your cause. It only proves what the French politicians have been saying, that Arabs are tribal and cannot rule an entire country themselves."

Bella knew what Nasser was saying made sense. He had come to the same conclusion, but he thought it more prudent to let Nasser lecture him as a father lectures a son. The Algerian Independence movement needed Nasser's help. Egypt was a sanctuary for the FLN and Nasser was well respected as a leader in the Middle East. The discovery of oil was still new to the Arabs and power had not yet shifted to Iran, Iraq and Saudi Arabia.

Egypt also had a seat at the United Nations and could plead the Algerians' case to the other world leaders. If France was to be pressured to give up Algeria, the pressure would need to be both internal and external. International opinion weighed greatly on the French government after their loss of Indochina. "The U.N. is on your side. Imperialism is out of fashion. Democracy and self-determination are the new international watchwords," said Nasser. "Your Arab brothers are on your side, but they won't stay on your side if you continue this foolishness with Messali and the MNA."

"We have made our point," said Bella. "We will stop the violence as long as he does not retaliate."

"I see little chance of that now that you have thrown down the gauntlet."

"It was one man."

"It was a public execution... and in Paris, no less," said Nasser. "Maybe if you offered him an olive branch."

"Such as?"

"The female assassin that shot his agent. Give her to Messali."

"Messali will have her killed."

"Yes. I would think so. But it may stop the war."

Bella considered for a long moment. He did not want to anger Nasser. "I will take the proposal to my fellow leaders," he said. "I do not know how they will respond."

"See that they respond in a positive manner, Bella. If your revolution is to be successful, you will need Egypt's help. You will need my help."

Nasser's message was not lost on Bella. He would see that the violence between he and Messali stopped for now. But he also knew that Messali would most likely retaliate and when he did, Bella and the FLN would be justified to respond in kind. The civil war would continue and that was exactly what Bella wanted.

Bella knew very well that any settlement between the Algerians and the French would need to be diplomatic. The FLN needed to weaken France's resolve to get them to the negotiating table as the Viet Minh had done. The FLN would need to turn public opinion against the imperialists, and the best way to do that was to increase the cost of colonialism through violence. Bella's little civil war in the cafés of Paris was the perfect platform to elevate French pain and he wasn't about to let it go… not even for Nasser.

On his way back to the safe house Nasser had arranged for him, Bella purchased a copy of Politiques Internationales from a newsstand. He read the article Brigitte had written on the assassination. He admitted to himself that her coverage of the event was fair in its portrayal. Bella was not interested in fair. Brigitte Friang was a celebrity and people listened to celebrities. He wondered if there was a way to turn Brigitte toward the Independent movement. She was smart and should clearly see the justice of their argument. And yet, she was French through and through.

Bella wondered if Brigitte might be used in another way to help the cause. Her death, especially if it were violent, would sent shock waves throughout France. The French public would mourn her as a fallen hero. Even a martyr perhaps. He didn't care what they thought of her. He wanted to cause France pain and Brigitte's death would be sure to do that. The more pain the French were forced to endure the more likely they would give up Algeria to avoid more pain in the future.

Of course, Nasser would never approve. They would risk losing Egypt's support for such a hideous act. But such a feat might push the scales in Algeria's favor, and Nasser loved to bet on a winner. Bella's mind was settled. It was worth the risk. He would take up the proposal of Brigitte Friang's assassination at the next meeting of the leaders of the FLN.

A cargo ship was docked in the Port of Oran on the western coast of Algeria. Oran was the closest major port to France, which kept it busy. Longshoremen worked twenty-four hours a day to unload the ships docked at the port. Another dozen ships were anchored in the harbor waiting their turn to be unloaded and loaded.

Algeria was a major supplier of raw materials and foodstuffs to France and other European countries. France shipped back finished goods to be sold in the Algerian markets. It was a typical colonial system of trade with France having the advantage of higher priced goods and the ability to tax. As unfair as the system appeared, it provided millions of Algerians with jobs which they might not have had if the country was left to his own devices. Imperialists were efficient at taking advantage of their colonists.

An Algerian stevedore loaded crates into a cargo net in the forward hold of a ship. He had been trained by his FLN handler to recognize the labels of weapons and ammunition heading for French Army bases. He filled the net and attached the net to the crane hook lowered into the hold. He told his supervisor that he was taking a quick break for a piss and a smoke. The supervisor nodded his consent. The stevedore grabbed the top of the net and put his feet on the ropes below. Riding the load was the fastest way to reach shore. It was also one of the most dangerous, especially if the load shifted. It could easily crush a man's hand or foot and leave him dangling for his life high above the cargo hold.

The cargo net carrying the stevedore rose out of the hold and swung over to the dock. The stevedore jumped off just before the crane set the load down. He pulled out a cigarette and signaled a vendor selling hot coffee to make him a double. He glanced back at the crates just unloaded and made a mental note of the number stenciled on the back bumper of the truck onto which the crates were being loaded. Then he walked to a dockside payphone and made a call to his FLN handler to notify him of the weapons and ammunition shipment. The FLN handler had another informant in the transportation office that would give him the schedule and destination of the truck.

The FLN needed weapons and ammunition to fight their war against the French and terrorize the pied-noir. The easiest way to acquire them was to steal them from the French. Ambushes were set up whenever a French arms shipment arrived in port. The rebels would wait until the supply convoy left the port facility on its way to the French Army bases. Once the FLN mobilized, few shipments arrived at their intended destinations.

The FLN's methods would vary. Sometimes they would feign an accident and ambush the convoy when it stopped to help. Other times they would arrange for road work to be done on the main highway between the port and the capital. When the convoy stopped for the sign-man, the rebels would pounce. The convoy drivers were usually spared, especially if they were Algerian and did not resist.

But their favorite tactic was to wait until nightfall, then dig a trench across the road and let the front wheels of the lead truck fall into the trench. An attack would follow and capture the arms and supplies.

The FLN had eyes everywhere. Young boys on bicycles relayed intelligence throughout the country. Bed sheets on rooftops became signals that a convoy had departed a port or base. Even Algerian radio broadcasts of seemingly nonsensical phrases were utilized to send signals as the British had done to notify the French underground of pending missions against the Nazis during the occupation.

In this way, the rebels were fed an endless supply of arms and ammunition by the French convoys. Their supply of arms would need to keep pace with the expansion of their movement. Nobody wanted to fight the French unless they were given the weapons to do so. Some of the weapons would be sold off to criminals and underground movements in other nations. Cash was always king and could be used to buy information or bribe officials when required.

Smuggling was also an effective method. The FLN had sympathizers throughout Europe and the Middle East. Raising money was easy and buying arms was even easier. Getting them into Algeria and past the French border guards was the difficult part. But the rebels were ingenious. Bullets were hidden in dried dates and figs from Egypt. A heavy machine gun was hidden in a secret compartment inside a wooden cross bound for an Algerian Catholic church. Pistols were smuggled in metal olive oil cans from Italy. Grenades and shells for their bazookas were hidden inside the day's catch by Algerian fishermen.

Once inside Algeria everything had to be stored in secret for the day when it would be needed. Mosques were often used. Local businesses had tunnels dug below their warehouses and factories. They even used Christian cemeteries where the Algerians would dig up an existing gravesite, remove the corpse for cremation later and rebury the casket filled with weapons and ammunition. Night was their co-conspirator and allowed the rebels to work without the prying eyes of the French.

The stevedore hung up the phone, bought his coffee and sat down on a load of wheat bags to finish his cigarette before returning to the ship. He watched the two French soldiers patrolling the docks as they passed by. *Soon they would be forced to leave and Algeria would be free,* he thought. *Very soon.*

SIX

Bruno wore his dress uniform with its multiple decorations and awards as he waited in front of the Palais Garnier. The baroque-style Opera House was nothing short of glorious with its stone-carved façade capped with golden statues and a green-patina roof.

Bruno did not own a suit, much less a tuxedo. His dress uniform was the best he had for formal occasions. He was hesitant to accept Brigitte's last minute invitation to escort her to the opening performance of *Cendrillon*.

Brigitte climbed out of a cab. She was a vision in her evening gown with her hair up. Coyle had bought the tickets because he knew Brigitte loved the opera but was called in to fly a brigade of paratroopers back from Hanoi when another pilot came down with the stomach flu. Brigitte mused that the last minute call for the Air Force dispatcher was suspiciously timed since she knew Coyle was not a fan of the opera... any opera.

Bruno was not a fan either but he liked to be seen with Brigitte on his arm and he couldn't think of a good excuse in time. Brigitte imagined that Coyle thought she would invite one of her female friends to accompany her. Inviting Bruno to escort her was a reminder to Coyle not to assume anything when it came to Brigitte.

Brigitte loved the opera… any opera. It was the pageantry that she loved most. Seeing everyone in high-society dressed to the nines.

Politicians liked to be seen at the opera. It made them seem cultured when their constituents saw their photos in the society columns of the newspapers and magazines. They put on airs and displayed their best manners. Brigitte found this amusing, but always played along. She knew that tomorrow they would be stabbing each other in the back. The opera was a great place to make and renew contacts. It was more difficult for a government official to refuse an interview when he knew he might run into Brigitte at a social function among their friends. Brigitte was a master at the game of social pressure.

Bruno saw her and walked down the curved stone stairs to greet her, "Brigitte, you look lovely."

"Thank you. You clean up pretty good yourself, Little Bruno," said Brigitte. "Is that a new decoration?"

"Yes. Yes. I had it sewed on at the last minute by my landlady. I thought you might like it."

"I like them all. They show your bravery and love for your country."

"Perhaps but I prefer action rather than bits of cloth to show my patriotism."

"You are too modest."

"Modest? I think not. Shall we go inside?" He offered her his arm.

They walked back up the spiral stairs toward the main doors. Brigitte always entered the opera house in the center doors even if it meant waiting a few extra minutes in line. On entering, the view of the grand staircase with its balustrade of red and green marble and the painted canopy ceiling above were breathtaking. The only room that could compare was the grand foyer, with its golden pillars, crystal chandeliers, and painted ceiling panels by Paul Baudry, to which the stairs led.

Across the street Marwa sat in the backseat of a taxi watching as Bruno and Brigitte entered the opera house. Marwa knew very well what Brigitte looked like from when their eyes met after Sami Djaout's assassination. Marwa was happy that Saadi and the council had changed their minds and now wanted Brigitte Friang assassinated. Marwa would be only too happy to comply with their wishes.

It wasn't that Marwa hated Brigitte. She didn't know Brigitte. It was that Brigitte represented everything Marwa hated about France. Brigitte dressed like a modern woman and did not cover her hair. Her dresses where too short and showed her ankles. She was confident and looked men in the eye. Marwa saw all of what Brigitte was as disrespectful to her culture and religion. Marwa felt it was her duty to protect the world from people like Brigitte Friang. People that wanted to abandon the old ways and embrace the new, unproven ways. People that had no respect for Allah, her God. Brigitte's death would be a symbol of Allah's will and power.

Marwa had agreed with Saadi that killing Brigitte at such a public event would have the greatest shock value and was sure to capture international headlines. But the police presence had tripled since her last scouting mission. She could not hope to escape once her mission was accomplished. Saadi had taught her that it was important to survive any attack if possible so she could fight another day and serve Allah well. There would be other opportunities, she thought. Brigitte was a very public person. Marwa ordered the taxi driver to take her back to the apartment Saadi had arranged for her.

Egypt was safe. Bella watched as his young fighters trained with the Egyptian Army. The Egyptians had excellent training facilities for their troops and Bella planned to take full advantage of Nasser's gracious offer.

Bella was not stupid. He knew that Nasser would want something in exchange for his support. Nasser had aspirations of becoming the leader of the Arab Nations as they broke free from their oppressors. Nasser would expect Bella and the other leaders of the FLN to support his bid for power once Algeria gained its Independence.

Nasser was a shrewd politician and understood the importance of keeping the military on his side. He made sure the Egyptian soldiers had the best facilities and weapons that the country could afford. The Army and Air Force generals were his most important power base and he knew his survival depended on their loyalty. They had backed him after the president's attempt to assassinate him and he made sure they were rewarded for their loyalty. The people could be charmed and convinced with rhetoric. The generals required cash and seaside villas.

Bella's ideas on training his soldiers were simple. Fifty FLN mujahideen would be trained in Egypt until they were proficient at military tactics and techniques. Those fifty would be dispersed throughout Algeria where they each would train ten more every three weeks. It was not safe to train more than ten at any one time in the country. Too large a group would attract attention from the French Intelligence units and their informants. Bella would need to be patient while he built his army.

In addition Bella would personally train five commando teams of four men each. The commandos would learn to strike hard at key targets, then disappear into the countryside or cities. Their missions would be less about killing and more about destabilization. Utilities, bridges, airfields, radio towers, and police stations were their focus. They would tie up large numbers of French soldiers assigned to hunt them down. They would lay booby-traps for the French soldiers and kill as many as possible. The commandos would only attack when the French forces were divided and dispersed. When French units were detached and small numbers of the soldiers could be isolated. Only when victory was assured.

Bella knew that his forces would be greatly outnumbered right from the start. He also knew that his army would grow when the people saw success in the struggle against their oppressors. Nothing was a better recruiter than success. The people would be willing to sacrifice their lives for the cause, but they did not want their lives wasted.

With luck the French would overreact against the planned attacks. Bella wanted the French to flex their military muscle against the Algerians. He wanted them to teach the people a lesson and keep them in line. The more military might the French used against the Algerians the faster his army would grow and the faster the revolution would progress. Bella needed to strike hard and enrage the French beyond reason. He would not make the same mistake the Algerians had made ten years earlier after the Setif Massacre and negotiate for better conditions. There would be no more negotiations until they had won their Independence. Once the fire was started he would pour on the oil until it engulfed the entire nation.

Coyle sat in the cockpit of the C-119 with his French co-pilot, navigator and engineer. None of them spoke English and what little French he knew was of little use. Instead, they communicated through a kind of sign language that they had made up. They had been flying for over four hours on their mission to ferry troops back to France. This time it was a demi-brigade of paratroopers. Coyle needed to urinate. He motioned to his co-pilot that he was going to pee by making an arc motion with his thumb and forefinger. The co-pilot nodded. He motioned that he had the wheel and was in control of the aircraft. Coyle got up and exited the cockpit.

There was only one toilet on the plane for the five crew members including the crew chief and sixty seven paratroopers that rode in the cargo hold on very uncomfortable canvas seats. There was a line. As pilot, Coyle had the right to jump the line, but he didn't. He wanted to stretch his legs. Since the cargo hold was filled with the paratroopers' gear and there was no place to walk, standing was the best he could do. He got in line with the others. "You are American?" said a voice.

Coyle turned to see a Lieutenant Colonel standing behind him. "What gave me away?" said Coyle.

"You are not smoking."

Coyle looked down the line of paratroopers and to the man every single one was either lighting a cigarette, smoking a cigarette or putting out a cigarette butt in the bucket of sand secured to the deck. "Oh, we Americans smoke. We just breath in-between," said Coyle.

"Very prudent," said the Lieutenant Colonel. "You fly for the French Air Force?"

"Kinda. I'm a subcontractor. I work for Civilian Aviation Transport."

"CIA?"

"I couldn't say."

"Of course not. Nice to know you can keep a secret. I am Roger Trinquier."

"Tom Coyle," said Coyle shaking his hand. "Is this bunch yours', Colonel?"

"Yes. My bunch."

"It'll be good to get home... to France I mean."

"Yes. But it would have been better if we were victorious. No parade, I think."

"Probably not. But good wine."

"Ah yes. The wine... and bread."

"... and the cheese. Don't forget the cheese."

"I would never be so bold. So, you flew at Dien Bien Phu?"

"Yeah. I was there."

"And you knew the two Americans that were lost?"

"Yeah. I knew them. They were my friends."

"Losing one's friend is always difficult. I am sorry for your loss. Pity. We could have used more pilots."

"I don't think it would have mattered."

"Really? Why is that?"

"They were more determined."

"The Viet Minh?"

"Yeah. They just kept coming. Didn't matter how many were killed. Their generals just replaced them and they kept charging up the hills until the garrison ran out of ammunition. It was inevitable."

"I don't think anything is inevitable. Even in war. It is like you say… a battle of wills. The side that is more determined has the advantage no matter the numbers."

"So, you think the French could have won the war?"

"Of course. We just were not prepared to go the full measure."

"The full measure?"

"To do whatever it takes to win."

"And what might that have been? An American atomic bomb?"

"Bombs are of little use when fighting a guerilla war. Information is the most effective weapon. He who has the most will usually win."

"That's probably true but useful information is hard to come by."

"It is when our leaders refuse to see the truth."

"What do you mean?"

"A terrorist that attacks civilians should not be treated as a criminal. He is a combatant and should be treated as a soldier."

"I would agree with that."

"The information that a terrorist possesses can often save dozens if not hundreds of civilian lives, especially if the information is revealed in the first seventy-two hours after capture when it is still relevant. There are times when extreme measures must be used for the good of public safety."

"You mean torture?"

"At times… yes. But there are other means that are also effective, such as coercion."

"Coercion?"

"Threatening a member of the terrorist's family for example."

"What if the family member is not guilty of any crime?"

"It is doubtful. However a threat alone will usually suffice. Actual mistreatment is rarely required."

"Rarely?"

"Monsieur Coyle, one must be prepared for collateral damage if one is to wage war effectively. Surely you must understand this as a former fighter pilot?"

"What makes you think I was a fighter pilot?"

"I doubt the CIA would recruit you if you were not accustomed to violence. Yes?"

The door to the toilet opened. It was Coyle's turn and he chose not to answer Trinquier's question. "I guess that's me," said Coyle.

"Nice talking with you, Monsieur Coyle," said Trinquier.

"Just Coyle if you don't mind."

"Of course, Coyle."

Algeria had become a main theatre of battle during World War II after the Germans invaded. Operation Torch featured both U.S. and British landings on the shores of the Mediterranean. To stop the retaking of previously captured territory, the German's had planted thousands of mines, some heavy enough to take out a tank. It was those heavy mines that Saadi sought when he entered a clearly marked minefield that had been left behind by the Germans.

The field had previously been a road leading to the forests in the mountains between the ocean and the Sahara desert. The road had long been abandoned as too dangerous when several locals had been killed on it. Saadi knew that the heavy mines would be deep so that only a tank weighing ten tons or more would trip the firing mechanism. It wasn't those mines that worried him. It was the vehicle and anti-personnel mines that made him apprehensive. They were shallow and a man's weight could set them off. Even after ten years of rain and rust, many were still active. The Germans believed in quality and it showed in the manufacturing of mines.

Saadi and the few men that he brought with him did not have a mine detector. Instead, they used long stiff wires to probe beneath the packed clay that made up the road. It was a painstaking process that was often interrupted by French patrol aircraft flying overhead. When one of the men found something hard below the surface, Saadi would order his men to back away to a safe distance and he would move in to uncover and defuse the mine, then scavenge the precious high explosives inside the mechanism.

After several days, Saadi was still alive and he had what he needed to carry out his mission. The explosives were packed and sealed in metal drums, then lowered into the storage tank on the back of a septic truck. Even knowing the storage tank was an ideal place to smuggle weapons and supplies, the

French soldiers at the roadblocks would avoid inspecting the septic trucks. The Algerians only used their precious fleet of stolen septic trucks for the most important contraband.

Saadi sat at a table in a windowless room behind his bakery. The door was closed and he was alone. Before him were the makings of several bombs and the tins of tea biscuits in which he would hide them. The tea biscuits were the perfect size for an anti-personnel device plus the metal container turned to shrapnel when it exploded.

The high explosives in the German mines had not lost any of their potency. At least that was the theory but Saadi didn't totally trust the explosives. They had been exposed to the extreme heat during the summer months and the bitter cold Algerian nights. He had a limited supply of French high explosive material that one of his insurgents had recovered from a bomb at an airfield during the arming of one of the French fighter bombers. Emptied of its explosives the bomb had fallen harmlessly during a practice flight out in the Sahara desert and the French thought it a dud.

Saadi knew he could count on the French explosives and decided to use one part French with three parts German explosives in each device he was preparing.

He had considered using a mechanical timing detonator in the package. It would be easier to set the timer on the device before the explosive package was handed to the person delivering it, but mechanical devices sometimes failed if they were jostled around too much. Instead he had elected to use a British pencil detonator. The British pencil detonator was one of the most reliable methods ever created to discharge a bomb. The chemical pencil would need to be crimped with a pair of pliers once the bomb was in place. He would need to carefully instruct the person planting the bomb on the correct procedure and on the timing of the explosion for maximum effect.

Crimping the pencil would break the glass vial of acetone inside which in turn would begin eating away at the tiny wall of material between the liquid and the small amount of explosives on the other end of the pencil. The thickness of the wall determined the amount of time before the chemical reaction occurred that exploded the device. When the acetone came into contact with the explosive material the pencil would explode. The small explosion would set off the high explosive material, creating a much larger explosion. It was a very simple device and its simplicity made it reliable.

Saadi would only prepare enough packages for one week's worth of underground warfare. He had eleven tea tins sitting on the table. It was going to be a long night.

His girls had been well trained on where to place the deadly packages. In the center of the target was best so the effect of the blast radius could be maximized. Never behind a wall or anything too solid.

During the last assassination attempt at the highly secure Wolf's Lair bunker, Hitler had been saved because the explosive package had been placed behind an oak table leg which deflected the majority of the blast away from him. Saadi had learned from others' mistake and had handed down his knowledge to his three sirens.

Everything up to that point had been preparation and training. Tomorrow would be the start of the war for Algerian Independence. In the beginning, the FLN had five hundred men at arms. The French Army in Algeria numbered over fifty three thousand.

SEVEN

November 1, 1954 was All Saints Day – a catholic festival honoring the lives and deaths of all the saints. It was also the day the FLN had decided to begin the Algerian War for Independence. The day would be renamed and remembered as Toussaint Rouge or Red All Saints Day in France and Algeria.

It was just past midnight when nineteen year old Francois Laurent was leaving the Cassaigne police station in the city of Oran. His friend had been in a bicycle accident and charged with assault. By the time Francois arrived to pay the required bail, his friend had been released, because the charges had been dropped. It was all for nothing and Francois had to work early in the morning. Fortunately his home was only a few blocks away.

He was unchaining his bicycle from the light pole when three men from across the street emerged from the shadows holding submachines guns. They opened fire racking the police station and shattering all the windows with a fusillade of bullets. Francois was caught between the gunmen and the building. He was hit six times and fell dead on the sidewalk. He was the first civilian casualty of the Algerian War. There would be more… many more.

Jean Vaujour, Prefect of the Algerian police, alerted the French district military commander of the incident and the death of the young man. Vaujour correctly predicted it was the beginning of a countrywide insurrection. His warning was ignored. He was informed that the soldiers stationed in Algeria would stay in their barracks and on their bases until the trouble had passed. The French government did not want to panic the public by using the military when they felt the local police could handle the few rebels in each of the districts. Vaujour had two thousand three hundred police officers under his command to control ten million Algerians. The rebel attacks were just beginning.

It was a cloudless morning in Algiers – the capital of Algeria and its largest city. The streets were filled with shoppers and Europeans on holiday enjoying the crisp Mediterranean air. Christmas was approaching and some of the shoppers were growing anxious to find just the right gift for their loved ones.

Saadi handed a shopping bag from a local tea shop to Nihad, one of his three sirens. He handed her a pair of pliers which she slid into her purse. He could see that she was nervous. He smiled to reassure her. It helped. She smiled back. He said a prayer and kissed her on the top of the head as a father would do. She turned and walked down the street.

Saadi watched her from a safe distance. He was discreet, only giving an occasional glance in her direction as he sat on the front stairs of an apartment building peeling and eating an orange.

Nihad walked into a plaza and sat down in a sidewalk café.

Saadi was displeased with the table that she had chosen at the edge of the serving area. He would need to instruct Nihad and the two other girls better when her mission was over and she was debriefed. He decided not to scold her. Nihad was young and impressionable. He knew that his opinion meant a great deal to her. He would be gentle in his rebuke. He would tell her that it was her first time and he had expected her to be a little nervous. She would do better the next time and pay more attention to the details she had been taught about where to place the bomb. This was all assuming that she did not blow herself up in the minutes that followed. Saadi said a prayer and hoped for the best.

A waiter came over to the table and Nihad ordered a tea with milk and sugar as the Europeans preferred. When the waiter left, Nihad picked up the shopping bag and placed it in her lap. She opened her purse and pulled out the pliers. She reached into the shopping bag and opened the lid on the tea biscuit box inside. She crimped the British pencil detonator as Saadi had instructed her and placed the lid back on the box. She put the pliers back in her purse and set the shopping bag back on the ground next to the table.

When the waiter brought her tea, she asked him where the toilet was located. He pointed to the back of the restaurant. She got up with her purse in hand and left the bag under the table.

She walked into the restaurant and toward the back where the toilet was located. She walked past the toilet and out the back door into an alley behind the restaurant.

One minute later the bomb exploded killing a European woman seated next to the girl's table and the waiter serving her a pastry and coffee. Twelve more civilians were injured from flying shrapnel. All the windows in the immediate area were shattered from the overpressure of the explosion.

Saadi was pleasantly surprised by the power of the blast. The German explosives were still very potent and the British pencil detonator had worked as he had imagined it would… flawlessly.

The bomb attack was successful and would make the front page of every major newspaper across Europe and even in the United States. Bombs were always headline grabbers and struck fear in the minds of civilians. There was no way to predict when a bomb would go off, or where. They were very effective terror weapons.

Hadj Saddok, a prominent leader in the M'Chouneche township outside of Algiers, escorted Guy Monnerot and his wife on a tour through the gorges of Taghit Nath Bou Slimane. The Monnerots were French and Saddok was considered a friend of France, believing the status quo between France and Algeria should be maintained with the addition of French citizenship for Algerians. It was for this reason the three were singled out by the FLN. The leaders of the FLN needed to make it clear to the Algerian Muslims that a person was either for the revolution or against it. There was no middle ground that one could straddle and stay safe.

The bus they were riding in with the other members of the tour group traveled through a tunnel and into the scenic gorge. Si Larbi stood in the middle of the road and flagged the bus to a stop. Armed with rifles and submachineguns six mujahideen under Si Larbi's command surrounded the bus and demanded that the occupants disembark and line up on the side of the road. The driver and the tour members obeyed and exited the bus. Holding three photographs, Si Larbi walked down the line of passengers and identified Saddok and the Monnerots. Si Larbi ordered the other passengers to re-board the bus. They obeyed. He then requested that Saddok and the Monnerots to walk with him back into the tunnel that the bus had traveled through. They complied.

When they entered the tunnel, Si Larbi told them that they were free to leave on foot but should not return. As they moved farther into the tunnel, Si Larbi stepped around the corner of the outer tunnel wall and tossed a live grenade at their feet. The explosion seriously wounded all three of them. Si Larbi walked back into the tunnel and riddled their bodies with his submachinegun.

To everyone's surprise Mrs. Monnerot survived the ambush and was transported to a nearby hospital. While this upset Si Larbi, the other FLN leaders saw this a benefit. She would tell her story over and over again to the press and in this case bad press was good press for the FLN. They had made their point – choose or become a target of the mujahideen.

The Egyptian government had allowed the FLN to set up their overseas shop in Cairo to gather supplies and collect funds for the revolution.

It was a little before four o'clock in the afternoon when FLN representatives broadcast from the Voice of the Arabs radio station in Cairo. They aired a proclamation throughout the Middle East, "Algeria is returning to the fight for the freedom of Islam. We are calling on Muslims in Algeria to join in our national struggle for the restoration of the Algerian state – sovereign, democratic and social – within the framework of the principles of Islam."

There were more FLN attacks around the country. In total seven civilians were killed and scores wounded on the opening day of hostilities. It wasn't seen as just another escalation of violence. This was something far more serious. The attacks would continue in the weeks and months ahead. Each day more and more people would die or be seriously injured.

The FLN was making it clear that they meant business. This was not lost on the members of the MNA who saw the FLN as taking real action to free Algeria while their own leaders continued to pursue diplomatic solutions with the French. Many followers abandoned Messali Hadj and the MNA after the initial attacks and joined the FLN.

A Citroën touring car drove behind two police motorcycles through the streets of Paris.

Brigitte rode in the back seat with Mitterrand. "Eight dead and over fifty wounded in over a dozen separate attacks. The FLN has made a strong statement, wouldn't you say?" said Brigitte.

"I assure you, Mademoiselle Friang, these attacks in Algeria are nothing more than a handful of street thugs. They will be dealt with like all criminals… swiftly and with a firm French hand," said Mitterrand.

"Not all the attacks have been in Algeria, Monsieur Mitterrand. Two weeks ago I myself was witness to an assassination of an MNA representative in a café on the Champs-Élysées."

"Mademoiselle, you exaggerate. There is no evidence that the attack was anything more than a common robbery that turned violent."

"Except that no words were spoken and the victim's wallet was not taken."

"These things happen even in our lovely city. I assure you, there is no connection between the robbery in Paris and the events in Algeria."

"And if a connection is found?"

"Then we shall jump off that bridge when we arrive. Until then it is just conjecture."

"If the FLN brings their fight for Independence to the mainland, how will you respond? Will you negotiate a truce with their leaders?"

"I will not agree to negotiate with the enemies of the homeland. The only negotiation is war!" said Mitterrand. "As a precautionary measure, the president has agreed to call up sixty thousand reservists."

"To be sent to Algeria?"

"Yes. They will join our existing armed forces already in place."

"Reservists are young and inexperienced. Is it wise to mix them in with a civilian population?"

"As I said, it is purely a precautionary measure."

"You mean a show of force to the Algerians?"

"They will see it as they will see it. Algeria is an integral part of France and has been for over one hundred years. There are hundreds of thousands of pied-noir and French citizens living there. We are not going to let it go. It is not Indochina. The Algerians must know this. And if they do not, we are prepared to remind them."

The driver slowed as traffic increased. "What is the hold up?" said Mitterrand.

"There seems to some sort of fire at a café up ahead," said the driver.

"Inform our escort to use their sirens. I am already late for my meeting."

"Yes, Monsieur."

The driver signaled the two police officers on motorcycles to clear the way. They hit their sirens and traffic moved to the side of the road allowing the Citroën to pass. In the distance a column of black smoke rose from a café.

As the convoy approached the column of smoke, Brigitte and Mitterrand could see a dozen dead and badly wounded patrons laying on the sidewalk in front of the burning café. Windows in all the surrounding buildings had been blown out. "Conjecture?" said Brigitte.

"It could have been a gas explosion. You don't know, Mademoiselle Friang," said Mitterrand.

"No, Minister. You don't know. I have eyes," said Brigitte. "Let me out, driver."

The car pulled over. "What about the interview?" said Mitterrand surprised that she would just leave.

Brigitte did not dignify Mitterrand's question with a response as she jumped out of the car and trotted to the crime scene.

Nearby, Saadi stood next to Ludmila dressed as a French lady out for an afternoon of shopping in the boutiques that lined the boulevard. They had watched as her handiwork unfolded. The bomb has been perfectly placed in the center of the café for maximum effect. Saadi was pleased with his pupil, but was careful not to overpraise her. He did not want her to become overconfident and make a mistake or make the other two girls jealous. Ludmila was, however, his favorite siren and she could see it in his eyes. She had performed exactly as he had taught her, and she knew it.

Ludmila had always wondered about her heritage when she looked in the mirror. Her face had never looked completely Algerian. A large portion of Algeria's population was made up of the pied-noir from Germany, Italy, Spain and other European countries. It was well known that many Algerian woman had been raped by the foreign colonists. It was not so well known that some Algerian woman had carried on secret affairs with the colonists. She wondered about her mother and her marriage to her father who had been killed during the Nazi invasion of Algeria during World War II. Her mother and father were married very close to the time Ludmila was born. She never counted the number of months between her parent's marriage and her birth. She was afraid of the answer. Ludmila was Muslim. She loved her country and her God. To her it was the love that one carried in one's heart that mattered. The murmurings of her neighbors and relatives would stop once she had completed her mission and proved herself loyal to Islam.

The flight from Algiers to Paris was short. Saadi and Ludmila had entered France under the cover story that they were recently married and were on their honeymoon in Paris. They had forged documents including a marriage license that backed up their story and they had stayed the previous night together in the same hotel room. Ludmila had slept on the couch and Saadi in the bed.

Ludmila had considered slipping into bed with Saadi in the middle of the night. She doubted that he would be able to resist her and she wanted him. She knew he was married and a father, but that only made him more desirable. She knew fornication before marriage was a sin, but multiple wives were permitted in Islam. In her mind, the forged marriage license that Saadi carried had been recognized by French officials and was therefore valid. She was sure he would agree after they had made love. The only thing that stopped her was their mission together. Like him, she wanted it to be a success and their desires for each other could interfere with that success. She decided to wait.

Saadi could tell that Ludmila wanted him. It was often the case that young subordinates fell in love with their superiors. He admitted to himself that she was beautiful and had the type of disposition that would make her desirable in bed. He also knew that he needed to put her life at risk to succeed in the war against the French. She was a valuable asset. He could not let his feelings for her interfere with his mission. He would wait until the war was won before allowing any intimacy between the two of them. For now, he would see her as a soldier in the struggle for Independence and if she needed to be sacrificed for the cause then so be it.

Brigitte showed her press pass to the police officers holding the crowd of onlookers at a distance. They let her by. She walked to the remains of the café. There were body parts and pieces of burning furniture scattered across the ground. The sidewalk was charred black.

Brigitte watched as a forensic team sifted through the wreckage. One the forensic inspectors used a pair of tongs to pick up the mangled remains of a metal lid. She had seen the lid before in her own apartment. It belonged to a popular brand of tea biscuits. She made a notation in her notebook.

Brigitte was exhausted when she opened the door to her apartment. She have interviewed over a dozen survivors from the bomb blast. Nobody was able to identify the bomber although there was some mention of a European looking woman with a shopping bag that had sat near the suspected center of the explosion. Brigitte wondered if it could be the same woman that had assassinated Sami or if the woman had been killed by the blast. She would need to visit the city morgue tomorrow morning to find out if the woman had indeed died.

As she entered her apartment she heard the gasps of a woman weeping. She entered her bedroom to find Linh sitting on the floor crying uncontrollably with a telegram in her hand. Linh had already made Brigitte's bed and didn't want to wrinkle the bedspread by sitting on it. "Linh, what's wrong?" said Brigitte kneeling by her side.

"My brother in Hanoi... he dead," said Linh.

"Tuan is dead?"

"Yes. He dead. The Communists... they find out he work for the French and kill him. They cut off his feet and hand. They hang him from post."

"Jesus. I'm so sorry. His family... are they okay?"

"I not know. I cannot find. My sister send telegram."

"We'll find them, Linh. I promise."

Brigitte had feared that there would be retaliation by the Communists when they took over North Vietnam. Elected officials, journalists and government workers would be their first targets. Intellectuals and schoolteachers would be next on the list. She had seen it before when the Viet Minh had taken over villages during the war. But Hanoi was a city of millions and the death toll from the purge could be very high.

Linh had worked as a secretary for the French magazine where Brigitte was employed at the time. Linh had helped her brother get freelance jobs as a photographer for the magazine until he was hired by the French government's public relations department. Brigitte worried about Linh's close connection with the French. She had brought Linh to France to keep her safe and hired her as her housekeeper until she could find work. She knew that there was little hope of finding Linh's brother's family. They would be in hiding if they were still alive and that was a big "if."

EIGHT

Oran was located on the Mediterranean like most of the large cities in Algeria. Unlike many coastal communities, the city's stone fortress was located on a point several kilometers from the city and was in surprisingly good condition.

Marche de le bastille, the city's main outdoor market, was located near the palace and was known for its fresh snails, fruit and vegetables. Everything one needed could be found under the market's canopies. There were clothes, hand woven carpets, tin lamps, and leather goods. There were baked goods, sweets and candies, spices galore, and freshly butchered chickens and goats. There were coffee houses where locals would gather to gossip and drink a hot tea or coffee before returning to work.

The market was frequently visited by local government officials during the late afternoon before they headed home. It was a good place to gauge the current temperament of the local population and pick up the ingredients for the evening meal.

Samuel Bazalgette was the French administrator for the city of Oran. Technically, he shared power with Sak Amrani, a Muslim representative of the Grand Chieftains. However Amrani was not very interested in the actual administration of the city and saw his job as more ceremonial. He was good at making speeches and objected to the French mandates just enough to the keep the Chieftains that elected him happy. That was okay with Bazalgette. He preferred taking command and was good at organization. Bazalgette knew he would get the lion's share of the credit from the French Foreign Office if the city was run well. After all, he was French and Amrani was Muslim.

It was important that the two were seen together in public and that they appeared amiable. They made it a habit of appearing together somewhere in the city at least once a week. Today, they decided a stroll through the market would be nice since Amrani's young wife had requested he buy some fresh dates on his way home from the office.

Amrani was known for his pro-French views. He didn't love the French culture or the people. He saw them for what they were, the overlords that stripped away Algeria's natural resources and treated the Algerians like second class citizens. However he was also practical and saw the benefits that they brought to the Algerians. The Oran hospital was one of the best in Northern Africa and there were medical clinics in most neighborhoods. The city had its own university and while schools were lacking in the poorer neighborhoods there were several good private schools that educated the children of the elite. Oran was a peaceful city and attracted many European tourists. The tourists brought money into the local economy and the hotels and restaurants they enjoyed provided jobs. The police did an excellent job of keeping the riff-raff away from the tourist areas where pickpocketing and muggings were at an all-time low. Many French families purchased vacation homes overlooking the Mediterranean and employed maids, cooks and gardeners during the warm fall and winter months when Paris was known for its overcast skies and cold temperatures.

It was late afternoon when Bazalgette and Amrani strolled through the market. They we escorted by two French soldiers that kept their rifles slung over their shoulders. They knew to keep out of the way unless there was trouble. Amrani was generous with his purchases and often bought candies that he immediately handed out to the children in the street. It seemed like he knew the name of every shopkeeper and was quick with the latest joke that would make them laugh.

Bazalgette was much more subdued. He listened more than he spoke. He liked the Muslims in Oran and found their culture fascinating but was keenly aware that they detested him. He knew it was nothing personal. He represented France and the Muslims wanted their Independence. Of course they would hate him. Still he tried his best to put on a good face and do his job the best way he knew how. *Efficient administration was the best deterrent against the opposition's outcry*, he thought as he walked through the crowded market.

Nihad stood by a vendor selling purses and women's shoes and watched as Amrani and Bazalgette flanked by the two French soldiers approached. She was nervous and was having trouble remembering everything Saadi had told her. He had placed a pencil detonator with a short time fuse in the explosives. She would only have ninety seconds to leave the area once she started the timer. She needed to time the approach of the two men and the French soldiers so they were as close as possible to the explosives when they went off. She did not know Amrani and Bazalgette. She knew that they must be important or Saadi would not risk her life. She set her shopping bag down in front of the vendor's table and pretended to look at a pair of shoes. She asked if she could try them on and the vendor gladly agreed. "Of course. They are from my family's workshop. Five generations we have been cutting leather," said the vendor. "You will not find better quality in all of Algeria."

She picked up a pair of shoes and knelt down beside the table to try them on. She reached into her purse and pulled out the pair of pliers. She placed the pliers around the pencil detonator. She looked around at where she would go once she started the chemical timer. The path she preferred was blocked by a cart picking up trash. She would need to walk in the direction of the two approaching government officials and the soldiers. They were getting close. She squeezed the pliers and broke the acid vial inside the pencil detonator. She stood up and started walking toward the two officials. "Mademoiselle, my shoes," said the vendor.

She turned and walked back to the vendor and picked up the shoes she had left by her shopping bag. "I am sorry. They do not fit," she said.

"I have many sizes. Where they too small or big?"

"No. Thank you. I don't want them."

She turned and walked away. The vendor looked down and saw her shopping bag. He called after her again, "Mademoiselle, you forgot your shopping bag."

The vendor picked up the bag and trotted after her. One of the soldiers saw the vendor chasing after her and stopped her as she walked past thinking she might have stolen something. "What is the matter?" said Amrani.

The soldier pointed to the approaching vendor with the shopping bag. "I don't want it. I don't want it," said Nihad trying to break free of the soldier's grip.

"Don't be silly, Mademoiselle," said Amrani taking the shopping bag from the vendor and offering it to Nihad. "It is yours."

Nihad's eyes went wide like the shopping bag was a coiled snake ready to strike and refused to take it. Amrani and Bazalgette both realized something was wrong and exchanged a knowing look. Amrani opened the bag and looked inside. He pulled out the tin of tea cookies and laughed.

The explosion ripped through the market instantly killing eighteen people including Amrani, Bazalgette, the two French soldiers, the vendor and Nihad. Thirty-three more were seriously wounded, three of whom would die in Oran's state-of-the-art hospital in the ensuing days. Most were Muslim and did not think good or bad of the French or the Independence movement. They just wanted to sell their goods or buy something for their family's evening meal.

Saadi was saddened and angry on reading of Nihad's death. He had spent a great deal of time training her and he knew her to be loyal to Allah and her country. He did not relish the idea of informing Nihad's family of her death. He hated the wailing of Algerian women. He decided to let someone else inform the family. He had no time to mourn and needed to stay focused on the mission at hand.

Nihad was not smart and her nervous temperament ill-suited for this type of work, he thought. *I will need to be more careful selecting her replacement.* He was at the beginning of a war and he did not have time to train a new siren right away. It would have to wait. In the meantime, Marwa and Ludmila would need to take up the slack left by Nihad's death. The Café Wars would continue.

The heat was merciless in the Northern Sahara. The sun beat down like a hammer on an anvil. A mixed crew of German and Italian pied-noir roughnecks operated a drilling rig in the middle of the desert. The camp where they lived during their three week shifts was set up next to the rig and had all the comforts of home, including a shower and working toilet.

Oil had been discovered in Algeria at the end of World War II. Foreign oil companies were quick to drill test wells and the results had been promising.

This was a mixed blessing for the FLN and Algeria. It meant that when Independence was achieved the Algerians would have more natural resources to replace the revenue lost by the French departure from their lands. The flip side of the coin was that the French were less likely to leave now that Algeria was about to become their nation's gas pump.

A caravan of Berbers appeared over the horizon and approached the rig and camp. It was unusual for the Berbers to pay any type of notice let alone visit the pied-noir. They mistrusted foreigners and disliked most city dwellers. The crew stopped working and watched as the camels and mules approached. "What do you suppose they want?" said a roughneck.

"How the hell I am supposed to know?" said the supervisor. "Maybe cigarettes. They like cigarettes. Probably want to trade a goat or something."

"I like goat."

"Shut up and get back to work. I'll deal with them."

The roughnecks went back to work. The supervisor walked to his tent and retrieved a carton of cigarettes. He didn't want their dirty goat but he knew better than to piss off the Berbers. They could be trouble when they were angry.

He walked back out and moved toward the first camel rider as they entered the camp. "Welcome," the supervisor said making sure they could see that he was holding a carton of cigarettes.

The Berber riding at the head of the column pulled out his sword and split the foreman's head down the center with one stroke. He fell dead. The remaining Berbers charged the roughnecks as they scattered into the desert running for their lives. They didn't get far. The women in the caravan let an ear-piercing shrill with their vibrating tongues claiming a great victory.

Si Larbi entered a coffee house filled with Algerian business men discussing deals with their suppliers and customers. Coffee houses were common places to do business and people talked freely. He moved to the back of the building and found Bella sitting at a table in the corner. Bella rose and hugged Si Larbi as was the traditional greeting. "You are getting fat," said Si Larbi.

"Nasser likes to talk business during dinner," said Bella. "I admit I have put on a few kilos. Too many dates I think."

"So he is still cooperating? Nasser?"

"Yes. He has turned out to be a reliable ally."

"He will want something in return."

"Of course. The council is aware. What he wants most is loyalty and he's willing to pay for it. We will take his money and use his influence as long as it benefits our cause, and no further."

"I thought we agreed you would no longer come to Algeria once the war started."

"We did. But the council and I felt it was important that we meet face to face to discuss the next phase."

"There has been a change in plan?"

"Yes. There are some on the council that feel we need to more drastic in our attacks."

"More drastic?"

"Yes. We need international allies to convince the French to abandoned their efforts against our Independence. We need to take action that will force the French to overreact. Their overreaction will bring about sympathy for our cause. We are rebels and are not held to the same standard as the French forces. They are a western army and have agreed to the rules of war. We have not."

"Even if we are the ones that start the conflict?"

"Newspapers have a funny way of twisting the truth to bring about the most dramatic news. They will deemphasize the origins of the conflict if they feel the French reaction will sell more of their papers. We will need something big and terrible that provokes the French."

"What are you thinking?"

"You suggested an attack on Philippeville…"

"Yes. It is manageable. It's not as big as Algiers and we have strong support in the Muslim communities in the city."

"How long will it take you to prepare?"

"A week… maybe two. Most of our Mujahideen are already positioned in the surrounding area."

"And the fellagha?" said Bella using the traditional term for the Muslim militia.

"Perhaps a thousand. But more will join if they know the Mujahideen will lead the fight," said Si Larbi.

"Good. Prepare your forces," said Bella. "I will be sending you some of my commandos to help occupy the police."

Bruno stood at the front of a lecture hall filled with young French officers. In the beginning, the young officers had worn their dress uniforms out of respect to attend Colonel Bigeard's lectures. Soon after, the entire class had changed to paratrooper jumpsuits as that was what Bruno wore on a daily basis.

Bruno was the epitome of what a French soldier aspired to be. He was a true warrior and had fought in almost every major battle in both World War II and the Indochina War. It didn't seem to matter that Bruno had lost the last battle at Dien Bien Phu which ended the war in a French loss. He had fought bravely until the end. He was a living legend.

The older officers disliked Bruno. Some loathed him. He was seen as a showboat. An officer that put his men in harm's way without true cause. Bruno, of course, didn't see it that way. He preferred to be the aggressor in a battle because he saw it as safer for himself and his men. Nothing strikes fear into a hunter like a charging lion. Bruno knew that winning a battle was rarely about destroying his enemy physically; it was about destroying their will to fight. He told his men to 'get them running and keep them running. A fleeing enemy is a lousy shot.'

While many officers believed it was correct to fight the soldiers under their command until they had sustained acceptable losses and ceased to function as a unit befitting their size, Bruno's men fought until they won their objective or could fight no more, usually because they ran out of ammunition.

Bruno was also known for refusing to obey orders that he thought stupid. He was often threatened with being court martialed. He didn't care. He refused to sacrifice his men because of stupidity and was prepared to defend himself in front of the fellow officers that would judge him during a court martial proceeding. While his commanding officers detested his insubordination, they wished they had more commanders like him. Bruno and his men were always assigned the toughest missions and that was exactly what Bruno wanted.

Soldiers were always fearful when told they had been transferred to a unit under Bruno's command. It meant that they would most likely bleed and possibly die. And yet his new recruits quickly grew to respect him and gave him their loyalty. It was hard not to follow a leader that was the first to jump out of an airplane and first to leap from a trench when facing enemy fire. Bruno made his men brave because he led by example and they believed they were being well led. If they were to be sacrificed, it would not be in vain, but for the glory of France. Bruno was what he wanted his men to be and they became him. The enemy feared Bruno and often put a bounty on his head. Bounties that so far had not been collected.

"Armor has always been a problem for paratroopers, mainly because we don't have any," said Bruno. "We travel light and that gives us speed and maneuverability. The only true weapon we possess is our aggression. Having a twelve ton tank wrapped around them makes the enemy overconfident. A well placed Molotov cocktail can turn a tank into a frying pan inside. A grenade through an open hatch can turn it into a blender. Patient aggression is the key to destroying armor. You must put yourself into a position in which you may effectively attack the beast and then wait for the best opportunity to kill it. But don't wait too long and make sure your strike is sure. With armor you will rarely get a second opportunity."

A young cadet entered through a doorway, saluted and handed Bruno a message. Bruno read it silently and responded, "Please inform the General I will be there as ordered."

The cadet saluted again and left. Bruno turned back to his audience and said with a wry smile, "Detention." Everyone laughed.

Brigitte, wearing a pencil skirt and matching jacket, entered the café and looked around. Coyle, seated at the back of the restaurant, watched her for moment. She was beautiful and he was proud to call her his own. He signaled her. She walked back, sat down and gave him a peck on the lips. She pulled out her handkerchief and wiped off the lipstick she had left on his lips, as she always did. "I ordered you a coffee," said Coyle. "I know you don't have much time."

"I can always make time for you," said Brigitte, her eyes continuing to survey the restaurant and its patrons, looking for potential threats. She paid especially close attention to the shopping bags sitting on the floor by the customers seated at tables in the center of the café. She wanted to look in each bag just to be sure the contents truly were what they represented – lingerie, shoes or a lovely blouse from a nearby boutique… and not a bomb. Coyle could see her eyes darting around the room. "Rough day?" said Coyle.

"No more than any other day," said Brigitte. "Another bombing this morning. Five killed and fourteen wounded."

"Any children this time?"

"A baby. Seven months old. She and her mother were killed. They don't seem to care."

"Who doesn't care?"

"The terrorists and their bombs. They don't care about gender or age as long as the victims are French or sympathetic to the French cause."

The waitress brought their coffee and a plate of cookies that Coyle had ordered. Every clatter of the plates and cups seemed to set off a series of twitches in Brigitte's facial muscles. Coyle could see that Brigitte was beyond nervous, like a cornered wildcat ready to jump out of her skin. "Are you okay, Brigitte?" he said.

"I am fine, Tom. I just have a lot on my mind."

Coyle decided to change the subject in hopes Brigitte would relax. "The French Air Force has asked me to switch routes," he said.

"Let me guess. They want you to fly troops to Algeria?"

"Yeah. How did you know?"

"I interviewed a woman that survived the bombing at café Mormont last week. She said her husband had been called up and was leaving this week for North Africa."

"More fuel for the fire, I guess."

"It seems the French Army is playing into the hands of the insurgents. The more troops we send the more the Algerians feel the occupation."

"So, what's the solution?"

"I am not sure there is one."

"I suppose you could just let them go and give them their Independence."

"You do not know the French, Tom. We are very stubborn, even beyond reason. Algeria is a matter of honor, especially after Vietnam. We cannot let them go and expect to maintain our standing in the international community."

"The British let the Americans go and it didn't seem to hurt them much. Now we are the best of friends. We even saved their asses from the Nazis."

"This is different. France considers Algeria part of the municipality. It is France, just as much as Normandy or Savoy. And where does it stop? Who else will claim independence… Corsica? Roussillon? Alsace? Before long France would be a shadow of its former self. And would those new countries be any better off? How would they defend themselves?"

How would they govern? With whom would they ally?"

"I never suggested it would be easy. But people have a right to self-determination."

"Really? Did you tell that to General Lee and his confederates?"

"You got a point."

"It's not some game, Tom. It's the survival of my country we are talking about," said Brigitte looking more agitated, her eyes continuing their search for a threat, her face looking more and more like a trapped animal.

"Believe me I understand," said Coyle. "Americans want France to survive and to be strong. They are our oldest ally. I am just not so sure hanging on to a Muslim country bent on Independence is the best way to ensure that survival."

"Not everyone in Algeria believes in Islam. There are hundreds of thousands of pied-noir that were promised they could settle and raise their families in peace. They trusted France would keep her word and protect them. What happens to them if France just walks away? How long would they last against ten million Algerians that have sworn vengeance against them?"

"Like I said, not an easy solution. Now, please, drink your coffee and relax for a few minutes. You're working too hard."

"I don't want to relax. You seem to feel I am yours to command. I assure you I am not," said Brigitte getting up and exiting the restaurant in a huff. Coyle considered running after her but thought better of it. She was an independent woman. That was one of the things he loved about her, even though she snipped at him now and then. Over the past year of living together in Paris he had begun to understand her and her needs. Right now she just needed space and chasing after her wouldn't help matters.

NINE

The mess hall at the Air Force base outside of Paris was packed with soldiers returning from Indochina and those on their way to Algeria. Bruno entered the hall and looked around until he spotted Coyle sitting at a table eating his breakfast with his crew, now missing its navigator. Bruno approached and said, "Coyle, do you have a minute?"

Coyle was surprised to see Bruno and said, "Sure. Pull up a bench. It's Thursday. Aren't you teaching at the institute."

"Yes. Of course. But I am on... how do you say... a field trip," said Bruno sitting across from Coyle.

"Where are you headed?"

"Algiers. If you have room."

"Oh. Sure. Cargo hold is full up, but they booted my navigator off my crew so you can have his seat in the cockpit."

"You lost your navigator?"

"Yeah. Apparently we are not allowed to get lost over the Mediterranean according to Air Force regulations. No navigator is required."

"So you can fly without one... a navigator?"

"Yeah. It ain't that far. Ya just gotta keep heading south once you hit water. You can use a compass, right?"

Bruno smiled and said, "Yes. The use of a compass is part of my skill set."

"Great. You're my navigator for this trip. So why the field trip to Algiers?"

"I am not sure. But when I am called by a general I go."

"Probably a good strategy. Hey, I met another para commander on his way back from Indochina. Colonel Roger Trinquier. Do you know him?"

Bruno's expression darkened on hearing Trinquier's name. "Ah yes. He was commander of the Maquis in Laos and the Vietnamese highlands."

"Maquis?"

"Guerilla units mostly from the highland tribes. Good fighters. They fought behind the lines and harassed the enemy."

"Why weren't they at Dien Bien Phu?"

"The Viet Minh hunted them down. Many were killed and their villages burned. They never made it to the garrison."

"We could have used them."

"Yes. But they served their purpose. They provided invaluable intel on Viet Minh troop movements and kept the Viet Minh from invading Laos after Dien Bien Phu fell. However their methods were… questionable."

"Questionable?"

"Yes. You must remember the hill tribes hated the Viet Minh and they did not believe in taking prisoners unless it was to extract information. They were very effective."

"You mean they used torture?"

"Yes. That is what I mean. Colonel Trinquier learned a great deal from his time with the Maquis. He was their commander, but also their student."

French Army headquarters in Algiers was located next to the Kasbah – an ancient walled citadel that included the city's main medina. Built on the side of a hill overlooking the city, the Kasbah was the heart of learning and religion. The citadel had originally contained over one hundred mosques, thirty-two mausoleums and twelve Zawiyas – religious schools and monasteries. Over the years of occupation, the French had destroy the majority of the religious buildings or converted them to Christian churches and military barracks.

The Kasbah had become a symbol of French oppression. The leaders of the FLN had taken up residency in the hundreds of abandoned buildings and hid among the thousands of Muslim homes within the citadel's walls. They could rely on support from the neighborhood and were given plenty of warning whenever a French patrol came near.

The French Army headquarters was a fortified compound with high walls, well-guarded gates and an abundance of machine guns placed strategically around the compound and surrounded by sandbags. The general's living quarters were built from a former Zawiya with its large courtyard where students would gather for prayer and drink from the center fountain. There were manicured gardens where the general and his staff could enjoy tea and relax while off duty. There was a large barracks for the troops that guarded the compound and patrolled the area immediately around it.

Bruno waited in the reception area outside the general's office until he was called inside by the secretary. It was an impressive office with twenty foot walls and two electric ceiling fans that kept the room cool during the repressive summers. General Jacques Massu sat in an easy chair enjoying his afternoon tea with Colonel Trinquier and Major Paul Aussaresses seated on a couch. They all stood to return Bruno's salute and shake his hand as Massu introduced them, "Thank you for coming, Colonel Bigeard. I trust your flight was not too bumpy?"

"It was fine, General. Thank you for asking," said Bruno as he sat down per Massu's invitation. Bruno was unsure why he had been called by Massu. French generals were not in the habit of interviewing Colonels for potential command or staff positions. Besides, he had only been at his present position at the institute for less than a year. He believed it was possible that the general wanted his advice on an upcoming para operation but when he saw Trinquier he knew that would be redundant. Trinquier was a well-qualified para commander with over a decade of combat experience like himself. Bruno knew he was not here to offer his opinion. Bruno was miffed.

"I believe you know my chief of staff - Colonel Trinquier?" said Massu.

"Yes. We fought together in the highlands of North Vietnam and in Laos," said Bruno.

"Good to see you made it out, Bruno," said Trinquier. "I heard it was quite difficult after the garrison fell."

"Yes, well… I survived. Many didn't," said Bruno. "Your ears must be burning, Roger. I was just talking about you with a friend."

"With whom might that be?"

"The pilot that flew me down. An American. Tom Coyle."

"Yes, I remember. He was with you at Dien Bien Phu," said Trinquier. "An American pilot of a C-119. Interesting…"

"Why is that interesting?" said Bruno.

"A boxcar can drop two platoons behind enemy lines at the same time. That makes it interesting."

"I am sure you two will have a lot to talk about later at dinner. I am not sure you if you know Major Paul Aussaresses, my head of intelligence," said Massu.

"I have heard of the Major, but I don't believe we have ever met," said Bruno.

"I imagine you are curious why I called you here. So I will get right to it," said Massu. "I am sure you are familiar with the current situation with the Algerians and the FLN."

"I am."

"We have reason to believe that there will be a major mujahideen attack on Philippeville in the coming days. We thought you might like to come along as an observer."

"As an observer?"

"Yes," said Massu and chose his next words carefully. "Bruno, this war is like no other that France has fought before. It is a terrorist action through and through. The atrocities that the FLN are committing to the pied-noir and even their own people are horrendous. They go far beyond even what we saw in Indochina."

"I have heard the stories," said Bruno.

"They have no regard for morality or common conventions. They are truly fighting a war of terror and it is only growing worse."

"And you want me to… observe this?"

"No, to be honest. We want to observe you."

"I do not understand."

"I am sure you have figured out that we are in need of strong commanders with combat experience. We all know you are more than qualified. What we don't know is how far you are willing to go to achieve victory."

"I would give my life for my country."

"As would we. But this war may require more than that… it may require your very soul. Our objective is to completely wipe out the FLN. To hunt them down like the animals that they are. We will give no quarter and we ask for none in return."

"The main problem is finding the bastards," said Trinquier. "They hide among and are protected by the Muslim communities. Like the Viet Minh they can attack our troops one minute and vanish the next. The Muslims feel it is their religious duty to help and hide them. They threaten to kill anyone who cooperates with our forces or the pied-noir. Money will not loosen their tongues, so we must use other means."

"I see," said Bruno. "How did you find out about the planned attack?"

"My counter-insurgence team has setup a network of informants within the population," said Aussaresses. "Some were agents for the FLN that we were able to turn. One of those agents works at the local semolina mill."

"Semolina?" said Bruno.

"It's the flour used to make the Algerian flatbread. It's a staple and eaten at almost every meal," said Trinquier.

Aussaresses continued, "About a week ago, one of my informants noticed that the mill's warehouse was empty. We checked with the local bakeries and found that they too were low on their semolina supply. So, where was all the semolina going if not to the bakeries?"

"We questioned the mill owner and found out he had sold a large quantity of semolina to a mujahideen quartermaster."

"He just told you that?"

"He did when we put a noose around his twelve year old daughter's neck and threaten to hang her."

"My God," said Bruno.

"The girl is fine. The threat was enough to obtain the information we needed," said Aussaresses.

"Information that will save hundreds of lives, Bruno," said Massu.

Trinquier continued, "We now know that the mujahideen have a large contingent camped in the mountains just above Philippeville. The semolina is being used to feed them. We also know they intend to attack the pied-noir community in Philippeville the day after tomorrow. We will be ready for them."

"We thought it prudent that you view our tactics first hand before committing to lead a unit under my command. We may not want the world or even France to know what we are required to do, but I will be damned if I will deceive my commanders," said

Massu. "If you decide to join us, it will be with open eyes."

"And if not?"

"Then you will keep your mouth shut about what you see. Is that clear?" said Massu.

"Yes, sir," said Bruno.

Bruno desperately wanted to command a combat unit again. Teaching at the institute was important but there was no comparison against the thrill of actual combat. Bruno was a warrior at heart and a born leader. He believed his training and experience were being wasted. He was a lieutenant colonel and after his next promotion he would not be allowed to fight with his combat unit. He would command at a distance like Massu. A desk jockey. The thought sickened him. Time was running out.

What Massu was offering may be his last opportunity to fight the enemies of France. He did not want to miss his chance to serve his country one last time on the battlefield. He knew what was being asked of him and that it went against his personal morals. Perhaps he could find a compromise and keep his hands clean. The only way to find out was to accept Massu's offer and let them observe him. He wasn't sure how he would react but a chance at a combat command was worth the risk.

Trinquier invited Bruno to join him for a drink in the garden after the meeting with Massu. Trinquier was like many officers and did not like Bruno but respected his ability as a fighter. It was well known that Bruno won the battles he fought. Trinquier knew he needed a bulldog to command his paratroopers.

"Your friend, Coyle, do you think he will fly for us?" said Trinquier.

"I don't know. In Vietnam he only flew cargo and occasionally troops for the Air Force. He once was a great fighter pilot but he has become a pacifist," said Bruno.

"And yet, from what I hear, he fought at Dien Bien Phu."

"Yes. For a woman."

"The journalist, Brigitte Friang?"

"Yes."

"She must be one hell of a woman."

"She is."

"So, you will ask him?"

"Me?"

"He is your friend."

Bruno considered for a long moment. Was this part of their test to see if he was fit for command? "All right. I will ask him but I cannot guarantee his answer."

"Ask nicely," said Trinquier with a smile.

Massu stared out his office window and watched Bruno and Trinquier talk. Aussaresses was still with him and said, "I don't trust him."

"You don't trust anyone. That's why you are so good at your job."

"Why he is so important?"

"He is a hero."

"Yes. And he will draw attention. Attention that we don't want."

"Now. No. But when all this is over and bombs are no longer killing Parisians during their morning coffee and the politicians have conveniently forgotten how they asked us to restore peace at all costs, the public will demand answers. There will be inquires as to what we have done and how we did it. The generals and politicians will demand a sacrifice. And who better to offer them than a hero?" said Massu.

TEN

It was the middle of the night when Si Larbi woke his Mujahideen fighters in the mountains above Philippeville. Fires were stoked and a big breakfast was cooked and eaten. It would be a long day and they would need their strength. He was patient to a point and then hurried his men along. They would need to reach the city before sunrise to avoid being seen by the pied-noir militia outposts.

Up to this point in the conflict the mujahideen had not concentrated their forces and stayed away from the cities that were well protected by the French Army and the pied-noir militias. He was surprised that FLN leaders had granted his request to attack Philippeville.

There was a large community of pied-noir in the suburbs of Philippeville and the ethnic tension was unusually intense, even for Algeria. Many of the Muslims had lost family members during the Setif Massacre ten years before. The entire region was a powder keg waiting to explode and the FLN was ready and willing to light the match. The pied-noir settlements would be an easy target for him and his men once they had killed the militiamen in the outlying outposts.

Café Wars

Like most settler communities the pied-noir of Philippeville did not rely on the French Army or police to protect them. They had learned from experience that the French were slow to react and French laws often got in the way of justice. Instead, the pied-noir of Philippeville had recruited their own militias and armed them using community funds. The militia trained like the army and many of its members were veterans from the armed forces of their native countries or the French Foreign Legion.

It was still dark when the column of five hundred mujahideen reached the bottom of the mountain. Si Larbi let them rest for a few minutes then ordered them to their fighting positions.

They spread out into a skirmish line and sent sappers out in front to take out the militia outposts. The fighters that had been fighting guerilla type actions for the last year were excited. They had never been part of a fighting force this large and it gave them confidence.

In addition to the mujahideen, there were over two thousand fellagha – former farmers that had turned to violence when the French government took away their farms and gave them to the pied-noir. The fellagha would attack the French garrison inside Philippeville and keep the four hundred soldiers that garrisoned the fort busy while the mujahideen attacked the pied-noir settlements.

FLN commandos were hidden in cellars around the city and would attack the government buildings, the police station and any police patrols in the operational area. Once the battle started, prayers would need to be postponed until after their victory but they were sure that Allah would understand and continue to protect them.

Si Larbi was anxious to get on with the attack but he knew he needed to be patient. There was a lot at stake. The eyes of men that would one day rule an independent Algeria where on him. This was his chance to impress them and ensure his future in the new government.

Tringuier had placed his brigade of paratroopers between the militia outposts and the city. He did not want to tip his hand to the unsuspecting mujahideen commander. The French were well dug in with the troops' foxholes at the base of a slope and supported by machine guns and recoilless rifles elevated on the top of the slope so that they could shoot over their troops' heads. Claymore mines were laid out in groups of three in front of the foxholes. It was a well-laid trap. The attack on the outposts would give the French troops fair warning that the enemy was near. There would be no surprise attack as the mujahideen had planned.

French reconnaissance units were the first to spot the mujahideen as they approached the pied-noir outposts. The recon unit commander radioed Tringuier to report his observations and give him a rough estimate of size of the mujahideen forces that his men were about to face. It was more than he had expected but he knew his men were well prepared and had the element of surprise on their side. Tringuier was not overly concerned. He told the radio operator to send out the go signal to all French forces.

It was dark as Bruno and Coyle waited on a military airfield beside Coyle's C-119. The two platoons of paratroopers and their commander were already inside and seated so the plane could take off the moment it received the radio message that would trigger the operation.

Bruno had convinced Coyle to fly for Massu by promising him that he would not be required to drop any napalm drums as he had at Dien Bien Phu. He told Coyle of the need to drop the two platoons behind the enemy lines once the battle had begun in order to cut off the enemy's escape. Only a C-119 was big enough to transport the required number of men in one load and Coyle's C-119 was the only one available in Algeria at the moment. Coyle was wary but had agreed, just this once. "I would like to ask you something but I do not want to offend you," said Bruno.

"Go ahead. I have a pretty thick skin," said Coyle.

"Why no combat? You were once a fighter pilot and I know you can handle yourself in a battle," said Bruno. "Do you not wish to serve your country?"

"Well, first… this ain't my country and this ain't my war. Second, I've seen enough violence to last a lifetime. I figure I've paid my dues and I'm due a break. Third, if America ever enters a war again I'll have to see how I feel at the time and if I'm really needed. There's usually lots of young fools willing to risk their lives for the glory of fighting for their country. I know. I was one of them. I just don't find it so glorious anymore."

"I see," said Bruno.

"Do ya? Or do you see me as a coward?"

"I know you are not a coward, Coyle. You proved that at Dien Bien Phu. I believe you just need the proper motivation to fight."

"I guess."

"Brigitte is the proper motivation."

"That she is."

The cockpit side window slid open. Coyle's engineer popped his head out and said something in French. "That's it. We are go," said Bruno.

Coyle and Bruno climbed through the side door and the crew chief buttoned up the aircraft by closing the back doors. The two engines were fired up and the plane taxied to the runway. The engines roared to full power and the twin-tailed aircraft took off into the dark sky.

The pied-noir in the outposts above the city were well trained and knew the mujahideen were coming that morning. They also knew that they would be the first attacked and most likely would not see the sunrise. It didn't matter. They were protecting their families and were willing to sacrifice their lives for their cause. They kept quiet and stayed low watching the hillside above. They could see movement but dared not open fire which would surely give away their position. Instead they would wait until they were attacked and kill as many of the Muslim fighters as possible before being overrun.

Café Wars

The battle for Philippeville started in the darkness of early morning. Si Larbi ordered his men forward. The mujahideen crawled through the grass as far as they dared, then tossed grenades into the pied-noir outposts. The explosions were a signal for those in the city to begin their attack. Most of the pied-noir in the outposts died before ever getting a shot off. Those that survived the grenade attacks were overwhelmed by mujahideen rifle and machine gun fire in less than a minute. The settlers had done their duty and died bravely for their community.

Si Larbi was pleased that few of his men had died or been wounded in the attacks on the outposts. The surprise of the attack now gone, Si Larbi ordered the rest of his mujahideen to rise up and move down the hill toward the city. He and his men were unaware of the French positions below and fell straight into the paratroopers' ambush.

The well-disciplined paratroopers waited until the mujahideen were just a few yards in front of their positions before setting off the claymore mines. Six hundred ball bearings were launched from each of the mines in the mujahideen's direction using shaped charges in the way that Napoleon's cannons used nails and bits of broken bottles to mow down his enemies. The effect was the same and two dozen mujahideen were ripped to pieces in an instant.

Si Larbi was lucky and was not injured. He yelled to his men to get down. The mujahideen hit the ground and lay as flat as possible as the French opened fire with their machine guns. Si Larbi ordered his men to hold their ground and return fire. Hearing their commander's voice, the mujahideen recovered from their initial shock and returned fire.

Inside the cockpit of the C-119 Bruno stood beside the paratrooper commander, a captain, and looked out the window at the battle below. The positions were clear with the French between the mujahideen and the lights of the city. The lines traded tracer bullets as the battle raged. Coyle pointed to where he thought would make a good landing zone for the paratroopers. The captain nodded in agreement. Coyle banked the aircraft toward the landing zone. The captain left the cockpit to ready his men for the jump. "Watch your top knot, Bruno," said Coyle.

"You have never explained what that means," said Bruno.

"Yeah, I know. Drives ya crazy, don't it," said Coyle with a smile.

"Americans," said Bruno turning to leave.

"French," said Coyle watching him exit the cockpit. Once the paratroopers had jumped Coyle would return to the airbase, pick up the rest of the captain's company, and return to the battlefield.

In the hold, the crew chief opened the side door on the back of the aircraft. The paratroopers hooked up their static lines on their captain's orders. Bruno slipped on his parachute. It was unusual for Bruno to carry any type of weapon into combat. He believed that a commander's duty was to lead his men, not fight the enemy directly. But today he had been invited to observe not command. He attached a submachinegun on to the parachute's harness above the backup chute. *Today I will fight if given the chance,* he thought. *I may never be given the opportunity again.*

The jump light turned green and the captain signaled his men. They jumped out the doorway and the captain followed. Bruno was the last to jump. He didn't like the feeling of following as he stepped through the open doorway. He was always the first to jump from the lead aircraft even when he commanded an entire battalion. He would talk to the captain later and explain his reasoning for jumping first but at the moment he was falling into a combat zone and needed to focus.

The paratroopers landed on the backside of the hill above the city. The mujahideen were too busy fighting the paratroopers already engaged to notice the two platoons disappear behind the top of the hill.

Bruno released his submachinegun and detached his parachute. He listened as the captain gave orders to his platoon commanders to deploy their men at the top of the hill overlooking the mujahideen positions. He was here to observe not to advise. Still he could not stand idly by as French troops risked their lives for the country when he knew they were being badly led. He waited until the captain was finished and the platoon commanders had left before he approached. "Why the top of the hill?" said Bruno.

"We will maintain the highest fighting position no matter how the battle unfolds. Plus the sun will be at our backs and blind the mujahideen," said the captain.

"Yes, but the bright morning sky will silhouette your men and make them easy targets. Why not deploy a few yards down the hill? You will still keep the advantage of the sun and the higher fighting position when the mujahideen retreat."

"And if we are attacked from behind?"

"Fight the enemy you see not the one you imagine."

The captain considered Bruno's advice. He knew his reputation and didn't doubt the wisdom of his words. He did not want his men to see him as unsure or incompetent and yet he did not want to endanger them any more than was necessary to achieve their mission. He swallowed his pride and nodded agreement to Bruno. The captain went off to update his platoon leaders on the new fighting positions.

Bruno thought highly of the captain. When confronted with the error, he had made the right decision to protect his men above any personal desires or needs. A good officer must learn from his mistakes and correct them when possible.

The grenade explosions on the hillside and the battle that followed were clearly visible from the city. The FLN commandos emerged from their hiding places. They were armed with submachineguns, grenades and Molotov cocktails. Their objective was not to destroy the French authorities within the city but rather to occupy them with fire bombings so they could not respond to the mujahideen and fellagha attacks. They gathered in a designated alley near the police station.

They moved as a unit to the front of the building. Three of the commandos lit and hurled Molotov cocktails at the barred windows. Two of the bottles of gasoline smashed against the iron bars and set the front of the building on fire. When police officers ran out to investigate, two commandos with submachineguns opened fired killing three police officers and driving the others back into the burning building.

One bottle made it inside and shattered on the tile floor in the commander's office. The police commander was engulfed in flames. He ran for the door but was overwhelmed before he could get it open. He fell to the floor and died.

The gunfight between the commandos and the police officers firing through the station's windows and doorway only lasted five minutes. The commandos had other targets that they needed to strike and broke off the attack. The police station was burning inside and out. The fire and tending to their wounded would keep the police tied up well into the morning. They would be of little use to the city's residents.

The leader of the fellagha had heard the explosions from the grenades on the hillside above the city. His men were gathered under the overhead tarps of the market nearest to the French garrison. They were not heavily armed like the mujahideen. What they lacked in munitions they made up for in numbers. Over two thousand men armed with axes, picks and spades were under his command. A few even had pistols and rifles left over from the Nazi occupation when they fought on the side of the French and British.

His men were not well trained and lacked discipline, but they were determined to drive the French and the pied-noir from Algeria and reclaim the farms they had lost. He hoped this was enough to keep his men fighting when the French opened fire with their machine guns and recoilless rifles. He ordered his men forward toward the garrison. Many carried ladders and ropes with grappling hooks that could be used to scale the steep walls.

He knew that the mujahideen would join them in their battle to take the French fort once they disposed of the pied-noir militias. His mission was to keep the French forces occupied and to take the garrison if possible. He was a veteran of World War II and had fought in the Foreign Legion against the fascists. He was getting older and had become a leader in his community. He wanted to prove himself to the FLN leadership in hopes of gaining a position in the new government once independence had been achieved. He would sacrifice his friends and neighbors and maybe even himself for the cause.

The four hundred French soldiers guarding the fort were waiting for the rebels. Their commander did not wait until the crowd reached the garrison's walls and gave the order to fire at will. The soldiers in the garrison complied. They killed six fellagha and wounded fifteen in the opening volley from their machine guns.

The soldiers defending the garrison walls quickly ran out of targets as the rebels sought cover down the alleys and disappeared into the surrounding buildings. The violence of the French counter-attack caused the farmers and their leader to reconsider. Why attack a well-protected garrison when there were plenty of easier targets throughout the city? The fellagha knew where the pied-noir communities were located and that those not in the militia would be defending their homes and shops. The rabble turned and marched away from the garrison to the outskirts of the city.

The commander of the garrison was baffled when the enemy broke off the attack. This was not part of the French plan. He radioed Trinquier and gave him an update on the enemy's movement.

The battle on the hillside raged between Trinquier's paratroopers and the mujahideen. The French had struck a powerful blow in their surprise counterattack but Si Larbi and his mujahideen were determined to break French lines and attack the city below.

Bruno watched from the hilltop above as the French paratroopers he had jumped with readied their defensive positions. He could see that the mujahideen were digging in and fighting just as fiercely as the battalion of paratroopers below them. He hated the idea of just sitting and waiting for the mujahideen to retreat. He crawled his way over to the paratrooper commander and said, "Captain, your platoons are well deployed, yes?"

"Yes. We should be able to fight anything they can throw at us when they retreat," said the captain.

"And you still have a squad in reserve?"

"Yes. Of course."

"Excellent. Why don't you let me take your reserve squad around the back of the hill and attack the mujahideen in the right flank? If your men can roll them up, the mujahideen will have no choice but to retreat into your firing positions just as you planned."

"But they are my reserves," said the captain.

"And they still will be. They will just be deployed in a different area of the battlefield. First sign of trouble they will break off contact and rejoin your lines."

"And what happens if the mujahideen overrun our position?"

"Once they break off contact with the para battalion below I doubt they will be in any condition to break through your lines. You said yourself you should be able to fend off anything they throw at you."

"Well, yes… that is true," said the captain unsure. What Bruno was suggesting was unorthodox and not part of the plan agreed to by his commander Colonel Trinquier. But Bruno was a commander the captain had studied in officer training, a hero among the paratroopers. He was known to be aggressive and win his battles. The captain wanted to win this battle desperately and Bruno could see that.

"Perhaps a better question is what happens if the mujahideen escaped without every falling into your trap? Would it not be better for your reserve to drive them to you?" said Bruno.

"I agree. You will lead them?"

"I will advise your squad leader."

"Very well. You may proceed, Colonel," said the captain.

"As you say, Captain," said Bruno as he began to move off to advise the sergeant in charge of the reserves. "Oh, one more thing… you might want to radio Colonel Trinquier and let him know we are coming. It would be a shame for your men to get caught in the crossfire."

"Wait. What?" said the captain. It was too late Bruno was gone and so were his reserves.

The mass of fellagha moved through the streets of Philippeville like a virus spreading through a human body. Everyone knew which buildings and storefronts were Muslim and which were French and pied-noir. Many in the mob secretly shopped at the French and pied-noir establishments because they had a wider selection and the quality of their products were usually better that the Muslim businesses. Most of the storefronts were buttoned up tight with iron folding gates across their doors and windows. When the mob came across a non-Muslim storefront they simply pried the gates from their anchors in the walls with their picks and spades. Looting was commonplace as were Molotov cocktails. The French and pied-noir businesses burned, sending black smoke into the sky. Business owners and employees were pulled from their cars and bicycles as they arrived to open their shops and offices. The French civilians and pied-noir were beaten and shot. A few Muslim business owners and employees were caught in the madness and killed before they could convince the mob of their loyalty.

The real bloodletting started when the mob reached the residential neighborhoods of the pied-noir. Front doors on homes were kicked in and the families inside were dragged into the streets. Apartment buildings were set on fire and the occupants were attacked as they fled the burning buildings. Those that resisted were immediately shot and killed. Those that chose not to fight fared far worse. Families barracked themselves inside their homes only to be burned alive by the torches and fire bombs of Muslims.

Women and children were not spared. All of the horrors of the world were unleashed on the pied-noir communities that morning. Over one hundred years of Algerian occupation and injustice boiled into a rage that could not be stopped. Decapitation was considered kind. Rape and disfigurement less so. Muslim farmers, miners and factory workers turned into monsters like wild beasts driven into a frenzy by bloodlust.

Trinquier was disappointed when he received the report that the fellagha had broken off their attack on the garrison after only light casualties. He had hoped for more. He was also concerned about where they would go next. From his vantage point on the hill he could see fires starting to spread on the outskirts of the city. He knew that this was where the pied-noir communities were located but it was too far away to determine their exact location. The battle on the hillside was fierce but his paratroops were well-dug in and were in no risk of being overrun by the mujahideen. He sent his recon platoon down the hill to investigate.

The French recon platoon moved down the hillside toward the city. They too could see the fires burning in the buildings, stores and houses. What they were not prepared for was what they saw as they moved closer – dismembered body parts and rivers of blood in the streets. As much as they wanted to enter the city and stop the violence it was not the mission of the recon to fight unless to defend itself. The unit commander's voice trembled slightly as he radioed Trinquier and reported the massacre.

Trinquier was busy winning the battle between the mujahideen and his paratroopers when he received the recon commander's report. At first he thought the recon commander was exaggerating but he heard the truth when the veteran commander's voice cracked. This was a man that knew violence and whatever he had just seen had shaken him. He ordered the commander to monitor the situation but not interfere. The French paratroopers would fight one battle at a time.

Trinquier was not anxious to report the massacre to Massu and decided to wait until he saw the evidence for himself. Besides, Massu would take the news much better once the battle on the hillside had concluded and he could give the general an accurate count of dead and captured mujahideen. Trinquier and his men were on the verge of a great victory but all that would be lost if the recon commander's report was true. His mission had been to protect the pied-noir and French citizens. He had failed. The massacre would make the headlines, not his victory against the rebel forces. Trinquier was a man of purpose and not one to dwell on his failures. He was mad as hell and his mood darkened.

The para captain above the mujahideen lines was the next to radio in. Trinquier became unglued when the para captain informed him that Bruno was leading one of his squads in an attack against the mujahideen right flank. He berated the captain for not obeying the orders he had been given and following the plan they had agreed upon.

Bruno led the squad of paratroopers around the backside of the hill and moved up on the flank of the mujahideen line. It was a fairly standard maneuver to roll up an entrenched flank where the enemy could only concentrate a small amount of its firepower. Bruno's forces on the other hand could spread out and attack with everything he had. This allowed a smaller force to attack a much larger one with a high probability of success. The key was to get the enemy to break and run before they could regroup and put up a viable defense on their flank under attack. Bruno knew that the momentum and ferocity of the attack was the best way to break the mujahideen units which would realize that they were being attacked from two sides. Nothing demoralized a soldier more than seeing his comrades running for the hills and leaving him behind.

Bruno suggested that the sergeant move his squad up until they were within grenade-throwing distance. The grenades could be followed by a brief charge using their submachineguns. The sergeant was a veteran of World War II and Indochina. He knew what Bruno wanted and agreed.

The paratroopers moved as close as they dared without being spotted by the mujahideen firing at the French below. They spread out into two parallel lines of eight men each and lay flat, waiting for the signal to attack. Bruno, the sergeant and three other paratroopers tossed grenades into the mujahideen lines.

The exploding grenades killed four mujahideen and wounded three others. Bruno was the first to leap to his feet and open fire with his submachinegun. He was joined by the sergeant and the squad of paratroopers. Bruno was in the center like the tip of an arrow and charged forward toward the side of the mujahideen line. He was not alone, the paratroopers on both sides of him kept pace while firing their weapons. Bruno yelled a battle cry and was joined by those that followed. It struck fear into the Mujahideen as Bruno had hoped.

The mujahideen in the firing line had three choices: they could continue to fire against the larger paratrooper force below them on the hillside, turn and fire on the paratroopers charging from the side and overrunning their lines or… flee. Most chose the latter and those that didn't were soon dead.

Si Larbi saw his lines falling apart as several of his men ran past him and down the hillside. He ordered the men to stop but it was too late. Fear had struck his men and it would be a complete rout if he didn't do something first. He ordered his men to retreat down the side of the hill away from Bruno's paratroopers. An orderly retreat would allow him and his men to put up a credible defense as they backed away from the enemy. It would save dozens if not hundreds of lives.

The mujahideen line rolled back on itself and the men that were fleeing again took up firing positions and rejoined the fight. The mujahideen resistance became stronger and held off the attacking French paratroopers. Si Larbi considered counterattacking.

He realized that his men's morale was shaky at best and if the French pressed them they could break once again. He decided to continue the retreat. The mujahideen forces leapfrogged backwards and retreated across the hillside toward their opposite flank.

The fighting slowed as the mujahideen disappeared and the French ran out of targets. The French para captain above would never have his chance at cutting off the mujahideen retreat.

Si Larbi and a large portion of the mujahideen escaped to fight another day.

Bruno could not see what was down the opposite side of the hill and as much as he and his men wanted to continue the pursuit it was not prudent. *Never turn a victory into an enemy ambush,* he thought. The French broke off the attack.

After a brief celebration and a patrol of the area to ensure the mujahideen were indeed gone, the individual paratrooper units combined into a battalion and moved down the hillside toward the city.

Bruno and Trinquier were leading. Trinquier said nothing about Bruno's imposition on his command. Bruno had won another battle but Trinquier would receive the credit for the victory on the hillside. It was his command after all.

The mujahideen had dispersed and were hiding in the Muslim sections of the city when the French forces arrived.

The French paratroopers were shocked as they entered the city and saw the gore from the massacre. Veterans of World War II and Indochina became visibly sick, especially when they saw the torn and disfigured bodies of women that had been raped and the severed limbs of little children. The Muslim mob had killed one hundred and twenty French citizens and pied-noir in the most brutal manner imaginable.

Bruno wanted to turn away but knew that his composure in the face of such violence would give confidence to the men around him, something they desperately needed at that moment. They followed his example and stayed alert as they moved through the streets. The French medics moved to help any civilians still alive. There were not many.

Trinquier ordered his radioman to put in a call to headquarters and request a conversation with General Massu. It took less than a minute before Massu was on the line. Trinquier reported the victory on the hillside with over fifty-six dead and twelve captured mujahideen. Massu congratulated him. "There was an unfortunate development," said Trinquier over the radio, "The fellagha mob that we thought would focus their attack on the garrison broke off their attack after only a few casualties. They turned around and attacked the pied-noir communities on the edge of the city. I am afraid there are quite a few casualties. Over."

"Don't dilly-dally, man. How many casualties?" said Massu breaking radio protocol.

"Extensive, sir. It will take time to count the limbs," said Trinquier not wanting to reveal the entirety of the massacre over the radio where others might be listening.

"I see," said Massu.

There was a long silence. Trinquier waited. "We cannot let this stand, Roger," said Massu. "It will embolden them."

"I understand, sir. I assure you, my men and I will do what is required," said Trinquier.

"Very well. See that you do. Out," said Massu and the signal went dead.

Trinquier handed the headset back to the radioman.

ELEVEN

The mountains of Algeria were peppered with valuable minerals. Mines generated a large portion of the tax revenue that the French needed to rebuild after the Nazi occupation that had destroyed many of their cities and much of their public infrastructure during World War II.

The El-Halia Sulfur mine east of Philippeville was owned by a family of Spanish settlers that had come to Algeria at the turn of the century. It was a small concern but it provided a healthy income and dozens of jobs for the surrounding communities both pied-noir and Muslim. It was a tunnel mine which was rare for Sulfur mines in Northern Africa. Open pit mines were safer and allowed for the use of heavy machinery to extract the mineral. However in this mine the vein of Sulfur ore was deep in a mountain side and required multiple shafts to harvest. It had to be mined by hand, and that meant jobs. There was, of course, ethnic tension between the two communities but they had learned to get along by simply staying out of each other's business and keeping to themselves.

The mine compound was surrounded by a barbed wire fence and only had one guarded entrance that was used both by the employees and the trucks that carried the Sulfur to a processing plant near the city of Constantine. Three armed guards patrolled the compound, and there was a stash of weapons that were kept under lock and key that could be used by the employees if the mine was every attacked by rebels or thieves seeking its weekly payroll. Many years had passed since anyone had been bold enough to attempt to break the security, and the miners carried on their day to day work without concern of outside intervention.

It was the yellow dust that really concerned them. It stung their lungs and assaulted their sense of smell. Rotten eggs and pig shit were the most common descriptions. One never really grew used to it, they would say. Being Sulfur and used in most munitions, the mineral was also quite flammable, especially in dust form. The miners went to great length to prevent open flames and sparks in the mine. Electric lights had been used since their invention and that greatly reduced accidents. Air was pumped deep into the mine where the miners worked. Vent shafts were cut into the rock to allow the yellow dust to be pumped out and prevent dangerous build-ups that could blind the miners and choke them to death.

The FLN sapper that visited the mine that day had penetrated the barbed wire fence the night before and stayed hidden from the morning patrol. Saadi had instructed him personally on how to enter the compound and where to go. The sapper waited until the miners arrived for the day shift. Unlike the night shift which was made up of mostly Muslim workers, the day shift was staffed with pied-noir miners. Both shifts preferred to be ethnically divided when they worked. It prevented arguments between the miners.

When the sapper was sure the last of the Muslim miners had left the compound, he crawled to one of the ventilation shafts and detached the metal hood leading to the air pump. He pulled out a Molotov cocktail from the canvas bag he had brought with him. He used the American lighter that Saadi had given him to light the end of the gasoline soaked rag and dropped the bottle down the shaft. Then he jumped up and ran for the perimeter fence.

A guard spotted him as he ran and opened fire with his submachinegun. The sapper was hit three times and fell into the barbed wire fence where he died just as the Molotov cocktail hit the bottom of the air shaft. The bottle broke and the burning rag ignited the gasoline just as Saadi said it would. A ball of flame ignited the yellow dust. It wasn't an explosion that killed the miners inside but rather a wall of flame that incinerated any in its path and sucked up all the available oxygen suffocating anyone lucky enough to avoid the fire. The destruction was complete and killed eighteen pied-noir miners.

The affect that the FLN had hoped for was not the death of the miners, although it did make the headlines of the Algerian newspapers, but the dividing of the community. The pied-noir blamed the Muslims just as the FLN had planned and exacted their revenge in a raid that killed four Muslim families, including children.

Trinquier was issuing orders to his company commanders when his radioman approached. "Colonel, I've picked up a distress call from a pied-noir colony at El-Halia mine twenty kilometers to the east. It seems there has been an explosion. Many settlers were killed and wounded. They are requesting military assistance."

"Jesus, can't these people do anything for themselves?" said Trinquier.

Trinquier considered for a moment and looked over at Bruno standing nearby. He did not want Bruno around to witness what was going to be required in Philippeville. He turned to the radioman and said, "Tell the miners we will be sending help."

"Yes, sir," said the radioman.

Trinquier walked over to Bruno and said, "Hell of a morning."

"Yeah. Hell is a good word to use," said Bruno. "Do we know who did it?"

"We have our suspicions. We will find out," said Trinquier. "I was wondering if you could do me a favor?"

"Of course. What do you need?"

"As you can see, my hands are quite full here with this mess. We just received a distress call from the El-Halia mine complex. I was hoping you could take a platoon up there and investigate."

"Absolutely," said Bruno.

"Excellent," said Trinquier.

It was late in the afternoon when the five truck convoy carrying Bruno and a platoon of paratroopers rolled up the hill toward the El-Halia community.

Black smoke rose from the mining complex. The fire inside the mine was yet to be extinguished and would probably burn for several more days until the surviving workers sealed off the entrance and air vents to starve the fire of oxygen.

The neighborhood next to the mine was quiet. Bruno found it strange that there was nobody on the street, not even children. Communities usually pulled together with families visiting each other for comfort after a disaster such as the one reported. But here… there was nothing… not a soul in sight.

The first truck pulled to a stop on the edge of the community and Bruno stepped out. He motioned for the sergeant to deploy the men. The paratroopers were formed into six fire teams and moved on to the community streets. Still nothing. The sergeant motioned for a corporal and his team to enter one of the houses.

The team moved up and the corporal knocked on the front door. There was no answer. He looked back at his sergeant and shrugged. The sergeant motioned for him to be more assertive. The corporal kicked in the front door and the team entered. Two minutes later they came back out. Another shrug from the corporal revealed that the house was empty.

The paratroopers kicked in doors and entered houses until they finally came upon a door that they couldn't kick in. They moved around the back of the house and found the back door too was blocked from the inside. They continued around the house until they found a bathroom window. It was too small for anyone on the team to fit through. They called the smallest paratrooper in the platoon to the house, broke the window with the butts of their guns and boosted the small paratrooper in through the opening.

He fell headfirst into the bathtub under the window. Fortunately, his helmet protected his skull from cracking against the porcelain. He gathered himself and cautiously moved through the house. He saw the problem right away. Someone had stacked all the furniture in the living room up against the front door preventing it from being opened. The same was true with the back door.

He moved down a hallway and opened the door to each room until he found one that was locked. He kicked it in, breaking the doorframe. He entered. It was dark, the curtains drawn tight. He moved around the end of the bed and saw a European woman huddled with her two small children. She looked terrified like she and her children were going to die. He tried to reassure her that he meant no harm. She asked one simple question, "Muslim?"

The paratrooper shook his head. She seemed to take a breath but kept her children tight in her arm. "I am going to get help," he said in French.

Her eyes went wide again and said, "Muslims?"

"No," he said. "No Muslims. I promise."

Tears streamed down her face and she heaved out a cry of relief. The paratrooper could not help but feel for the woman. He moved back into the hallway, wiped the tears from his eyes with the sleeve of his uniform and cleared the furniture from the front door.

Within an hour, Bruno felt he had a pretty clear picture of what had happened in the little community of El-Halia…

When the dust had cleared from the initial mine explosion, the security guards found the body of the dead sapper. He was clearly North African and the Quran in his pocket demonstrated that he was a practicing Muslim. There were no other identification papers on the man and no way of knowing who, if anybody, had sent him to destroy the mine. But the guards and the pied-noir that gathered around the corpse had already drawn their own conclusions.

The peaceful relationship between the Muslim miners and the pied-noir miners had been disintegrating over the last year, especially as the cry for Independence increased. The pied-noir were afraid that Independence in a Muslim state would mean the destruction of their way of life and potentially the death of their families. The Muslims had argued that they all could live in peace once the French had gone. The pied-noir believed they knew better.

The French government had taken the best farms away from Muslim families that had lived on them for generations. The Muslims were compensated but not until after the land was auctioned off at a sharp discount to the colonists as an incentive for settling in Algeria. The Muslims were not allowed to bid on their own farms in a public auction.

Once Independence was achieved the Muslim families would surely want their land back. The pied-noir had worked hard to improve the land and weren't about to give it back to the Muslims. It would mean civil war in which the pied-noir militias would be vastly outnumbered and outgunned.

Fist fights had broken out between the miners and had to be broken up by the mine's security guards. Things had gotten so bad that the mine owner had demanded that all weapons within the community be locked up until things had settled down. He was the only one with the key.

In a weekend boxing match sanctioned by the mine as a way to blow off steam the Muslim community pitted their best fighter against the pied-noir's best fighter. The pied-noir fighter was a mountain of muscle from Northern Germany. He beat the Muslim fighter to a pulp before the referee and three other pied-noir pulled him off the unconscious fighter. The Muslim fighter died two days later.

The pied-noir were smug. They had made their point. And it was the Muslims that now feared them. So much so, they had blown up the mine with a large portion of the pied-noir inside so they could even the odds in the village. It was obvious to everyone. It was also untrue. The FLN had sent the sapper with the mission to blow up the mine and divide the community. He had succeeded.

The pied-noir were enraged by the attack and had retaliated against the Muslims killing several in a most brutal manner. The Muslims vastly outnumbered the pied-noir. A mob of over one thousand Muslims descended on the pied-noir community and killed everyone they could find. Only six Pied-Noir families had survived by barricading themselves inside their homes and putting out the fires from the Molotov cocktails hurled through the windows.

Café Wars

The European woman's husband tried to sneak out and go for help. He had been caught in the streets and torn apart by the Muslims. She wept over his remains when she finally found what was left of him. It was more than she could take and later that night when she was alone in her home, she hung herself in her kitchen orphaning her two small children.

Bruno radioed in his report to Trinquier. He told the colonel the story of El-Halia as best as he could piece it together. After the massacre the majority of the Muslims had fled the town and hidden in the hills afraid of French Army reprisals. Slowly, they were coming back and occupying their homes. They were very wary of the paratroopers that patrolled their streets. The Muslims' anger had turned to fear.

Trinquier repeated the words he had been told by Massu, "We cannot let this stand."

Bruno knew what he meant. Justice needed to be swift and overwhelming to keep the Muslims from being emboldened and continuing their attacks on the pied-noir community, and to keep the Independence movement from growing.

Bruno was a patriot and loved his country of which Algeria had been a part for over one hundred years. It was not unlike the American Civil War where a large segment of the country had grown distasteful of the union and wanted to go their separate ways. He believed in democracy and the right to self-determination. They were principles that had made his country the envy of Europe and the world.

He had fought the Viet Minh in Indochina because they wanted to leave the French Union. Cambodia,

Laos, Tunisia and Morocco were in the process or had all already left the union. But Algeria was different. It was considered part of France not just a colony. And now the Algerians too were fighting for their freedom. France was falling apart. It was at war with itself, fighting against the very principles on which the new Republic had been founded.

Bruno knew that he needed to act quickly if he was going to take action. He avoided letting his desire for a combat command influence his decision. He was not afraid to disobey orders from his superiors if he thought they were unjust or just plain stupid. In fact, Massu and Trinquier were not his commanders. He was still considered an observer. Part of him wanted to go back to Paris and forget this ever happened. But that was a coward's path and Bruno was no coward.

As the sun rose the next morning, Bruno issued orders to the platoon to round up as many of the Muslim men as could be found. Within an hour, one hundred and fifty prisoners were herded into the town square.

The trials were quick, often only lasting a minute or two. Evidence was shallow at best. Blood stains on the hands or shirt were enough to convict a man. Bruno ordered them all to be hanged.

The women wailed and shrilled their tongues in unison as they watched the French paratroopers carry out Bruno's orders. Bruno stood at parade rest the entire time with eyes staring straight ahead and his face solemn and unmoving... except for a slight twitch on the left side of his face that he could not control. He was showing the Muslims French justice and determination. He was the face of France.

TWELVE

The battle at Philippeville seemed to be winding down. There was still sporadic gunfire when French forces cornered one of the FLN commandos. The commandos were exceedingly brave. They did not surrender but chose to fight to the death.

Trinquier stood in a café with his unit commanders and his staff gathered around. The café was a pied-noir bistro owned by an older Spanish couple that had been running the establishment for over thirty years. Their bodies lay on the tile floor. The man had been disemboweled and the woman violently raped until she died of shock.

Trinquier had left the bodies in place to make his point. "I cannot let this stand," Trinquier said to his men. "If you love France as I love France you will not let this stand. The FLN and their Muslim collaborators have murdered your brothers and sisters; French citizens. They have murdered the colonists we have sworn to protect. They have murdered their own kind for remaining loyal to the French cause. They have murdered police officers for doing nothing more than their duty. They have attacked our garrison. This uprising will not stop unless we stop it. Here. Now. We cannot let this stand. You are authorized to use all measures at your disposal to bring justice to this city. We must retaliate ten-fold for what they have done if we are to bring peace back to this community. They must know that France will fight fire with fire. That our judgement is swift and complete. We will not let this stand. Vive la France!"

"Vive la France!" said the men.

"You have your orders. Dismissed," said Trinquier.

The officers saluted and moved off. The captain of the paratroopers that Bruno had jumped with was slow to leave. Trinquier took note. "Perhaps you would feel more comfortable if your orders came from Colonel Bigeard?" said Trinquier.

"No, sir," said the captain.

"Do you duty, Captain," said Trinquier with an unwavering firmness.

"Yes, sir," said the captain saluting and moving off with more zeal in his step.

The paratroopers had seen the carnage on the streets and in the homes of the pied-noir neighborhoods. Many were sickened by it. Others enraged. Their commanders repeated the words of Massu and Trinquier, "We will not let it stand." and ordered them to use all means necessary. They were unleashed like hounds chasing a fox and their vengeance was complete.

Café Wars

The FLN leaders knew the French would retaliate against the Muslim citizens of Philippeville. They had planned on it. The mujahideen put up a token resistance just so they could say they tried to stop the French. But that was not what they wanted… to stop the French. Philippeville would become the symbol of French oppression. It would reveal the true nature of the French and the pied-noir. Newspapers would focus on what the French had done not the FLN. The FLN were rebels. The French were civilized or at least that is what the world had thought until Philippeville.

The final body count was never reported. The French admitted to twelve hundred Muslim citizens being killed. The Muslims claimed ten times that number. The truth was somewhere in between. But it wasn't the number of Muslims killed that shocked the world. It was the way they were killed.

Bullets and grenades were not the weapons of choice that day. They were the bayonet and the rifle butt. The French paratroopers used the same methods the Muslims had used against the pied-noir and some additional methods they had learned from the Viet Minh. Nobody was safe within the Muslim neighborhoods and nobody was spared when caught. Those that could, fled the city. Those that could not, died.

The paratroopers did not set fire to the city as the FLN and Muslims had done. They did not want the fire to spread. Fire was indiscriminate, the paratroopers were not. Their focus against the Muslim community was sharp as a razor's edge.

When Trinquier called Massu on the phone to give him the final report, Massu stopped him before he started and said, "Colonel, I have been following the reports from our intelligence group and I am well aware of the situation. I think it would be best to accurately detail your attack on the mujahideen on the hillside and the fellagha attack against the garrison and the pied-noir communities."

"And what followed?" said Trinquier.

"Less detail in the official report on the actions later in the battle would be prudent," said Massu.

"Perhaps you are correct, General," said Trinquier.

"You can give me your report in person when you get back," said Massu. "But even then it is not necessary to report every last detail. You are the commander of your battalion and your discretion is accepted."

"Very well, sir," said Trinquier. "I look forward to seeing you, General."

"And I you, Colonel." Massu hung up.

Several hours later, Trinquier received Bruno's phone call to report on the events of El-Halia. Trinquier repeated Massu instructions about leaving out unsavory details and assuring Bruno that his command of the platoon and their actions were acceptable. "You are saying that I should lie in my report?" said Bruno with his usual frankness.

"No. Of course not. But the world and the French public may not understand the actions needed to keep the peace," said Trinquier.

"I will not cower under the umbrella of ignorance. Your men and I have performed as you requested with honor. We have nothing to hide. My report will reflect the truth of the events and nothing else. You may do with it as you wish."

It is as I feared, thought Trinquier. *Bruno is going to be a problem.*

A formal dress laid on the bed. Brigitte had six pairs of shoes sitting on the floor in front of the dress. Nothing seemed to match. She was not usually this picky about what she wore. She liked to look attractive but was often too busy to spend time fussing. She had learned to be a minimalist when it came to hair and makeup. She never wore perfume in combat for fear the enemy might pick up her scent, endangering herself and the men around her.

She had worn the dress before to receptions at several embassies and government functions but this was different. She was to be the guest of honor at a dinner hosted by the soon-to-be president of Egypt, Nasser. She decided to leave early to the airport and pick up a new pair of shoes on the way. *It is a special occasion and requires special shoes,* she thought.

Coyle had offered to accompany her but then got the call from Bruno asking him to fly the paratroopers into Algeria. She understood the importance of his mission and said that the dinner was nothing more than a gathering. She lied. She was hoping Coyle would see through her deceit and demand to go with her. He didn't. She was disappointed when he told Bruno he would take the mission. She hid her emotions from Coyle. She was good at hiding emotion. She believed it was what a professional woman needed to do to be respected. She believed it was one of the reasons Coyle was attracted to her. She could stand toe-to-toe with anyone, man or woman.

She glanced at her wristwatch and did a quick calculation in her head. There was plenty of time before her flight for a quick shopping trip downtown. She could leave her luggage in the taxi and have the driver wait while she ducked into her favorite shoe boutique. She knew she was overestimating her decision-making ability when it came to shoes but she didn't care. This was important.

She called a cab and asked the dispatcher to have the driver come upstairs to her apartment to help with her luggage. She was quite capable of carrying her luggage down to the street but this was Paris not the northern highlands of Vietnam. She did not want to break a sweat before shopping and the long flight to Egypt. She finished packing.

The taxi driver loaded her luggage into the trunk while Brigitte climbed into the back seat of the cab. The driver climbed in and said, "Airport, Mademoiselle?"

"Yes, but first I need to make a quick stop downtown to pick up a pair of shoes."

"Very well, but I will run the meter," said the driver.

"Do as you please. I will only be a few minutes."

"Of course. It is just a pair of shoes. Yes?"

"You are being impertinent."

"I am a taxi driver and that makes me a realist," he said starting the engine and pulling into the street.

Brigitte did not see the sedan pulling out and following the taxi. The driver was a young Algerian man. Marwa sat in the passenger seat. She reached down and pulled a submachinegun from a canvas bag and laid it in her lap. There was not enough room on the street for two cars to drive side by side in the same direction. She would need to be patient and wait until the taxi pulled onto the four-lane boulevard that led to the airport.

A few minutes later both cars pulled onto the boulevard just as the assassins expected. The driver of the sedan changed lanes and accelerated to parallel the taxi. Marwa rolled down her window and chambered a round into the submachinegun just as Saadi had shown her.

Brigitte was completely unaware of the danger as the sedan gained speed and moved closer. She was thinking about Coyle. How could he be so dense and not see that she needed him by her side? Yes, his mission was important but this was a dinner in her honor being hosted by the leader of Egypt for Christ's sake. If he was going to be in a relationship with her he would need to learn to make sacrifices.

She reflected for a moment and softened. She thought about Dien Bien Phu where Coyle had risked his life to parachute into the garrison in hopes of protecting her. He was almost killed by enemy fire. McGoon, Coyle's best friend, was killed during the flight. *Tom has sacrificed for me,* she thought. *He has lost a great deal and it still haunts him. I must admit… I did tell him that the dinner was not important and that he should go on his mission. After all, he is just a man not a mind reader.*

The sedan pulled up alongside the taxi. Marwa placed the barrel of the submachinegun out the window and rested it on the doorframe. She pointed the gun at Brigitte's head and reached for the trigger.

Brigitte was lost in thought and oblivious to what was happening.

It was only sheer luck that the taxi driver turned down another intersecting boulevard along the shopping district before Marwa was able to fire her weapon. The sedan drove past the intersection. Marwa screamed in anger. The young driver was startled and slammed on the taxi's brakes skidding to a halt. He jammed the gearshift into reverse and attempted to back into the intersection. The traffic was too heavy. Cars honked and blocked his way. He shifted into first and made a U-turn but it was too late. The taxi carrying Brigitte had disappeared in the traffic and all the taxis appeared the same. Marwa was furious and let the young driver know her anger in no uncertain terms cursing him with every oath she knew. She had lost her opportunity to serve Allah and Saadi. Shoe shopping had saved Brigitte's life.

Nasser was hosting a traditional Egyptian dinner in Cairo's Presidential Palace. He and his guests were seated on short stools with thick pillows around a hand-woven carpet. A roasted lamb surrounded by rabbits and pigeons made up the centerpiece. Ful medames with hard boiled eggs and slices of lemons, kasari with its mix of rice, lentils and chickpeas topped with a spicy tomato sauce, and kofta – meatballs of minced chicken and beef mixed with regional spices and onions - were laid out on the platters sitting on the carpet. There were no individual plates or utensils. As was Arab tradition, guests were

expected to use aish baladi - the Egyptian pita bread –
to scoop up mouthfuls of the various dishes and eat
with their fingers.

As the guest of honor, Brigitte was seated next to
Nasser. She knew that Nasser was a man of the 20th
Century and that the traditional feast was for her
benefit. Nasser was trying to impress her. Why, she
did not know. Her past articles about Nasser and
Egypt had been considered disparaging by the Arab
community. "If you wish I can arrange for a fork or
spoon. We are not complete barbarians," said Nasser.

"No. This is fine. The food is excellent," said
Brigitte scooping up a piece of pigeon with her pita
bread. "Your excellency, there are many in my
country that feel your pan-Arab rhetoric is stoking the
flames of revolt in Algeria."

Nasser chuckled at the question, "Imperialist
powers rarely see nationalistic points of view as
anything but reactionary."

"But isn't pan-Arabism just another form of union
such as currently exists between France and Algeria?"

"Yes but between Arab nations not the Western
nations that have enslaved them. The Arabs have
common traditions and cultures. Only Arabs can truly
understand Arabs."

"You believe the Algerian people should be
allowed self-determination?"

"Of course. Shouldn't we all."

"I don't have to remind you that Algeria has been
part of France for well over one hundred years."

"Time does not equate justice."

"And the Israelis… shouldn't they be allowed self-
determination?"

"The Israelis have stolen their nation from the Palestinians that they now enslave."

"Not according to the United Nations."

"Ah, well... I doubt the United Nations can agree upon anything when pressed."

"They agree that the Suez Canal and the Straits of Tiran should remain open to the ships of all nations, including Israel."

"Yes but the Suez does not belong to the United Nations. It is Egypt's."

"Britain and France would disagree. French investors built the canal and Britain purchased Egypt's interest long ago."

"A consortium of western investors is allowed to profit from the canal through an operational company but the canal itself has always been owned by Egypt. As a nation we will continue to protect Egyptian soil and water."

"So it is Egypt that determines who has the right to use the canal?"

"Yes. We will do with it whatever we see fit."

"Including denying Israeli ships freedom of navigation?"

"If it is our desire."

"And is it?"

"Yes. For the time being. Until Israel finds a just solution to the Palestinian problem... or ceases to exist. Whichever comes first."

"Back to the Algerian question. The French military claims you are sheltering the FLN and giving them aid. Are you?"

"The French military makes many claims. Their generals all want to become politicians. They say what the people want to hear."

"So, you deny helping the FLN?"

"Algerians are free to come and go as they please in our nation. We welcome all Arabs."

"Do you allow them to broadcast on your radio stations?"

"You know we do, Mademoiselle Friang. I would think a journalist like yourself would appreciate the right to express one's views."

"Even when that view promotes violence?"

Nasser smiled instead of answering the question and said, "Have some more roasted lamb. It's an old Arab recipe and quite tasty."

"Your excellency, why am I here? You know my views are not sympathetic toward Egyptian claims and pan-Arabism."

"Mademoiselle Friang, you have become the latest flavor of ice cream to the French public. They read your articles. They listen to you. Egypt does not seek confrontation for the sake of confrontation, especially when journalists are involved. I believe your negative attitude toward Egypt is because you have never understood Egypt. The same goes for Algeria."

"You believe I do not understand my own country?"

"Have you ever been to Algeria?"

"Of course."

"I don't mean the French façade built in the European quarters of Algiers. I mean the real Algeria; the Muslim neighborhoods and the shantytowns, Algerian schools and hospitals. They are… a different world than the world you know. They will challenge your assumptions. As a journalist in search of the truth, don't you feel they are worth a visit?"

"Perhaps. But what does that have to do with Egypt?"

"We are all Arabs. The way your government treats Algeria reflects on France's relationship with the rest of the Arab nations, including Egypt. The Arabs want peace but only through respect and dignity... which can only be offered when you truly understand us. Peek behind the veil, Mademoiselle Friang. Peek behind the veil."

A messenger walked into the hall and approached. He handed Nasser a message. Nasser's countenance darkened as he read in silence.

"I hope everything is okay," said Brigitte, probing.

"I am afraid not, Mademoiselle Friang. You will have much to write when you return to Paris. There has been an uprising in Algeria. French troops and colonist militias have just slaughtered twelve thousand Muslims in Philippeville and the surrounding communities," said Nasser. "I fear the time for understanding has passed."

Brigitte was crestfallen. She had to remind herself that Nasser was a shrewd politician and was not beyond orchestrating an intricate lie to further his intentions. She would need to find the truth for herself and she couldn't do that sitting on an expensive rug eating pigeon. "Your Excellency, if you will excuse me, I must leave," she said.

"Of course," said Nasser. "I will have my limousine take you back to your hotel."

Brigitte could feel her hands shaking and did her best to hide them as left the room.

A taxi pulled to a stop in front of Cairo's International Airport. Brigitte exited the cab. She waited until the trunk was unloaded and her luggage was handed off to a porter before paying the driver. She was irritated and curt with everyone that came in contact with her. Her mind was racing considering the angles of what Nasser had told her about the massacre. She could not allow herself believe it and decided to not pass any kind of judgment until she investigated.

Brigitte did not notice the sedan pulling up behind and dropping off a man dressed in a suit without luggage. The man looked Egyptian with coal black hair, dark eyes and a dark complexion but could have been Algerian or even French. His suit was not expensive and he wore a black tie over a white shirt. When Brigitte entered the airport the man followed her at a discreet distance.

Brigitte approached the airline counter and spoke to the ticket agent, "I'd like to change my ticket to include a stop in Algiers."

"Yes, ma'am. How long will you be staying in Algiers?"

"Just the day," said Brigitte. "I'd like an afternoon flight to Paris the following day."

"Very well. The flight for Algiers leaves in twenty minutes. You will need to hurry," said the agent.

"That's fine," said Brigitte.

The agent changed the ticket and collected the increase in fare before handing her the two new tickets. She watched the porter tie the destination tag onto her luggage and hand it over to the ticket agent. She tipped the porter and moved off toward passport control.

The man tailing her watched her move through passport control. He walked to an employee gate and showed the guard his badge. The guard let him pass into the international waiting area of the terminal without a passport. He followed Brigitte to the gate and waited until she boarded her flight. Then he went to a nearby payphone and called Nasser on his personal phone line. Nasser did not want a journalist like Brigitte loose in his country, especially not now. The time for his bold move was drawing near and Nasser knew that secrecy could very well determine his success or failure.

Trinquier sat waiting in the reception of Massu's office. He was still wearing his battle fatigues from earlier that morning in Philippeville. He noticed a small speckling of blood on his left pocket. "Do you have a tissue?" said Massu to the lieutenant sitting at the desk.

"Of course, Colonel," said the Lieutenant and handed Trinquier a small stack of tissues from a drawer in his desk.

Trinquier wet one of the tissues with his tongue and cleaned the specks of blood off the pocket as best he could. *I should have taken the time to change*, he thought.

Bruno entered the reception area and saw Trinquier. He did not salute as was the custom to a senior officer. Trinquier and Bruno were both Lieutenant Colonels but Trinquier had received his promotion first and was therefore considered senior. Trinquier could have been considered Bruno's commanding officer because of his temporary command of the paratroopers in El-Halia but Bruno chose not to see it that way. "I am afraid you will have to wait your turn," said Trinquier, standing.

Bruno grabbed Trinquier and pushed him against the wall, "Is it true? Twelve thousand?"

"Come now, Bruno. You knew there would be blood," said Trinquier.

"Yes but not in rivers," said Bruno. "And not women and children."

Trinquier smiled and said, "Your report of El-Halia was quite telling."

"I did my duty as ordered," said Bruno.

"And what makes you think I did not do mine… as ordered?"

Bruno was stunned by the revelation that Massu might have ordered the killings.

The Lieutenant at the desk ducked into Massu's office without knocking. Major Aussaresses was sitting across from Massu. "I'm sorry, General. There is an… incident in the reception area that you may wish to supervise. Colonel Bigeard has arrived," said the Lieutenant.

Massu knew immediately what the Lieutenant meant and moved quickly into the reception area.

Massu saw Bruno with his fists clenched around Trinquier's uniform. Massu gave a quick glance at the Lieutenant. "Attention," said the Lieutenant. "The general has entered the room."

Bruno released Trinquier and saluted. Tringuier straightened his uniform and saluted. They remained at attention. "Colonel Bigeard, I do not know your last commander but I seriously doubt he would have approved of such comportment. I am technically not your commanding officer and am not required to report such an event. However Colonel Trinquier may feel otherwise," said Massu. "Colonel Trinquier?"

"It was just a misunderstanding between fellow officers, General," said Trinquier. "No need to report anything."

"Very well. At ease, gentlemen," said Massu. "We shall resume our conversation in my office."

Bruno and Trinquier followed Massu into his office. They sat. "Before we get started I want to make it clear to both of you. I am not interested in body count at this point in time. You are commanding officers in the French Army. I trust you have exercised proper restraint over the men under your command and have only done what was necessary to fulfil your missions," said Massu. "Is that understood?"

"Yes, sir," said Trinquier.

Bruno took a moment to consider Massu's words. Massu was sweeping the entire affair under the carpet including Bruno's own actions in El-Halia. Bruno knew he was part of it all, whether he agreed with it or not. He did not doubt his actions in El-Halia but questioned how the public would interpret what he and his men had done, should they find out. What Trinquier had done was on a completely different level of barbarity. But what did Bruno know for sure? He had only heard rumors of the events. He had left Philippeville before the massacre. And now Massu was ordering them both to remain silent. Perhaps Massu was right. These were extreme times that called for extreme measures. Bruno believed that one should fight fire with fire. He responded, "Yes, General."

"Good. Now that we understand one another," said Massu. "It is important to recognize that blood runs hot during and after battle. We are warriors and we are required to inflict violence on our enemies. I will wait until I read your full reports on the events of the preceding days before making any recommendations or commendations but I want you to know that I understand you both did what you needed to do. The insurgencies in Philippeville and El-Halia have been turned back and peace has been restored. France owes you both a debt of gratitude."

Massu took pause to let the words sink in and then continued, "Colonel Bigeard, I am offering you command of the 3rd Colonial Parachute Regiment. Your mission, should you chose to accept it, is to take the battle to the countryside and root out the mujahideen rebels hiding in the mountains, the desert and the forests. You will have a fleet of helicopters at your disposal that should be used for your initial attack and followed up by para drops that will bring in additional units to support the attack. Speed and maneuverability will be your allies and help ensure your success. Do you need time to consider, Colonel?"

"No, General. I am honored and I accept," said Bruno.

"Excellent. You will be under the command of Colonel Trinquier, who is being promoted to full colonel," said Massu.

Bruno tried to hide his wince on hearing that Trinquier was to be his commanding officer. "Major Aussaresses and his unit will provide the necessary intelligence as to the enemy's whereabouts.

Congratulations, Colonel Bigeard. You are once again the tip of France's lance."

Bruno was leaving the headquarters compound when he saw Brigitte at the main gate arguing with the sergeant in charge. "I am a member of the French press. I have a right to ask questions of the general and his staff," said Brigitte.

"You can ask all the questions you wish, Mademoiselle Friang, when you have an appointment," said the sergeant.

"It can take over a week to go through proper channels to get an appointment," said Brigitte. "By then this story will be old news."

"I wouldn't know. I don't read much," said the sergeant.

"Clearly not," said Brigitte.

"Brigitte, what are you doing here?" said Bruno as he approached.

"Oh, thank God," said Brigitte. "Bruno, please ask the sergeant to let me pass."

"I am afraid that is not possible," said Bruno.

"Not possible?" said Brigitte.

"The complex is on lockdown. There have been several terrorist attacks."

"That's why I am here. There is a wild rumor that French forces have massacred twelve thousand Muslims in Philippeville. I just want to get the facts so I can dispel the rumors before things get out of hand."

"I understand, Brigitte. But I cannot let you inside the compound without the general's permission."

"So, go get the general's permission," said Brigitte.

"It's not that easy, Brigitte. The general is a busy man. Perhaps you could ask for an appointment through his office?"

"If anyone says appointment to me again, I swear I will claw their eyes out with my fingernails."

"Is that a threat?" said the sergeant.

"She's not threatening anyone, Sergeant. She is just venting her frustration."

"Sounded like a threat to me," said the sergeant.

"Tell the sergeant you were just venting, Brigitte."

Brigitte stood her ground and remained silent. "Tell the sergeant you were just kidding or he will arrest you and throw you into the brig, Brigitte," said Bruno. "I do not have the keys to the brig and it will take me some time to get you out. Perhaps a week or two."

Brigitte still stood her ground.

"I understand there are cockroaches and the occasional rat in our brig," said Bruno.

That broke Brigitte's silence, "While I have faced much worse than cockroaches and rats, I will admit that I may have overreacted in my comments."

"Not much of an apology," said the sergeant.

"Let it go, Sergeant," said Bruno.

"Yes, sir," said the sergeant.

Bruno stepped past the gate and pulled Brigitte to one side, out of earshot of the sergeant. "Brigitte, what in the hell are you doing? You can't just barge in and ask questions about ongoing operations like you did in Vietnam. Things are different now."

"Why should they be different? I am just trying to get at the truth, Bruno."

"I am not so sure that is a wise idea," said Bruno.

"What are you talking about? Of course it's a good idea. I am a journalist. The people have a right to know what their military is doing."

"Do they?"

Brigitte was taken aback by Bruno's question. She considered the implications and said, "The rumors are true then?"

"I didn't say that."

"No. But your silence infers it is so."

"You can suppose whatever you wish. As you have always done."

"Just answer the damn question, Bruno. Did French troops kill twelve thousand Muslims?"

Bruno considered long and hard before answering. He knew Brigitte was like a dog with a bone when it came to researching a good story. "There was an action at Philippeville. I do not know the exact number of casualties. I left before..."

"You were there?"

"I wasn't part of what happened in the city. I was part of the battle on the hillside overlooking the city. Then I was ordered to another place."

"They didn't want you to see what they were planning?"

"I don't think they were planning anything. They were reacting. Things may have gotten out of hand. I don't know. I wasn't there when it happened, Brigitte. I swear it."

"How could they do such a thing?"

"There are two sides to every story, Brigitte. The Muslims slaughtered pied-noir families including woman and children."

"How do you know? You said you weren't there."

"I wasn't. But one hears things."

"Just more rumors?"

"I suppose. Yes."

"That's why I have to get in and interview the general, Bruno. He knows the truth."

"Maybe. Maybe not."

"What do you mean?"

"A general will only hear what he wants to hear."

"He's going to try and sweep twelve thousand Muslim deaths under the rug like bits of dust?"

"I don't know what he is going do. He's a general. I'm a colonel. I obey orders."

"That is a sorry excuse, Bruno."

"Yes. But it is the only one I have. I am sorry, Brigitte."

"I will not let this stand. Not until the truth comes out… all of it," said Brigitte.

"I wish you luck. I really do. But I must go now," said Bruno moving off and leaving Brigitte in front of the gate.

THIRTEEN

Bruno stood on an airfield and spoke to the eleven hundred men in his new regiment. He was wearing his jumpsuit as were the soldiers standing before him. There was a large stack of bricks to one side of the columns of men and a burlap sack at the end of each line. "You know who I am and what is expected. You are now a member of Bigeard's Regiment. You soon will be the elite of the elite. I will not fail in my duty and neither will you. We will not wait for our enemy to attack. We will take the battle to them. If you die, you will die with honor. When the enemy hears our helicopters and sees our parachutes they will fear you. Some will run. Most will fight. It is no matter to us. We will own the battlefield. We will complete our mission. The one promise I will make to you is that I will never ask you to anything that I will not do myself," said Bruno and turned to his executive officer, Major Bour. "Major, issue the day's ration."

Major Bour ordered the regiment's Sergeant-Major to carry out Bruno's command. The Sergeant-Major barked out orders to soldiers as the end of each line. They picked up the burlap sacks and passed them down each line of troops. Each soldier pulled out a raw onion and passed the sack down the line. "What is this?" asked a young soldier.

"Breakfast," said a veteran.

"But our wine ration?"

"Ain't no such thing in this Regiment. Colonel says it slows the stamina. And believe me… you're gonna need your stamina."

The passing of sacks continued until every soldier in the regiment held an onion, including Bruno. "Bon appetite," Bruno said and he took a large bite out of his onion.

His men followed his example. "Once you have finished your breakfast we will begin what I like to call the Grand twenty-five. You will each load twenty-five kilos of bricks into your rucksacks. With your rucksack on your back you will do twenty-five pull ups, twenty-five squats and then we will go on a twenty-five kilometer forced march. When not fighting, we train. You will be the fittest soldiers in the French army. And when we fight you will not tire. You will learn to love battle because it is the only time when you will not be exercising," said Bruno.

Bruno finished his onion and walked to the brick stack. He loaded his rucksack with bricks and slung it over his shoulders. His men followed his example. All of the officers under his command joined in the forced march. Bruno had one guiding principle for the commanders in his regiment – You lead by example or you do not lead. "Follow me," said Bruno as he set off at a brisk pace.

His men followed. Most puked up their onion before the first ten kilometers. Bruno smiled. He was known for a brutal sense of humor and joked freely with both the officers and the enlisted men under his command. He did not penalize his men for struggling as long as they didn't quit. Over time they would become strong and confident like him and they would love him for it. They would become Bruno's men.

Brigitte entered the reception area of the French interior minister's office and approached Mitterrand's secretary. The secretary recognized her from previous visits and considered warning Mitterrand but Brigitte was too quick. "How may I help you, Mademoiselle Friang?" said the secretary.

"I'd like to see Minister Mitterrand," said Brigitte.

"Of course," said the secretary opening up the scheduling book.

"You needn't play your game. I don't have an appointment," said Brigitte.

"I see. Unfortunately the minister is fulling booked this entire week. Perhaps I could schedule you in for next week? Say Thursday after lunch?"

"Please inform the minister I am here. I am sure he can make time to answer a few questions."

"May I ask what it regards?"

"You may not."

"I see," said the secretary. "If you would like to have a seat?"

"Thank you," said Brigitte and she sat in a chair that had a good view of the door to the minister's office. The secretary called Mitterrand on the phone and spoke in a hushed voice. He nodded several times and hung up the phone. "The minister suggests you make an appointment."

"Please inform the minister that I will camp out in front of his house if he does not grant me an interview."

"I am sure that will not be necessary. If you will just—"

"He knows I'm not bluffing."

"I am sure you are not. But I assure you he has a full schedule and—"

"Never mind. I'll tell him," said Brigitte jumping up from her seat and marching toward the office door.

The secretary jumped in front of the door to stop her. "You cannot enter without being announced."

"So… announce me."

"Will you promise to wait here?"

"Yes… for one minute."

"Fine," said the secretary as he returned to his desk and called Mitterrand. Mitterrand did not answer. "Merde."

"Time's up," said Brigitte as she opened the door and marched inside. The secretary followed her.

Mitterrand was sitting at his desk reading the newspaper when Brigitte entered. "Busy?" said Brigitte.

"Brigitte, why are you in my office?" said Mitterrand.

"I'm sorry, Minister," said the secretary. "She insisted."

"Yes, yes. One of her tantrums. I am very aware of Brigitte's tactics," said Mitterrand. "Brigitte, do you know I could have you shot?"

"Philippeville," said Brigitte.

Mitterrand considered for a moment and motioned for his secretary to leave. The secretary exited closing the office door behind him. "I can't talk about it, Brigitte. It's a military matter."

"Bullshit. You are the military."

"You flatter me but no I am not. And even if I were, I would not be at liberty to talk about an ongoing operation."

"Ongoing operation? They already slaughtered twelve thousand civilians. How far did you plan on letting them go?"

"That is an exaggeration."

"So you do know something about it?"

"I have read a few preliminary reports. Yes. But I will not comment to you or anyone else in the press about the events in Philippeville until I have a full understanding of what happened."

"François, we have known each other a long time. How could something like this happen?"

"Off the record?"

"All right. Off the record."

"I don't know. I was as shocked as you were when I heard."

"Is it twelve thousand?"

"I doubt it, but it is significant by what I have been told."

"Jesus. If the Algerians ever lacked a reason to demand Independence they've got one now."

"Yes. I believe we have just woken the desert lion."

"The U.N. will hate France."

"Tell them to get in line."

"You know I cannot stop until I find the truth… on the record," said Brigitte moving back toward the door.

"I would expect nothing less," said Mitterrand. "You are one of the few that keep us somewhat honest."

"Somewhat?"

Mitterrand shrugged.

"You will let me know once you have finished your investigation?"

"Of course," said Mitterrand. "I am pretty sure I have your number someplace."

Brigitte laughed and left his office.

Brigitte sat in Damien's office. "I have tried every minister and general I know. Nobody is willing to talk about it," said Brigitte. "I've got to go to Philippeville, Damien."

"I don't think that would be very wise at this point," said Damien. "I am not sure the French Army could protect you, given the current state of affairs."

"Probably not but I've run out of ideas."

"We got a report that a French soldier was arrested for rape and murder of a teenage Corsican girl while on leave in Oran. He is being held at the Blida Military Prison just outside of Algiers awaiting court martial."

"I don't have time to work on another story, Damien."

"No. I didn't think you would. The prisoner was with the 10th Para Division under General Massu. He may have been at Philippeville," said Damien writing down the soldier's name on a slip of paper and handing it to Brigitte.

"Damien, you are a godsend," said Brigitte, collecting her things and moving toward the door.

"Would you mind telling that to my wife?" said Damien. "She thinks I'm a heathen because I don't go to church."

"I tell you what. I'll marry you if this works out," said Brigitte exiting his office.

"Oh good. Polygamy. Just what I needed to make my life more simple," said Damien to nobody in particular.

Coyle stood in front of a H-21 Shawnee helicopter surveying its long narrow body and tandem rotors. Coyle grunted as Bruno emerged from the helicopter's side door having completed his initial inspection.

"I wouldn't worry too much. Your boxcar can still carry three times as many troops," said Bruno. "And it's considerably faster than the helicopter."

"...and it needs an airfield. You can land this puppy anywhere. I know the future when I see it," said Coyle.

"Well, you could always learn to fly one."

"No thank you. I'm a fixed wing man and I plan on staying that way."

"That's the spirit," said Bruno slapping Coyle on the back. "Ride that pony into the sunset."

"It's a horse, Bruno. Ya ride a horse into the sunset. Not a pony."

"Oh? I thought they were the same thing."

"Ya thought wrong. How many of these things they give, ya?"

"Twelve of the Shawnee troop carriers and four Sikorsky gunships. We can drop two companies right on top of the enemy."

"And you still want me fly with you?"

"You are good luck. Besides, I would miss your American sense of humor."

"And you would see less of Brigitte."

"I don't think she wants to see much of me."

"Still in the dog house?"

Bruno looked puzzled. "What is 'dog house'?"

"Means you're up shit creek without a paddle."

"Oh, that doesn't sound pleasant."

"It's not."

"She does not say anything about me?"

"I am smart enough not to ask. I am sure she will get over it eventually."

"You Americans never cease to amaze me. You always believe things will work out."

"Yeah. It keeps us moving forward. When is the first mission?"

"We wait for Major Aussaresses to tell where we can find the enemy."

"And how is he gonna do that?"

"I don't dare ask."

Coyle looked at Bruno with concern.

"And you shouldn't ask either, Coyle," said Bruno. "Sometimes life is better not knowing."

"That don't make it right, Bruno."

"No. It doesn't. But it is the truth, my friend," said Bruno, and he walked away.

It was a windowless room with a concrete floor. There was a drain grid in the middle that was used to wash away the blood, piss and vomit. Aussaresses stood back and watched as a French corporal attached electrodes to the genitals of the mujahideen soldier that had been captured during the attack on Philippeville. The genitals were one of the most sensitive areas on the human body and responded well to electrical current.

The electrodes' wires were attached to a regulator which in turn was attached to a hand-cranked generator. Aussaresses was well aware that he could have used a car battery or the electricity from a wall socket but he liked the drama of the hand-cranked generator. The victim knew what came next once the handle started turning and the whirling sound only enhanced the feeling of terror. A knob on the regulator determined the amount of shock produced. Aussaresses had no desire to physically harm the mujahideen and ensured that his men were careful not to overstimulated the nerve endings beyond what they could endure. Torture was a time consuming process and patience was required.

This particular mujahideen was of interest because he was from the village of Ain Sefra in the Naama Provence. Ain Sefra was considered the gateway to the Sahara and a key strategic point. The French garrison in Ain Sefra had suffered multiple rebel raids and had lost a large cache of weapons a few months back. It was believed that the mujahideen were recruiting young Berber men to their cause as the caravans passed through the area on their way to the Sahara.

Aussaresses wanted the location of the mujahideen camp in the surrounding mountains. He would spend as much time as necessary to break the mujahideen prisoner and extract the information he desired. Aussaresses was a patient man. It was his patience that made him so unnerving.

Café Wars

Aussaresses was an officer and did not need to get his hands dirty. He had trained his men properly in the techniques he had learned in the French Army's anti-insurgency academy and in Indochina. He had studied the Viet Minh's interrogation methods by interviewing French soldiers that had been captured and later escaped or had been released at the end of the war. The Viet Minh were very effective at extracting information from prisoners in the first seventy-two hours when the information was fresh and most useful.

Aussaresses had an analytical mind. He had learned to compartmentalize the emotions he felt and the information he was gathering. Many of the men he spoke with had their spirits crushed and would never be the same again. They were no longer the warriors they had been trained to be. They had become docile. They had become shadows of their former selves. He found that interesting and made note of it in his extensive logs.

This was the mujahideen prisoner's fifth session and Aussaresses was hopeful. The man had been allowed to eat and drink between sessions. Aussaresses wanted him to retain his strength and for his body to regenerate so that it could endure more pain. It was usually the fifth or sixth session when the prisoner realized that the torture would continue indefinitely unless he was to give up the information his captors desired. The prisoner realized that he was being kept alive not because it was the humane thing to do but just the opposite – he was allowed to live to feel pain. He was like a man washed overboard in a storm. He was alone. There would be no rescue. Wave after wave would hit him as he struggled to stay afloat. Each time coughing out the seawater only to be hit by another wave. It was the fifth and the sixth sessions when most men began to feel deep despair and break. Although he had complete faith that the men under his command would do their duty, Aussaresses decided to attend the session personally.

After the ninth crank of the generator, the mujahideen blurted out a phrase, "Djebel Aïssa." The interrogator exchanged a glance with Aussaresses. Aussaresses looked at a map of the surrounding mountains. Djebel Aïssa was the highest peak in the Ksour Range in the western most part of the Saharan Atlas Mountains. The Berber caravan trails passed below the peak. It made sense that the mujahideen would locate their camp in such a place.

Aussaresses motioned for the torture to stop. He needed to know if the man was lying to avoid pain or if he was truly broken. Aussaresses removed a large envelope from his briefcase and removed the contents – three photographs. He walked over to the prisoner and showed him each photograph – one of his wife, one of his daughter and one of his son. He had the translator explain that his family had been picked up from his home in Ain Serfa late last night. They had been brought to this prison where they were waiting in the next room to meet him as a reward for telling the truth. If he was lying they would suffer the same fate as he was suffering until they were dead. He however would not be allowed to die and would continue living in pain and knowing what happened to his family.

Aussaresses and the translator waited for a moment as the prisoner heaved up his breakfast. The translator asked the prisoner if Djebel Aïssa was the location of the mujahideen camp. The prisoner's eyes filled with tears and he nodded. He knew he had just betrayed his country, his brothers and his God. Aussaresses knew he was telling the truth.

It was early morning when the sixteen helicopters lifted off from their staging area. Bruno's fleet was flying at full capacity and carried over two hundred paratroopers into battle. The twelve Shawnee troop carriers were flanked by the four Sikorsky gunships nicknamed "Choctaws." The Choctaws were each armed with a 20mm cannon, two rocket pods and two 12.7mm machine guns mounted on the sides of the fuselage. There was also a 7.5mm machine gun for the door gunner. The armament and ammunition overloaded the underpowered Choctaws and they had trouble keeping up with Shawnee troop carriers. While they were slow, they did provide a powerful mobile punch.

The helicopter pilots stayed close to the ground as they flew over the hills. They had learned from experience that flying low gave the enemy on the ground less of a chance to get a shot off. The Shawnee with their dual engines were heavily armored and tough. They were known for taking multiple hits and continuing to complete their missions. In addition to being slow, the Choctaws were also under armored. A single well placed bullet could put the aircraft out of action.

The mujahideen hidden on the slopes of Djebel Aïssa had no idea that the French were coming that morning. They had just finished their morning prayers and were preparing breakfast when they heard the sound of helicopter blades. At first they didn't know what to think. They had never heard the heavy whopping sound of a helicopter's blades.

The Choctaws swooped in and opened fire on the camp. The mujahideen scattered, many without their weapons. There was little cover on the mountainside. The mujahideen that remembered their weapons fired back until they learned that firing back at the Choctaws revealed their position and made them an instant target of the gunships.

While the Choctaws kept the enemy pinned down the Shawnee dropped off their troops on a small plateau on the opposite side of the mountain peak. It was a tricky maneuver. Only one helicopter could unload at a time and it took twenty minutes to complete the drop. As always Bruno was the first soldier out the door of the first helicopter. Two hundred paratroopers had been placed in the heart of the battlefield and there was nothing the enemy could do about it. Bruno was growing very fond of his helicopters.

Bruno radioed Coyle and gave him the go to take off with another two platoons of paratroopers. Bruno figured that Coyle's C-119 would arrive just as the mujahideen made a run for it. Coyle's drop of paratroopers would be the trapdoor to cut off the enemy's escape. But first Bruno needed to figure out which way they would run. He ordered his men forward.

The French attacked from the two sides of the mountain peak in a pincer movement. Bruno was gambling on surprise by breaking his force in two.

The mujahideen outnumbered the French two to one. But the French paratroopers understood the value of aggression and speed. They poured fire into the mujahideen, still unorganized and hiding from the helicopters. Most of the Algerian fighters broke and ran for the valley below. The paratroopers swept up anyone that stood their ground.

At the base of the mountain the mujahideen regrouped and formed battle lines. The paratroopers had the high ground and the advantage. The four Choctaws swooped into the valley one after another. They unleashed the last of their ammunition in strafing runs down the mujahideen's lines. When the Choctaws finished and headed for home, the paratroopers charged down the hill. The mujahideen had had enough. They broke and ran.

Coyle flew overhead in his C-119. He didn't need instructions from the ground on where to drop his load of paratroopers. It was obvious. He chose a hilltop at the end of the valley directly in the path of the fleeing enemy. The mujahideen lost all heart when they saw the parachutes floating down and cutting off their retreat. They threw down their weapons and surrendered to the French closing in on all sides.

Bruno was pleased with his first air mobile cavalry assault and made sure his men were well rewarded with plenty of wine, cigars and beef steaks that night.

Zaki, the shoeshine boy, was putting the finishing touches on a pair of loafers worn by a Swiss man on vacation. He didn't have any requests that day from his FLN handler but he still kept a close watch on the passport control exit gate. He saw Brigitte following a

porter carrying her suitcase on a luggage cart. Zaki
had no specific instructions to watch for the famous
journalist but he knew what she looked like from the
newspapers and he thought his handler would want to
know that she was in Algiers. He took his time and
finished the Swiss man's shoe. The Swiss man paid
for the shoeshine but didn't leave a tip.

Zaki told the shoeshiner next to him that he was
going to the toilet and would be back in a couple of
minutes. He wanted to make sure he didn't lose his
place in the queue for customers. Zaki walked to the
payphone and made a call. He told his handler about
Brigitte and was told that the information would be
passed on and that he was correct in reporting it. He
hung up the phone.

It was only forty-six kilometers from Brigitte's hotel
in Algiers to Blida but it took almost four hours to
reach by taxi because of the traffic and goat herds
blocking the road. Brigitte was convinced the driver
was taking her the longest way possible to run up the
fare as he weaved his way through the streets avoiding
the congested boulevards.

Brigitte hated to be taken advantage of by anyone
but when she was finally dropped off in front of Blida
Military Prison she decided not to argue with the
driver. Instead she asked him to wait until she was
finished so he could take her back to Algiers. He
happily agreed but asked for payment for the first trip
so he could refuel his taxi and get something to eat
while he waited. She paid him.

Brigitte did not have permission to visit the
prisoner and it was not the French Army's custom to

allow non-military visitors for soldiers waiting for court martial. She was forced to use every trick she knew to win approval from the French captain in charge of the prisoners.

Brigitte sat in an interview room waiting for over an hour while the prisoner, Corporal Garbis La Torre, was processed and brought into the room. His wrists and ankles were shackled. A separate chain was attached between the ankle and the wrist shackles. The short chain prevented the prisoner from taking a swing at a guard. The MPs sat him down and locked his ankle shackles to a steal ring in the floor. "Is that necessary?" asked Brigitte.

"Just a precaution, Mademoiselle," said the MP. "Corporal La Torre is going to behave himself. Aren't you, La Torre?"

La Torre didn't respond. The MP pulled out his baton and gave La Torre a light rap in the back of the head. "Aren't you?" said the MP.

"I'm always a gentleman with the ladies. You know that," said La Torre.

"Best stay on your side of the table, Mademoiselle," said the head MP as they exited the room and closed the door.

"Thank you for seeing me, Corporal La Torre," said Brigitte.

"Do you have any cigarettes?" said La Torre.

"Yes. Of course," said Brigitte pulling a carton of cigarettes from her purse and placing them on the table. She opened the box and pulled out a pack. "They're American. I hope that's okay?" she said opening the pack and handing him a single cigarette.

"It's fine," he said.

She lit his cigarette with her lighter. He took a deep draw and she could see that he enjoyed it. "You'll leave the carton," he said.

"Let's see how the interview goes," she said.

"You think you can buy me with a carton of cigarettes? I'm not a whore. I'm not like you."

Brigitte knew to be careful. She had to maintain control of the conversation if she was ever to find out what he knew. "No. I don't think I can buy you for a carton of cigarettes or with anything else. I don't think I need to buy you at all."

"What do you mean?"

"I think you want to tell your side of the story."

"The story? I didn't do it. The bitch wanted it. Things just got out of hand. It was an accident."

"I'm not here about the rape and murder."

"Then why are you here?"

"Philippeville."

La Torre chuckled, "Figures. You're a bleeding heart liberal that cares more about a bunch of ragheads than your own people."

"I care about the truth."

"The truth? What the fuck do you know about the truth of Philippeville?"

"Why don't you set me straight?" said Brigitte moving the open pack of cigarettes across the table. La Torre reached out and grabbed her hand. Brigitte pulled her hand back gently so as not to cause him to resist. He let go. "Your skin is soft... like hers," said La Torre.

"Tell me about Philippeville, Corporal La Torre. What happened at Philippeville."

"We taught those ragheads a lesson. That's what happened."

"And no one tried to stop you?"

"Tried to stop us? We were under orders."

"Someone ordered you to kill civilians?"

La Torre laughed and said, "That was a day to remember. That's for sure. The French beast was unleashed."

"Who ordered it… unleashed?"

"I ain't saying."

Brigitte considered her next words carefully. "Do you believe in God, Corporal La Torre?"

"God? What's God have to do with that bloody mess?"

"If you are convicted of the rape and murder of the Corsican girl, you will hang. I would think you would want to clear your conscience before you face the Almighty's judgment."

"The Almighty's judgment? You're a little late for that, sister. The devil already has a nice room reserved for me."

"Don't let the truth die with you."

"I ain't gonna die. They've got nothing on me."

"Then do it for France."

La Torre stopped for a moment and considered. "I did do it for France. Like I said… we were under orders."

"Tell the world that. Let that be how you are remembered… as a patriot serving your country. Serving France."

"Show me the pink," said La Torre.

"The pink?"

"Your tits. I bet your nipples are pink, not brown."

"You're an animal."

"I am what your God made me. You want to know what happened at Philippeville? Show me your tits."

"Who gave you the order?"

"Fuck you, bitch. We're all whores. I demand payment if you want the truth."

"I hope they do hang you."

La Torre jumped up and lunged forward at far as his chains would allow. He was just a few inches from Brigitte's face. "Let me bite your nipples, whore," said La Torre snapping his teeth.

The MPs heard the commotion and rushed into the room. They grabbed La Torre and pulled at him. He was strong and did not move.

Brigitte spit in his face. He licked her saliva off his upper lip with his tongue. "That a girl," he said.

The head MP pulled out his baton and hit La Torre behind the knee. His leg buckled. He elbowed one of the MPs in the nose with a loud crack. The MP fell back and blood flowed from his nostrils. The head MP hit La Torre again and again with his baton. The second MP rejoined the fight and helped wrestle La Torre to the floor. La Torre continued to struggle. The MPs beat him with their batons. "Tell me who gave the order?" shouted Brigitte above La Torre's grunts. "Was it Colonel Bigeard?"

"Bigeard's a pussy. He wasn't even there when it happened. Besides, he didn't have the balls to give an order like that," said La Torre as the MPs kept whaling on him with their batons and he kept struggling, throwing his elbows.

Brigitte was relieved but she still didn't have the truth. "Who was it then? Who gave the order?" said Brigitte.

"I'll tell the devil when I see him. You can ask him," said La Torre. "Come on, boys. You're hitting like girls. Show me what ya got."

The head MP struck La Torre hard across the head and it stunned him. He collapsed. It was over. They unlocked his shackles from the floor ring and dragged him out of the room. Brigitte picked up the carton of cigarettes and left, stepping between the pools of blood on the floor.

Brigitte flew back to Paris the morning after her conversation with Corporal La Torre. She had considered surprising Coyle in Algiers but after what she had heard at the prison she was in no mood for romance. Besides, she wasn't sure she wanted Coyle to know everything about the story she was putting together. She trusted Coyle with her life but there were times she felt he was a little naïve. It was one of the things she liked about him. He was like a breath of fresh air when the gloom of reality clouded her mind. But she thought he might inadvertently say something to Bruno or one of the other French officers. It was better just to stay silent on the matter or, if he pushed her, to change the subject. She was good at changing the subject. Especially with Coyle.

She sat in Damien's office, having just told him about the interview with La Torre. They both were silent as if reluctant to speak. The path forward wasn't clear. "I think I need a brandy," said Damien.

"Pour me one too," said Brigitte.

"I've never known you to be a morning drinker," said Damien.

"I am. I just hide it from you."

Damien shrugged, poured Napoleon brandy in two snifters and handed one to Brigitte. "You of course realize the danger in reporting the story," said Damien after taking a long sip.

"Yes. I think I do."

"You would have to make sure you have all your facts well documented."

"I will.

"The magazine also has exposure. We could be shut down for national security reasons… or at the very least they could censor us."

"They won't dare."

"They might. The government is very sensitive at the moment. The empire is falling and nobody can seem to stop it. The generals and politicians are circling the wagons as the Americans would say. They will not appreciate an attack on their reputations."

"I don't really care what they appreciate or don't appreciate. The French Army killed thousands of Muslims. Somebody needs to take responsibility."

"Right now you only have the word of an accused rapist and murderer. You need more than that if the magazine is going to stand behind you."

"I'll get it," said Brigitte.

"All right, said Damien sipping the last of his brandy to muster his courage. "What do you need?"

Trinquier sat with Massu finishing breakfast on the patio of Massu's office. It was a casual conversation. More catching up than planning. "And how is morale?" said Massu.

"The men are in good spirits. There is a feeling that they are making a difference," said Trinquier.

"That's good, and they are. The number of attacks on the pied-noir communities have been greatly reduced in the last week. Things seem to be calming down a bit."

"Let's hope so. I don't think any of us want a repeat of Philippeville."

The mention of the incident at Philippeville produced a tick in Massu's face. It was as if it was a taboo subject and by bringing it up Massu's body had reacted unconsciously.

Trinquier found Massu's reaction curious and took note of the tick. Even though the two had never discussed the details of what happened, Trinquier was sure that Massu's intelligence group was giving him updates on what they learned about the incident. *He is as much a part of it as I am and he knows it,* thought Trinquier. *He feels responsible. I may be able to use that in the future.* Trinquier decided to change the subject. "Were you aware that Brigitte Friang visited the prison at Blida?" he said.

"Yes. She interviewed Corporal La Torre."

"I thought you gave instructions that the corporal was not to have visitors."

"I did. She convinced the idiot captain at the prison that she wasn't a visitor."

"How is that?"

"Mademoiselle Friang can be very persuasive."

"And that doesn't concern you?"

"Why should it? Whatever information she was able to pry out of La Torre is bound to be suspect. Besides, he will probably be convicted in a few days and his execution will eliminate any testimony he might give in a court."

"I see."

"I don't think it's wise to chase after every lead she might find. Acting on our concerns just makes her think she's on to something. It is in everyone's interest to let things rest and carry on as if nothing unusual has happened."

"I'm not sure she would agree."

"No. But she may be convinced. Both the American and Colonel Bigeard were involved in our operations. When the time is right she will need to be reminded of that. She will not want to hurt either of them no matter what she finds."

"So in the meantime we just let her keep digging?" said Trinquier.

"Yes. But we don't have to make it easy for her. We do have rules, you know," said Massu.

FOURTEEN

It was night and thick clouds obscured the heavens over Dien Bien Phu. Coyle, dressed in a Foreign Legionnaire uniform, descended from the dark sky on his parachute. He could hear the gunfire and explosions below. He looked down and the valley was on fire in many places. Huts and rice fields burned. It seemed like the ground itself was red-hot beneath the clods of dirt. Tracer rounds streaked across the battlefield from all directions. It was impossible to determine which were the French trenches and which were Viet Minh. He didn't know where to steer his parachute. There was a fifty percent chance he would land on or behind enemy lines and be shot or taken captive. He was dropping fast. It would not take long before he knew his fate.

He could see some of the soldiers and nurses that he jumped with floating down and landing only to be shot by Viet Minh patrols tasked with hunting down the new recruits attempting to parachute into the French garrison. The Viet Minh took advantage of their helplessness as they became tangled in their parachute lines. Coyle had parachuted several times before when the plane he had been piloting was hit by enemy fire and he was forced to abandoned it before it crashed. He guessed that it was good he had jumped with others not as experienced as he in parachuting. They would keep the Viet Minh occupied while he landed and hopefully escaped. He felt guilty at the thought. He wasn't afraid to die. He had faced death many times before but he wanted to survive so he could save Brigitte. She was down there someplace in that hell hole and he needed to find her... to protect her.

He saw a series of trenches across a hill and the burned ruins of a building that he recognized on top of the hill. It was the mayor's mansion where Brigitte had been living while reporting on the siege at Dien Bien Phu. He pulled his parachute's cords and steered toward the hill. He could see French troops in the trenches firing their weapons at the Viet Minh as they charged the barbed wire perimeter. The French were too few and the Viet Minh too many. It would all be over soon. The French garrison would be overrun. He had to find Brigitte fast if he was to have any hope of saving her.

He landed on the hillside and slid downward when his parachute fluttered in the wind and pulled him toward the enemy lines. He pulled out his knife and plunged it into the wet ground to stop himself from sliding. He released his parachute harness with his free hand. The parachute floated away. He crawled back up the hillside until he reached a trench. He pulled himself over the edge and dropped into black water at the bottom of the trench.

The trench was still and the floor had turned into a thick mud covered with water. The smell was putrid and it made Coyle want to vomit. He didn't. It was pitch dark and he couldn't see anything but the occasional glimpse as a stream of tracer bullets from a French machinegun passing overhead. He tried to stand but his arms and legs were stuck deep in the mud. He pulled one of his arms free and reach up to find something that would give a handhold so he could pull the rest of body out of the mud. His hand felt something but it wasn't very stable. He decided it was better than nothing and he pulled on it. His other arm came free. He used it to grasp the side of the trench and again he found something that was unstable. A parachute flare launched from a mortar ignited high above the trench. He looked over at the wall of the trench and found instead of dirt the rotting corpses of French soldiers. He reached down and grabbed one of his legs with both his hands. One by one he pulled his legs free of the mud. More corpses rose up from the mud and floated in the black water. He wished for darkness again and the flare went out. He waded through the corpses and the black water until he again found the soggy bottom to the trench and gained good footing. He wanted to get away from the stench of death as fast as possible but knew he would be an easy target if he left the trench. He moved along the trench until he found an intersection that took him up the hill. He followed the new trench line until he reached the top of the hill and pulled himself out.

Before him stood what was left of the mayor's mansion after almost two months of constant Viet Minh artillery fire. He called out in a hushed voice for Brigitte. There was no response. He moved forward in the darkness and called out again. "She ain't here," said a voice. Coyle couldn't see who it was but the voice was familiar. He moved in the direction of the voice. Another parachute flare ignited above. He saw the owner of the voice… "McGoon?" said Coyle.

"Hey, Coyle. How they hanging?" said McGoon in a weak voice.

"They're hanging fine. What are you doing here?"

"The Daisy Mae crashed."

"I know. I saw it. And I saw you die."

"Oh, that's not good."

"But you're okay. You're alive."

"I'm not sure about that."

"What do you mean?"

"My gut hurts."

"Yeah. You got torn up something awful."

"I was afraid of that."

"Have you seen Brigitte?"

"Yeah. She helped me after the crash. She carried me up here."

"Brigitte carried you up the hill?" said Coyle knowing that McGoon weighed over two hundred and fifty pounds.

"Yeah. She's really strong for such a small thing. Said she'd be back latter to check on me."

"Where did she go?"

"The hospital."

"Brigitte's at the hospital?"

"Ain't that what I just said? You really need to have your hearing checked, Coyle. I think you may be getting old."

"I'll do that McGoon. Right now I've got to get you off this hill."

"I don't think that's a very good idea."

"Why not?"

McGoon moved his hand away from his stomach and revealed a long gash with his intestines popping out in places.

"Oh my God," said Coyle.

"Yeah. That's what I said the first time I saw 'em."

"I gotta get you a medic."

"I don't think there's much they can do. My guts keep falling out every time I try to get up. It's really annoying. I think it's better I just sit still."

"You can't, McGoon. The Viet Minh are coming up the hill. They'll be here soon."

"Ah, that's okay. I still got my survival pistol. I'll fight 'em off."

"I ain't leaving you, McGoon."

"You got to, Coyle. It's the only way you can save Brigitte."

What McGoon was saying seemed to make sense to Coyle. *"Yeah. I think you're right,"* said Coyle. *"Is there anything I can do for ya before I go?"*

"No. I'm good. Thanks for stopping by. I was getting a bit lonely."

"I'll come back once I find Brigitte."

"That'd be swell. Maybe you could bring a couple of beers with ya."

"You got it, McGoon," said Coyle as he moved off toward the back of the hill.

An artillery shell exploded nearby throwing dirt up into the air. "You'd better hurry, Coyle. I think they're coming."

Another shell slammed into the wall next to McGoon and exploded. McGoon caught fire and screamed. Coyle ran back toward him but the distance between them kept growing until McGoon and the ruins of the mansion were completely out of sight.

Coyle found himself next to the entrance to the garrison hospital. There were a thousand wounded French soldiers sitting and lying around the entrance waiting their turn. One was missing a head as his body waited patiently. More shells rained down exploding and kicking up great clouds of dirt and rock. Coyle knew he was dreaming but he didn't dare wake up until he found Brigitte. He entered the underground hospital.

The underground hospital was more cave than a structure. The engineers had dug out dozens of tunnels and rooms into the hillside. Water was seeping through the walls of the tunnel and mixing with the blood from the wounded. The mixture was turning the ground into a reddish-brown sludge. The air was thick with flies and smelled like the trench he left earlier. The wounded patients leaned against the wet walls and those that couldn't stand sat in the mud on the floor. Many had hacking coughs while others groaned from pain.

Coyle walked down the tunnel looking inside each of the rooms for any sign of Brigitte. Doctors and nurses operated on the wounded under the most abhorrent conditions. The bottom of their surgical gowns were covered in mud and the tops were *covered in blood. They had run out of morphine several days ago but their scalpels and saws continued to cut. It was the only way to keep their patients alive. Many died.*

Coyle rounded the corner to one of the side tunnels and he saw Brigitte leaning over a Viet Minh soldier trying to calm him down. "It's okay. I'm here to help you," said Brigitte.

The soldier babbled something in Vietnamese like he was delirious and hallucinating. "Brigitte?" said Coyle.

Brigitte turned and smiled. "You came," she said.

"Of course I came," said Coyle as he embraced her and held her tight. "I thought you might have died."

"I can't die, Coyle. I have too much to live for."

"Yeah. Me too."

The Viet Minh reached into his jacket and pulled out a grenade. The pin was already out. He loosened his grip and the spoon flipped off the grenade activating the timer. "Brigitte, we have to go," said Coyle with panic in his voice.

"I can't leave, Coyle. It'll make such a great story," said Brigitte.

The grenade exploded.

Coyle woke screaming. He was alone in his C-119 sitting in his pilot's chair. He had dozed off after parking the plane. It took him a moment to get his bearings. He was still in Algeria at the military airfield. He rose and left the cockpit.

Coyle thought about Brigitte and what his dream meant. He climbed out of the plane and walked across the tarmac. He entered the terminal below the control tower.

He walked to the payphone and called Brigitte. "Hey," he said when she answered.

"Is everything okay, Tom?"

"Yeah. Everything is fine. I just needed to hear your voice."

"That's sweet. When are you coming back to Paris?"

"Soon. I just have a couple more missions I need to fly."

"With Bruno?"

"Yeah, plus a troop transport to Nice. Are you okay, Brigitte?"

"Yeah. I'm fine just really swamped at work."

"Sure. I understand. Me too."

"We need to find time for each other, Tom."

"We will. I love you."

"I love you too, darling. Good night."

"Good night," said Coyle and hung up.

He doubted he would get much sleep but he was sure he could find a stiff drink at the officer's club. He needed it.

Saadi and Marwa rode in the back of a taxi through a business district in Paris. Marwa had a shopping bag sitting beside her on the floor. Saadi instructed the driver to pull up in front of an office building. "I will just be a few minutes, darling," he said to Marwa.

"We'll wait," said Marwa.

"You know I must charge you for the waiting time?" said the driver.

"Of course," said Saadi as he stepped out of the taxi leaving Marwa in the back seat.

Saadi walked into the office building. He continued through the lobby and slipped out the back.

There was another taxi waiting in the alley behind the building. Saadi climbed in the back where Ludmila was waiting with an identical shopping bag sitting on the floor beside her. "Hello, darling," said Ludmila.

"Thank you for picking me, darling. We will have a nice lunch. I have the perfect place," said Saadi and gave instructions to the driver to take them to a shopping district. The taxi drove off.

Inside the taxi at the front of the building the driver glanced in the rearview mirror at Marwa. She didn't like that he could see her in the mirror. She picked up the shopping bag and moved over directly behind the driver's seat. The driver grunted as if insulted. Marwa watched out the window and waited.

The taxi holding Ludmila and Saadi pulled to the curb in the shopping district. Ludmila stepped from the taxi holding the bag. "I just need to return my shoes, darling. I will only be a minute," said Ludmila.

"We will wait," said Saadi.

"I will need to charge you for waiting time," said the driver.

"Of course," said Saadi as he watched Ludmila trot through a crowd of pedestrians and into the front entrance of a shoe boutique.

Three minutes later, Ludmila came back out without the shopping bag and hopped in the taxi. The taxi drove off and turned down a busy boulevard. "Oh, no. I forgot my wallet at the office," said Saadi. "Driver could you please go back to the office where you picked me up?"

"Of course," said the driver and turned down another street heading back the way they came.

The explosion at the shoe boutique killed everyone inside. It also seriously injured twenty pedestrian hit by flying shards of glass when the front windows shattered. Burning shoes tumbled out onto the sidewalk. Smoke poured from the burning building.

Brigitte felt the explosion in her office and the windows rattled. She looked out the window and saw the black smoke from a fire billowing up into the sky. *It's close,* she thought as she grabbed her purse and headed out the door.

The taxi holding Marwa also shook from the explosion. "Feels like another of the those damn bombs went off," said the taxi driver.

"Yes indeed," said Marwa as she reached into her purse and pulled out a pair of pliers.

Brigitte ran out the front of the building and looked around. She saw the parked taxi and waved to the driver.

In the backseat of the taxi, Marwa already had the top of the tea biscuit tin open, exposing the explosives inside. The driver could not see her in his rearview mirror. She crimped the pencil detonator and closed the lid. "I've changed my mind. I will join my husband inside," said Marwa handing the drive the fare plus a big tip. "Keep the change."

She pushed the tin back into the shopping bag and pushed the bag under the back seat. She stepped out of the taxi and walked into the building. Saadi and Ludmila would be waiting in the alley behind the building. Saadi had killed the taxi driver with a wire garrote so there would be no witness of the three of them together.

The taxi driver in the front of the building saw Brigitte waving at him and pulled up. He felt fortunate to find a fare so quickly. Brigitte got in and told the driver to head for the shopping district. The taxi drove off. "Where are you going?" said the taxi driver.

"Just follow the smoke," said Brigitte.

The driver looked at Brigitte in the rearview mirror and said, "You're that famous reporter, yes?"

"Yes. Please watch the road and hurry."

"I've read your articles. The ones on the siege in Vietnam. They were good."

"Thank you. Watch the road please."

A fire truck sped through the intersection in front of the taxi. The driver slammed on the brakes to avoid hitting it. Brigitte threw up her hands to keep from hitting her head on the back of the front passenger seat. "That was a close one," said the driver.

"Just follow the fire truck," said Brigitte slightly peeved.

The driver did as she said and turned down the intersection. Brigitte glanced down at the shopping bag that had slid out from underneath the seat. "I think one of your customers left their shopping bag back here."

"Probably that curly-haired lady. I'll go back and give it to her once I drop her off."

"Curly-haired?"

"Yeah. Beautiful long black curls. Natural I think. Ya don't see that much anymore. Women are always cutting it short. Easier to care for I guess. Not my wife. I tell her to keep her hair long."

Brigitte looked down at the shopping bag and saw the edge of the tea biscuit tin. She reached down and carefully pulled it out. It was the same lid as she had seen in the aftermath of the other bombing. She carefully opened the lid exposing the bomb inside. "Pull over!" she said.

"But we're not there yet," said the driver.

"NOW!"

"All right. All right. Don't get your knickers in a bunch. I'm pulling over," said the driver slowing down and pulling to the curb.

"Get out of the car," said Brigitte opening the back door.

"What? Why?"

"You've got a bomb in the back seat."

"Where?" said the driver as her turned around and looked into the backseat.

"Get out of the car," said Brigitte running from the taxi. "Everyone run. There's a bomb in the taxi," shouted Brigitte to the pedestrians on the sidewalk.

"Merde," said the taxi driver seeing the explosives in the tea biscuit tin.

He grabbed the door handle and swung the door open. He was stepping from the taxi when the bomb went off, killing him instantly.

Brigitte was thrown to the ground from the explosion's overpressure. Shrapnel flew everywhere as the taxi was blown to bits. Most of the pedestrians were running away from the taxi when the bomb exploded thanks to Brigitte's warning. Only the taxi driver and an old woman were killed. Nine others were seriously wounded. Brigitte was lucky. She had run the right way. An iron trashcan sitting on the sidewalk by the curb shielded her from the shrapnel. Her only injuries were a scraped knee and a slight concussion. It made a great article for her magazine.

FIFTEEN

Aussaresses and his group of interrogators had done well with the prisoners taken by Bruno and his paratroopers. They were able to get several younger mujahideen to become informants within the larger group when they threatened to cut off their penises with a rusty pair of pruning shears. The pruning shears were actually quite dull and would have made a mess if the interrogators actually attempted what was threatened but the visual of the curved blade was enough to convince the young men that the French meant business.

It was decided to allow the prisoners to gather as a group for their meals so they would talk more freely among themselves. One of the young informants overheard a mujahideen leader talking about his wife's cousin who was part of another band of rebels. The cousin had participated in several successful raids along the eastern coast. The tales of the cousin that caught Aussaresses attention was a pet that the cousin kept back at the group's base camp – a Barbary Macaque.

The Barbary Macaque was a small ape that had almost been hunted into extinction by early European settlers. The surviving members of the species only existed in two forests both along the eastern coast of Algeria. The forests would be a natural hiding place for a mujahideen camp because the tree canopy would provide cover against French scout planes.

The cousin was brought in for further interrogation, but he died when too much electricity was used, and his heart stopped. Torture was a tricky business.

Aussaresses was confident enough in the information that he decided to share it with Bruno and suggested that he send in a reconnaissance team into each forest to determine the rebel camp's location.

Bruno also liked the information and decided on a more direct approach since a reconnaissance mission risked tipping off the mujahideen that the French were looking for them in the forests. The two forests were close to each other and only forty minutes apart by helicopter. Bruno would split his forces and search both at the same time. Reports from the coastal raids put the mujahideen force at no more than three hundred men, a force that the paratroopers could easily handle, even when split in two.

The plan was to use the helicopters to drop two companies of paratroopers in one forest then return to the staging area, pick up two more companies and drop them in the second forest. Once both groups of paratroopers were in place they would proceed with their searches. The helicopters would stand ready to pick up one of the two groups of paratroopers if the enemy strength proved to be larger than expected and carry it over to the battlefield.

Coyle would take off at the beginning of the search and fly in circles between the two forests. When one of the groups of paratroopers encountered the enemy, Coyle would drop two platoons behind the enemy's line and cut off their escape, as he had done on the previous assault. The four Choctaw gunships would supply air to ground support if needed.

Aussaresses suggested that he attach three of his interrogators to each of Bruno's companies. Information was most useful when it was fresh and actionable. Aussaresses knew that the mujahideen forces were planning several more raids on the coastal cities. He also knew that the mujahideen were getting help from collaborators in those cities; Muslims that would identify anyone that had sympathies toward the French. Those helping the French would be sorted out and executed by the mujahideen – or worse. Like the French the mujahideen were very effective at torture, although their methods were antiquated and often involved flaying the prisoner's skin.

Bruno was hesitant. It was one thing for Bruno to turn over his prisoners. That was part of war. What happened to the prisoners after his men had turned them over was up to the commanding general. It was not Bruno's concern. Bruno did not agree with Aussaresses' method and was concerned about the effect it would have on his men if Aussaresses' interrogators were allowed to exact information in the field. At the same time Bruno realized that he and his men had greatly benefited from Aussaresses' intel. The major was rarely wrong which was more than

Bruno could say about the majority of intelligence officers he had encountered during his career. Bruno agreed to Aussaresses' suggestion but asked that discretion be used if possible. Aussaresses smiled and said, "Of course."

Brigitte sat in the navigator's chair behind Coyle in the cockpit. She was far from happy, and let Coyle know it several times during the flight. "This is insane. I have reported on three wars. I can take care of myself," she said.

"I know you can," said Coyle. "But I can't do my job properly while worrying about you. Besides it's just for a couple of days until I can find a qualified bodyguard."

"What is a bodyguard going to do against a bomb?"

"I don't know. Shield you from the explosion I guess. Look you've been saying that we should spend more time together."

"That's the stupidest thing you have every said."

"No. I'm pretty sure I've said something more stupid."

"I cannot get my work done while I'm flying around with you."

"Sure you can. You have sixty-three paratroopers in the cargo hold about to parachute into battle. What about a human interest story?"

"Now you are telling me what to write?"

"I ain't telling you anything. I am merely making a suggestion."

"It was a stupid suggestion."

"I thought it was pretty good as suggestions go."

Brigitte considered for a moment and said, "All right. I'll take you up on your suggestion."

"Really?"

"Why not? Sitting behind you in the cockpit is just a waste of time," said Brigitte getting up.

Coyle was suspicious when Brigitte exited the cockpit. Brigitte could be convinced by a good argument but she didn't usually give in that quickly. Coyle had to wear her down. He knew she still had a lot of fight in her and wondered what she had planned.

Brigitte walked into the cargo hold and approached the crew chief. "The captain wants me to put on a parachute. He says we're entering a war zone and I should be ready if we are hit by enemy fire."

"He's expecting heavy enemy fire?" said the crew chief, alarmed.

"I guess. What do I know? I'm just a woman."

The crew chief handed her a parachute. He was surprised when she slipped it on and attached all the straps correctly like a veteran paratrooper. Brigitte moved off and approached the paratrooper captain by the cargo hull's back doorway. She knew him from Dien Bien Phu. He was a good man and an experienced warrior. "Captain, do you mind if I join you and your men?"

"I would be honored, Brigitte," said the captain. "But I am afraid it will be less eventful than Dien Bien Phu."

"Let's hope so," said Brigitte.

The captain motioned to the soldiers nearby to make room for Brigitte. She sat and waited. She could feel the adrenaline rushing through her body and smiled to herself. It felt good to wear a parachute again. This was her true nature.

Bruno dropped with the first two companies into a small valley ten miles from one forest. He didn't want his prey to hear the sound of the helicopters that terrified them. It was hot, and a long hike uphill before they entered the tree-line. Bruno was in excellent shape as were his men. Even with their thirty-five pound rucksacks and weapons they covered the distance in three hours.

Once they reached the trees Bruno let his men rest for twenty minutes and eat a cold meal from their MREs. He did not want them fatigued if they crossed paths with the mujahideen.

Bruno respected the mujahideen. What they lacked in training they made up for in courage and they could shoot well. Most mujahideen in Algeria had grown up in the countryside where hunting was a way of life. Guns and knives were a cultural tradition and every man was expected to be proficient at both.

Bruno ordered his men to their feet and they moved deeper into the forest. He sent skirmishers out on both of his flanks and scouts far in front of his main force. He did not want to fall into an ambush. The trees on the gently sloping mountain were mostly oak with thick trunks and deep green leaves. Oaks provided excellent cover for snipers because their branches were strong and allowed a sniper to climb high into the treetops. There were many patches of brush that could hide machinegun nests or recoilless rifles. He remembered the effectiveness of the Viet Minh recoilless rifles against his troop at Dien Bien

Phu. He had no desire to see that carnage again and ensured that his men keep a sharp eye out on the terrain they were approaching.

Bruno's paratroopers had learned to walk softly without making a lot of noise. They avoided small twigs that could snap and dried leaves that could crunch under boot. Two hundred men moved in two parallel lines stretched out across the mountainside like a fisherman's trawling net.

The forward scouts spotted the mujahideen camp as they climb over the top of a slope. The camp was in a tree-covered valley with a creek running through the center. The French scouts were well trained and quickly identified the location of the mujahideen lookout posts.

The scouts reported back to Bruno. He formed a plan and radioed Coyle where to drop the additional paratroopers that would cut off the mujahideen's escape. It was a fairly simple plan since the mujahideen only had two directions to travel if they wanted to avoid the French helicopter gunships. They would need to stick to the trees which ran along the creek from one end of the valley to the other. Bruno and his men would position themselves on one end of the valley and drive the mujahideen into Coyle's paratroopers once they were in position.

The sound of the creek helped mask the movements of Bruno's men as they formed a crescent shaped line that started at the top of the hillside, stretched down through the valley, over the creek and up the opposite hill. He anchored the two ends of his line with his light machine gun squads. His mortar squads were placed on the back side of the mountain were they would be out of danger from enemy fire but close enough to hit any position in the valley. His snipers would take out the mujahideen lookouts and their gunshots would signal the beginning of the assault. Coyle would drop his paratroopers at the beginning of the battle. Bruno's men would keep the mujahideen occupied while Coyle's paratroopers regrouped and moved into position.

Bruno gave the signal and four para-snipers fired their weapons in unison. It would have been a great embarrassment if any one of the snipers had needed to chamber another round to finish the job. They didn't. Four bullets dropped all four mujahideen lookouts. Two of the lookouts fell from their perches in the trees. One fell but his boot caught in another branch and he hung upside down. The forth simply leaned his head against the tree trunk and died.

The mortar and the machine guns were next to fire. The anti-personnel shells from the mortar exploded in the camp sending hot shrapnel everywhere and setting several tents on fire. The machine runs raked the mujahideen as they ran for their weapons. Twenty-two mujahideen were killed in the first minute of battle. Bruno's troops fired too but he kept them in line formation rather than letting them charge as usual. He waited until the mujahideen lines formed. He was gaining more confidence in the Choctaws gunships abilities and wanted to give them clean lines to strafe the enemy. It worked. The mujahideen took heavy losses when the gunships unleashed their rockets, cannon and machine guns.

In the sky above, Coyle flew over the opposite end of the valley and dropped the paratroopers in a clearing that he had spotted.

Café Wars

Unknown to Coyle, Brigitte jumped with them. Her chute deployed as expected and she floated down. She landed with her knees bent and tumbled to the ground. She gathered her chute and placed it with the others to be retrieved at a later time. She moved up beside the captain along with the other troops. She had learned through experience to keep her mouth shut and listen. The paratroopers took their business very serious and did not have time to explain anything to a civilian. There would be time for questions later once the battle was finished and, God willing, the paratroopers had won the day.

The paratroopers spread out across the mouth of the valley between the two mountain ridges. Their machineguns anchored the ends of their lines just as Bruno had done. Their job was simple. Wait and let the mujahideen come to them. It didn't take long.

The Choctaws strafed the mujahideen lines as planned, killing dozens. When their firing ceased, Bruno ordered his men to charge. The paratroopers were mostly running downhill. They moved quickly and methodically killing anyone in their path that did not immediately throw down their weapon and put their hands high into the air. Those that didn't surrender broke and ran toward the opposite end of the valley and right into the line of paratroopers waiting for them.

The entire battle lasted less than fifteen minutes. Over two hundred mujahideen were taken prisoner. The prisoners were brought back into the village where they were searched and tied with their hands behind their backs. Their weapons were stacked into a large pile. The camp was searched thoroughly and the tortured bodies of six French civilians were found.

Aussaresses' interrogators picked out several of the leaders and moved them to a grove of trees outside the camp. It was their way of being discreet as Bruno had requested.

Brigitte entered the camp with the captain. "Little Bruno," she said approaching Bruno and giving him a hug.

"Brigitte what are doing here?" said Bruno.

"It was Tom's suggestion," she said with a shrug. "I didn't think you would mind. You don't, do you?"

"You shouldn't be here, Brigitte."

The screams of those being interrogated could not be stifled by their interrogators. Bruno and his men were unsettled as were the rest of the prisoners. Brigitte was shocked. "What's going on, Bruno?" said Brigitte staring in the direction of the screams.

Bruno remained silent. "You can't allow this, Bruno," said Brigitte. "This is your command. This is your responsibility."

"You shouldn't have come, Brigitte," said Bruno turning and walking away.

Tears welled up in Brigitte's eyes as the screams continued.

Bruno was ashamed. Brigitte was right and he knew it. It was his command and by letting it happen he was condoning it. He stood by a tree at the edge of the village.

The mujahideen that had been taken prisoner were unnerved by the screams of their comrades. One of the prisoners, a young man, was able to wiggle out of the rope used to tie his hands. He decided that he would rather die fighting than be tortured. He jumped up and rushed one of the paratrooper guarding the prisoners. He grabbed for the soldier's submachinegun and they struggled. The machine gun fired a burst before the paratrooper pried it free from the young mujahideen and hit him across the head knocking him out.

Bruno had heard the scuffle and the gunshots. He turned to see what was going on and felt a twinge of pain. He looked down and saw the left side of his uniform turning red. He had been hit in the chest by one of the stray bullets. He wanted to say something but everything sounded silly to him. He collapsed to his knees and leaned back on the heels of his boots. He remained upright. The captain saw him and couldn't believe his eyes. "Medic," he yelled.

Brigitte turned and saw Bruno kneeling on the ground with the blood stain that centered over his heart growing on his uniform. She screamed and ran to his side. She didn't know what to do. There was so much blood. He wanted to say something that would make her laugh and stop crying. Something that would assure her that he was okay. He couldn't think of anything so he smiled as he looked into her eyes and fell over. Brigitte wailed uncontrollably and pulled his head into her arms. The medic arrived, knelt down and pulled his shirt open. There was a bullet hole near his left nipple. Blood was pouring out the hole. The medic placed a large square of gauze over the wound and pressed down firmly. The gauze turned red and was saturated with blood in less than a minute. "We've got to get him to a hospital now," said the medic.

Bruno was carried in a rubber poncho by four of his paratroopers. Brigitte ran beside him. They loaded him into a waiting Choctaw in a forest clearing. Brigitte climbed in after him along with the medic. "Too much weight," said the pilot. "One of you has to get out."

There was no discussion. Brigitte climbed out and the helicopter lifted off. She collapsed to the ground in tears as she watched the helicopter climb over the mountains and disappear.

Bruno was lucky. The medic was an experienced veteran of two wars and had seen his share of chest wounds. Bruno's was bad but to the medic's surprise Bruno was still alive. He was strong and in excellent physical shape. The medic didn't have much hope but he and the other doctors and nurses would do everything in their power to save him. Everyone knew of Bruno and the role he had played in the final battle at Dien Bien Phu in the Indochina War. It was bad form to let a hero die under your care.

The helicopter landed at an airfield. Coyle's C-119's props were already turning. Bruno was transferred to the back of the plane where two nurses and a doctor were waiting in a makeshift triage center. It had been decided that the only chance Bruno had of living was to fly him to Paris where a team of heart surgeons were waiting.

As the crew chief closed the cargo hold doors, Coyle looked back through the cockpit door and saw Bruno lying helpless. Emotion flooded Coyle's mind and his eyes teared up. Bruno was his nemesis and friend. Bruno couldn't die. Not like this. The doctor ran forward and said, "You've got to keep your altitude as low and steady as possible. His blood pressure is extremely low and fluctuation in altitude could kill him."

Coyle nodded and climbed into the pilot's seat. He throttled up the engines, taxied onto the runway and took off into the cloudless sky.

Aussaresses' interrogators produced the desired results. Thirty-six mujahideen collaborators were rounded up and arrested in the cities along the coast. Those thirty-six produced the names of another one hundred and seventy collaborators throughout Algeria, most of whom disappeared after being taken into French custody. The mujahideen and the FLN were taking a heavy toll from the paratrooper assaults. News of Bruno's grave injury traveled fast and gave the underground leaders hope.

Bruno disappointed them and lived. The bullet had missed his heart by less than an inch. It had nicked an artery which would have killed a normal man. But Bruno was far from normal. The surgeons in Paris had worked on him for six hours before closing his chest and even then they were unsure of the results.

Bruno remained in the hospital for two months. Brigitte visited him almost every day. Coyle visited when he wasn't flying missions in Algeria. They played cards, told stories and laughed. The laughing hurt Bruno for the first month as his chest cavity healed but he didn't let on that anything was out of the ordinary, except for the occasional wince which he couldn't help. It was only when he started doing his morning workout of squats, pushups and sit-ups in his room that the doctors finally released him. They had never had a patient like Bruno. He wasn't like other men. He was extraordinary.

With his duffel bag beside him, Bruno stood by the C-119 on the airfield. Coyle and Brigitte approached. "Anxious to leave us?" said Coyle.

"Not you but I am looking forward to getting back to my command. All of this bread and butter is making me fat. I am setting a poor example to my men," said Bruno as Brigitte kissed him three times on opposing cheeks as was the French custom.

"You do realize it has only been two months since you were shot in the chest?" said Brigitte.

"Yes, yes. Bad things happen. It is war," said Bruno.

"Well I've got a plane to check out. I'll leave you two to talk." Coyle moved off to inspect his plane.

"I hope you don't mind me seeing you off?" said Brigitte.

"No, no, Brigitte. You are always welcome," said Bruno.

"I thought we should clear the air before you go. I don't know when will be the next time I see you. I don't want there to be bad feelings between us. Life is too short and one never knows what could happen. I just want to…"

"Apologize?"

"No. Acknowledge that there are times when I walk into a situation and I don't know the whole story. It's an occupational hazard."

"You do not need to apologize, Brigitte."

"Again, I'm not apologizing."

"Have it your way. You don't need to acknowledge anything. You are the bravest woman I know. You and I have traveled a long road together."

"Exactly. I know you love France as I love France. We want what is best for our country and its people. This war in Algeria… The bombings in Paris… I am not sure I understand what is happening."

"War is changing, Brigitte. You can no longer recognize the enemy."

"It is no different than what we faced with the Nazis or the Viet Minh."

"Maybe not, but the scale is different and their methods are madness. They torture and kill entire villages. Women and children. The young and the old. French and Muslim alike. There is no distinction. They are not just collateral damage. They are the target of their attacks, not the military. It seems their goal is just to cause as much pain and suffering as possible until we have had enough. Until we surrender."

"There has always been an enemy willing to attack civilians to accomplish its goals."

"I agree but there's no logic in what they are doing. It is anarchy. Chaos for the sake of chaos."

"That is why it is so important that we act civil. We cannot stoop to their level."

"No, Brigitte. We must fight fire with fire. If we do not, we will surely lose."

"And if we do as you say and fight fire with fire. What do we win? What will we have become?"

"I do not know. I am a soldier. I follow orders. I will leave it to politicians to decide who we are."

"That's an excuse, Bruno."

"Yes, but a good one."

"You are a human before you are a soldier."

"I am not so sure anymore. It seems I have been fighting all my life."

"Maybe it's time to stop."

"I would be lost. It is all I know," said Bruno as the engines on the C-119 started to turn and cranked to life.

Bruno kissed Brigitte three times on the cheek and said, "Au revoir, Brigitte. Take care of yourself and your crazy American."

"Au revoir, Little Bruno," said Brigitte with a smile. "Don't forget to duck."

Bruno picked up his duffel bag and moved off toward the plane. Brigitte watched until the plane started to taxi to the runway. She blew Coyle a kiss through the cockpit window. She smiled as she turned and walked back to the airfield main gate.

The Saharan sun was hot and merciless. Two Berber scouts lay hidden on the defile side of a sand dune, sharing a pair of binoculars. They watched a team of roughnecks operating a drill – threading pipe extensions so the carbon steel bit can penetrate further into the bedrock below. They surveyed the surrounding area for any signs of security. A lone guard stood watch with a rifle slung over his shoulder. The stacks of crates of tools and supplies were covered with canvas tarps to keep the grit out during the frequent sand storms. There were several tripods of rifles leaning against each other near the oil rig.

The Berber scouts slid a few yards down the dune then climbed to their feet and ran down the sandy hillside. At the bottom of the dune was a raiding party of fifty Berber warriors mounted on camels. There was a quick discussion with the scouts and the raiding party's leader. He ordered a sniper with a long rifle to take out the guard and the rest of his men to mount up and attack.

There was a crack from the sniper's and the back of the guard's head exploded. The roughnecks stopped their work and stared out at the surrounding dunes.

The fifty camel riders appeared over a distant dune and raced toward the roughneck's camp and drilling rig.

The roughnecks ran for their weapons. Several were killed by long shots from the charging riders. The Berbers were excellent marksmen even from the back of a galloping camel or horse. The roughnecks grabbed their rifles and moved behind the crates as the camel riders closed their distance.

The roughnecks pulled off the canvas tarps from crates and revealed two light machine guns armed by French paratroopers. Behind the machine guns and stacks of crate were three mortar positions. Bruno appeared from behind a stack of crates weaponless and defiant. He ordered his men to open fire. The machine gunners fired first and took a terrible toll on the Berber riders.

Camels and riders fell at full gallop and their blood mixed with the sand. The roughnecks joined in the massacre and fired their rifles.

The charging camels broke and the riders pulled at their harnesses to stop them from running wildly from the battlefield.

The mortars followed the machine gun barrage with their familiar thumps as the shells were launched from their tubes.

The shells landed and exploded behind the surviving camels and riders cutting off any hope of escape. It was mayhem, as the last of the riders tried to get their camels under control. It only took another minute before there were no more camels or riders standing. The mortars and machine guns ceased. The roughnecks cheered and ran out onto the battlefield to finish off any wounded Berbers.

Bruno wanted prisoners but knew better than to get between the roughnecks and the Berber raiders. The roughnecks wanted their revenge and were pitiless just as the Berbers had been with their long knives and rifles. There were no enemy survivors that day.

SIXTEEN

Algiers airport was crowded in the late morning as overseas tourists left their seaside hotels and caught their flights back home. Zaki finished a customer's shoes and raced off to the toilet. He didn't want to miss out on business but he really needed the toilet. He had eaten at the airport's food kiosks, and that was never a good idea.

Zaki finished using the toilet and went to wash his hands at the sink. He reached for a paper towel, but the dispenser was empty as usual. He turned to see two French Army soldiers standing behind him. He didn't react. He started to move off when one of the soldiers grabbed him by the arm and said, "Not so fast, Zaki. You need to come with us."

"Come with you?" said Zaki. "I thought all French men liked young girls."

"Shut the fuck up," said the soldier squeezing his arm tighter.

"Okay. Okay. I'll go," said Zaki. "Just promise to use a little olive oil."

Zaki was wearing a pair of German Army boots he had bought in the night market. He placed the edge of his right boot just below the soldiers knee and pushed down as hard as he could. His boot slid down the soldier's shin. The soldier screamed in pain and let go of Zaki's arm. Zaki made a run for it out of the toilet doorway. The soldiers ran after him, one limping badly.

Zaki sprinted across the terminal. His handler had warned him that one day he might need to elude the French and that he needed a preplanned escape route. He knew that there was little chance of escaping out the front of the terminal. The airport was on the outskirts of the city with lots of open space and few places to hide. There would be a car or jeep waiting to pick up the soldiers and their suspect. Even if he could find a taxi driver willing to give a young Algerian a ride, the French soldiers would force the taxi to pull over and nab him.

Zaki needed to put distance between himself and his pursuers before he reached the outskirts of the city. He ran behind the airline ticket counter and the ticket agents. He leapt over the stacks of luggage dropped off by passengers. The soldiers followed. They were big and burly. They crashed into the ticket agents and tripped over the luggage.

Zaki pushed through a door leading into the terminal operations area. There was a maze of luggage carts waiting to be loaded onto the departing planes. Zaki considered hiding behind one of the carts stacked high with mail bags. He decided against it. Too much of a chance of the soldiers enlisting the help of airport personnel to search the area. He ran through an opening that led out on to the tarmac.

The soldiers entered the operations area and saw Zaki run through the opening.

Zaki ran between the planes parked on the ramp and across the taxiway. He crossed the grass that separated the taxiways. The soldiers followed, the one with the scraped shin lagging behind.

A pilot revved the twin engines on his plane and released its brakes. The plane accelerated down the runway. There was nothing the pilot could do when he saw Zaki running across the runway in front of the plane.

The two soldiers saw the plane roaring down the runway toward Zaki. They stopped at the edge of the runway. They could see that if Zaki kept running he would be directly in the path of one of the plane's props when it reached him.

Zaki saw the plane approaching. He knew he would not make it all the way across the runway before the plane reached him. He also knew the soldiers would not venture out onto the runway while a plane was near. Zaki waited until the last possible moment before he dove to the ground. The plane's prop went directly over him and the wing's landing gear missed his head by less than a foot. As the plane passed Zaki jumped up and continued to run across the runway.

The two soldiers continued their pursuit until Zaki reached the perimeter fence on the far side. He climbed up and over the fence.

The two soldiers had had enough and gave up their chase. Zaki was gone.

Zaki stood in the shadows of the alley across from his family's home – a two-story with a courtyard in the center and thick plaster walls to keep out the heat in the summer and cold in the winter. He could see his mother moving around through the kitchen window. It was almost dinner time. Zaki was hungry. He had been watching the surrounding area for over two hours.

There was no sign of anyone watching the house. He tried to remember who he might have told at the airport where he lived. He was fairly sure he had never mentioned it to anyone. But he wasn't positive. So he waited and watched. He needed to get to his mother and warn her not to mention anything about Marwa or himself. His mother didn't know much, because Marwa and he had agreed not to tell her anything about what they were doing for the FLN. There was no need to worry her and the less she knew the safer she would be. Still the French were very good about putting bits and pieces of information together. His mother was naïve and could say something that might lead to Marwa's location.

He decided he had been watching long enough. Emerging from the alley, he walked down the street away from his house to look around. He saw nothing that made him feel suspicious. He turned and walked the other way. He passed his house and continued another two hundred yards up the street. Still nothing. He walked back to the front of his house and peeked through the windows. Nothing looked out of place. He moved to the front door and took one last look around. It was clear. He opened the door and went inside, careful not to make any noise.

The entry way and the living room were empty. He could hear his mother in the kitchen. He kept quiet and walked up the stairs. He took a quick look around in the bedrooms. They were empty and undisturbed. He walked back down the stairs. He could smell the evening meal and his stomach growled. He moved down the hallway and entered the kitchen, still cautious. His mother was at the sink cleaning a bowl of vegetables and didn't see him enter. He did not see his little sister, Rania, but that didn't worry him. She spend much of her time at her friend's house playing and learning how to bake the cookies she loved. "Sorry I'm late," said Zaki. "I got held up at work."

His mother turned around. She did not smile and Zaki was worried that she was angry. "Where's Rania?" said Zaki, trying to break the ice.

It was his mother's eyes that gave her away. A quick glance to the pantry doorway. Zaki knew they were not alone. He thought about running out of the house but he couldn't leave his mother and sister alone with whomever was in the house. He was not a coward. He felt the presence of someone moving up behind him in the hallway.

Zaki took two steps into the kitchen and looked into the pantry. The soldier with the skinned shin was standing in the pantry with his hands on the shoulders of twelve year old Rania. No gun was necessary. A man his size could easily break her neck. The second soldier that had chased him appeared in the hall doorway. Zaki looked at a carving knife on the counter next to him. He considered picking it up and fighting the two soldiers but he knew his family would suffer even if he won, which wasn't likely. He knelt on the tile floor and put his hands behind his head to show he would surrender without a fight. The soldier in the doorway walked forward and slugged him in the face. Everything went black when his head hit the floor and he fell unconscious.

Aussaresses took a personal interest in Zaki's interrogation. The politicians in Paris had been putting substantial pressure on the commanding generals of the Army to do something about the terrorist attacks that plagued their city. The bombs were scaring off the tourists, and France needed their money to rebuild and pay off her war debts.

In turn the commanding generals were putting pressure on Massu. Massu told Aussaresses to use all means necessary to find information that would reveal the location of the terrorists. *Shit always rolls downhill,* thought Aussaresses.

Aussaresses knew that Zaki was a low-level spy for the FLN. Zaki was never told why his handler and those in command wanted to know when certain people entered or exited Algeria. He didn't need to know to do his job. In fact Zaki didn't know much beyond the identity of his handler and even that was probably an alias. Hardly worth Aussaresses' time. But Aussaresses understood the concept behind a crack in the damn and Zaki was just the crack he needed.

With Zaki in custody the leaders of the FLN did not know what he would reveal, if anything. They didn't know how the French would use what information they learned against the rebels. The longer Zaki stayed in custody the more the FLN would worry and that was what Aussaresses wanted.

He wanted the members second guessing each other. He wanted them to panic. Aussaresses would make great use of Zaki, even if he didn't know anything. But first Aussaresses wanted to know what Zaki did know and Aussaresses was an expert at pulling information from a prisoner's head.

After three days without sleep, a person loses all track of time and begins to hallucinate. They don't know if it is day or night unless they see the sun or the moon which their interrogators deprive them of as soon as they enter prison. They begin to forget what they said and can't remember what they didn't say. A skilled interrogator can twist the prisoner's mind into believing he or she has already told them everything they wanted to know even when in reality the prisoner has told them nothing. The prisoner is forced to use the interrogator as a gauge of what is real and what is not real. Sleep deprivation is a very effective tool in discovering the truth.

Zaki had been awake for almost sixty-nine hours when he dozed off and his head nodded down. The bucket of cold water that hit him in the face woke him. Zaki was strapped to the armrests and legs of a wooden chair with baling wire. It had already cut deep into the flesh around his wrists and ankles. It cut further when Zaki jerked from pain.

Aussaresses sat in the corner reading the newspaper and sipping a café as if he wasn't paying any attention to Zaki or the interrogator. Zaki had never seen the French officer before and wondered why he was there. It was hard for Zaki to focus and reason. "Give us a name and you can sleep," said the interrogator.

Zaki said nothing. The interrogator turned back to Aussaresses as if asking for permission. Aussaresses looked up from his paper and seemed to quickly survey the situation. He gave a small nod to the interrogator and went back to reading his paper. *The officer controls my fate*, thought Zaki.

"Two," said Aussaresses without looking up.

The interrogator picked up a pair of pliers from a table. Zaki whimpered. He knew what came next. He had already lost two of his fingernails. The interrogator placed the jaws of the pliers on the tip of one of Zaki's fingernails. "Slowly," said Aussaresses without looking up from his newspaper.

Zaki's wrists and ankles jerked against the wire as the interrogator slowly pulled off his fingernail. "Marwa!" said Zaki without even knowing what he had said. Anything to stop the pain.

Aussaresses was surprised at hearing the name of Zaki's sister and motioned for the interrogator to stop. The interrogator released the pliers. Zaki gasped for breath. Aussaresses set down his newspaper and considered. *Why would Zaki say his sister's name when asked for a name?* According to the two soldiers that captured Zaki, the mother had explained that her daughter had been offered a job in a woman's shoe factory on the outskirts of Paris where she was now living. The soldiers had assumed that the mother was telling the truth, because she was too afraid for her young daughter Rania to do otherwise. Aussaresses also believed the mother was telling the truth as she knew it. But Aussaresses also knew that children did not always tell their parents the truth, especially when they thought their parents would be angry or worried. Aussaresses had sent an agent in Paris to check out the mother's story but the agent had not yet returned to report on the results of his inquiry. The mother had said her daughter had left nine months ago which was right around the time of the first bombing in Paris. Aussaresses was intrigued by the possibilities. "We already know about your sister," said Aussaresses. "You'll need to give us more if you want to the pain to stop."

"Marwa," Zaki said again and then passed out.

There it was again. The name of the sister. Like it had value. Something that would save him. "Give him some food and water and let him sleep. And for God's sake hose him down. I think he shit himself," said Aussaresses getting up and exiting the room.

Aussaresses sat at his desk reading a report when his phone rang. It was his agent in Paris. It was as Aussaresses thought... there was no Marwa working at the factory. If fact, there was no factory at the address given. Just a barbershop. *So where was Zaki's sister and what was she doing?* He instructed his agent to pull Marwa's duplicate photo from the passport office and give it to the police prefect in Paris to issue a bulletin to apprehend and bring Marwa in for questioning.

When Zaki woke, his mind was clear. He couldn't take any more and would do anything to avoid pain. He was broken. He told Aussaresses everything he knew about his sister. He knew she had been specially trained by an FLN leader but he didn't know the leader's name or the type of training his sister had received. "When can I go home?" said Zaki.

Aussaresses smiled and said, "Get some more sleep. You're a growing boy."

Zaki's trial was held in secret and lasted less than five minutes. There was no jury and no witnesses. The defense attorney assigned to represent Zaki only asked that the death penalty not be allowed because of the defendant's young age. The judge denied the motion but did show some mercy when he pronounced the guilty verdict and sentencing. The guillotine would be used to remove Zaki from this earth.

As horrible as the device and its operation appeared the guillotine was actually considered a humane method of capital punishment by the French. They had designed the device during the French revolution and it was used often in the purge that followed. It was, of course, much more efficient than death by hanging, especially if the neck of the person being hanged did not break when dropped from the gallows. It was far less traumatic for the members of a firing squad that were ordered to carry out a prisoner's sentence and far more accurate. The guillotine never missed. Once the guillotine's blade separated the prisoner's head from his body he felt nothing and there was no question that he was dead. It did however occasionally malfunction which could bring about horrific results. It was also true that some doctors believe that the victim was still aware for several seconds after decapitation because there was still a small amount of blood in the brain but that was pure conjecture since nobody survived the guillotine to relay the experience. The guillotine represented a finality of justice in these enlightened times.

Zaki was one of twenty-four prisoners that had been sentenced to the guillotine that sunny day in the prison courtyard. Executions were no longer public affairs but a few journalists were allowed to witness the event.

Zaki thought it was good that his mother and sisters would know about his death; that they would have closure. He hated the thought of disappearing like so many of his friends had done; their families never knowing what happened to them. He waited his turn in line. Each execution took about five minutes. It was the clean up after each decapitation that took most of the time. The guillotine was messy and the French thought it rude that a prisoner to be executed suffered the indignity of lying in another person's blood. They were not barbarians, after all.

It was a surprisingly orderly occasion. There were twenty armed guards supervising the line and surrounding the platform on which the guillotine sat. If one was going to die, the guillotine's blade was by far quicker and less painful than several bullets in the back. And even if you survived the bullets they would still cut off your head with the guillotine once you had healed enough to be ruled healthy. There was no escaping at this point in the process of justice. Just death.

Zaki's turn came and he was escorted up the stairs to the platform. The executioner's assistants lay Zaki face down so he would not see the blade dropping.

Zaki did not struggle. He had been told by other prisoners that struggling only made it worse and could cause the guillotine to malfunction. Zaki was sure he didn't want that to happen. The assistants secured his neck within the device by using a metal plate with a half-mooned cutout on one end.

Many say that when a person knows they are about to die their lives flash before their eyes. Zaki's life had been so short he was worried that he would run out of things to think about. Instead, Zaki thought about the time his father had taken him into the mountains to hunt deer. Zaki never got a chance to shoot a deer because they never spotted one, but it didn't matter. He loved just spending time with his father. The sunlight through the trees of the forest and his father's smiling face was Zaki's final thought when his head was severed from his body.

Marwa was awoken by a knock on her door. She looked at the wristwatch Saadi had given her. It was four-thirty in the morning. She slipped on her robe and walked to the door of her apartment. She picked up the revolver that sat on the hallway table and pressed the barrel against the front door as Saadi had shown her. The security chain was already on the door but she knew it would not prevent a determined intruder. She put her foot ten inches behind the door to stop it if the person on the other side tried to force their way into her apartment. She opened the door until it rested against her foot and peered out through the gap.

Saadi was on the other side of the door with a folded newspaper under his arm. Marwa closed the door and pulled off the security chain. She opened the door again and let Saadi enter. "What is wrong?" said Marwa as she closed the door and replaced the security chain.

"We must talk," said Saadi.

"Should I make tea?" said Marwa.

"Yes. I think tea would be good," said Saadi.

"Please. Sit," said Marwa as she moved off toward the kitchen.

Saadi sat on the couch and placed the newspaper on the coffee table.

Marwa prepared the tea. She knew something bad must have happened for Saadi to visit her so early. She brought the tea out on a small tray along with four biscuits and set it on the coffee table. She poured a glass for Saadi and one for oneself. "Why are you here, Saadi?" said Marwa with a small quiver in her voice. "Is it my mother?"

"Your mother is fine," said Saadi as he handed her the newspaper. "Page six near the bottom."

Marwa opened paper to page six and saw a list of the Algerians that had recently been executed for terrorist crimes against France. She saw Zaki's name at the bottom of the list and gasped. "Oh my God." Tears welled up in her eyes.

"The French caught him at the airport," said Saadi. "I'm sorry."

"Did he suffer?"

Saadi remained silent. Marwa broke down and wept. "My mother?" said Marwa.

"We have sent someone to comfort her. They will make sure she is okay."

"I must see her."

"And you will. But we have a mission that must be fulfilled. You swore an oath."

"Yes. Of course."

"Zaki died a martyr's death and is assured a place in heaven. We will avenge his death together."

Marwa nodded.

Aussaresses decided he needed to supervise Marwa's arrest in Paris. He didn't know when his intelligence unit would have another opportunity like this and wanted to ensure there were no mistakes. He also wanted to ensure that proper credit was given to her captor, namely him.

He knew Massu would take the credit if given the chance. Of course Massu would mention Aussaresses' name as a minor player in the intricate web that Massu had designed to capture the notorious terrorist. Massu was a shrewd politician and Aussaresses would expect no less of him. Aussaresses had his own political aspirations. This was most likely Aussaresses' last war and he needed to enhance his reputation as much as possible.

Aussaresses did not notice the motor scooter following him to his hotel. He was an officer and therefore not expected to stay on base when visiting. He used his per diem plus a supplement to pay for a small room at the Hotel George V just off the Avenue des Champs-Élysées. Most officers chose to stay in less expensive lodgings and pocketed the majority of the per diem. But one did not run into high-level diplomats, generals, and politicians in flop houses.

Café Wars

The George V had three excellent restaurants in which Aussaresses ate his breakfast and lunch. For dinner he preferred La Maison du Caviar which was easy walking distance from the hotel. He knew the maître d' well and always tipped for a seat that gave him a view of the reception area. He liked to know who was entering the restaurant. It was a popular spot with high society, famous musicians and movie stars. The restaurant's specialty was Russian caviar which always impressed his dates and smoothed the way for a more enjoyable evening.

The dining room was crowded when Aussaresses arrived with his date - the hostess at a local nightclub that he frequented when in the city. The maître d' gave him a signal that the required tip for a good table would be twice what he normally gave. He paid it, not wanting to look cheap in front of his date. She was very attractive.

They were escorted to their table and the maître d' took their drink order as was the custom. Aussaresses ordered a medium-priced champagne. His date was beautiful but he was sure she would not be able to tell the difference between a high and medium-priced champagne. The bubbles looked the same and that was what was important to her. He pretended to seem interested as the girl babbled on about the time she met Jerry Lewis in the lounge at Le Dome. Aussaresses kept glancing at the front door as each person entered to see whom he might want to run into at the bar on his way to the toilet. The waiter walked over and informed him that there was a telephone call for him. He was surprised, as he couldn't recall telling anyone that he was here this evening. Many on his staff knew that he frequented the restaurant, but they knew better than to disturb him unless it was a true emergency. He excused himself and moved to the end of the bar where the house phone was located. He picked up the phone and said, "Hello."

The line went dead and he hung up. *A joke?* he thought. *But whom?* When he turned to go back to the table he saw that a beautiful woman was behind him. It took him a moment to realize that he had seen her before... in a photograph. It was Marwa.

Saadi had instructed her to use her revolver and to fire two shots into his chest followed by a coup de grace to the head once he had fallen to the floor. She had decided that bullets were far too kind for the man responsible for Zaki's death. She had stolen a steak knife from one of the tables.

Marwa raised the knife above her head and swung downward toward Aussaresses' chest. He instinctively put his hand up to deflect the blow. The knife plunged through his palm and the tip of the blade pierced the back of his hand. The knife had been stopped. Aussaresses cried out in pain and cursed.

Marwa was furious. She kicked his shins and pushed forward with all her weight keeping her hand on the knife. Aussaresses tripped and fell backward. She held onto the knife's handle and followed him to the floor landing on top of him. She grabbed the handle of the knife with both her hands pushed the blade towards his face. The tip of the knife sliced his eyebrow open and slide down into his left eye. He screamed. A waiter and the maître d' pulled her off him but the damage was done. He was blind in one eye and badly disfigured. His date shrieked on seeing him.

Café Wars

Marwa was kept in a cell with a single light bulb that shined day and night. Loud music was played over a loudspeaker whenever she dozed off. If the music didn't wake her the guards soaked her with a fire hose. She was a wreck after three days of no sleep.

She was removed from her cell and dragged into an interrogation room. She was stripped naked. Her hands and feet were tied with baling wire. She was hung by the baling wire around her wrists from a meat hook on a steal pipe overhead. Her feet dangled a few inches off the concrete floor. Copper clamps on the ends of wires were attached to each of her nipples. The wires led to a hand cranked generator. The guards left the room, leaving her alone with her thoughts... *What comes next?*

She hung from the pipe for what she thought was three hours. In reality it was only thirty minutes but one tended to lose track of time in these types of situations. The door opened. Aussaresses entered with a gauze patch over his left eye. The bleeding had stopped after the second day. Soon he could be outfitted with a leather eye patch which he thought would give him a rouge look and amplify his mysterious reputation. The wound was not ideal but not the end of the world either. He sat down in the room's only chair and stared at her silently.

Marwa was unnerved by his one good eye moving up and down her naked body. "You, fucker. I'm gonna kill you," she said.

"No. You had your chance. It's my turn now," said Aussaresses.

He rose and walked over to the generator. He flipped a switch to "ON" and gave the generator's handle a whirl. Marwa screamed as the electricity coursed through her nipples. Her body convulsed and the baling wire dug deeper into her wrists and ankles as she jerked. The generator handle slowed to a stop and the generator wound down decreasing the voltage as it slowed. Finally it stopped and Marwa gasped for breath. Aussaresses stared at her again with a kind of curiosity. He wondered why the nipples were the most effective location on a woman's body to place the clamps of the electrodes. He had studied the human body during medical school and he knew that a woman's vagina had far more nerve endings than the nipples. But still he and others like him found the nipples to be more effective on a woman. He surmised that it was probably the smell of burning flesh so close to the nostrils and the visual of seeing smoke rising from her nipples that struck such terror in a woman's mind. It didn't really matter what the reason as long as it was effective, but he was naturally curious. "I am going to need the name of your handler," said Aussaresses.

"Fuck you," said Marwa.

"That's my girl," said Aussaresses. "It will get better once you start sweating."

He gave the generator's handle another whirl and Marwa screamed. The echo bounced off the concrete walls in the hallway and struck fear in the other prisoners waiting their turn in their cells.

The session continued until Marwa finally fell unconscious for the fourth time and Aussaresses waved off the guard with the fire hose. He would let her rest for a bit before continuing. He didn't want her to die of shock before revealing the name and location of her handler. Aussaresses was a patient man.

Marwa woke a few minutes later her arms still hanging from the pipe. She was exhausted and her body glistened in cold sweat. Her beautiful black curls were clumped together in long strands. She knew she would eventually reach a breaking point and reveal Saadi's name. It wasn't that she was worried about Saadi. He could take care of himself. She just didn't want to give Aussaresses any kind of victory over her... over Zaki. She was resigned to her fate but determined to pick the manner of her death. She turned her head to the side and used her tongue to draw the first strands of hair into her mouth. She swallowed without chewing.

After a coffee and a visit to the toilet, Aussaresses went back to the interrogation room with his newspaper tucked under his arm. The pain medication he had been given was wearing off and he felt a stinging sensation in his eye. He lightly pressed on the gauze for a moment and the pain went away. It would be back. He pulled a small bottle of medication from his pocket and opened the lid which contained an eyedropper. He used the eyedropper to place two drops of medication on his tongue. It was bitter. He wished he'd brought a cup of coffee with him to wash out the taste. *Next time,* he thought and made a mental note to himself. He opened the door to the room and entered. He found Marwa's lifeless body hanging from the pipe. Several strands of hair led into her mouth and disappeared. Her eyes were bulging and her face was blue from lack of oxygen. She had suffocated to death.

Aussaresses was disappointed but did not let his emotions get the best of him. He grunted and pulled out his notebook from his shirt pocket. He used a small pencil to make an annotation for later reference – Cut Off Female Prisoners' Hair.

Saadi stood on the rooftop of his bakery as the sun set. He was upset that he hadn't heard from Marwa after the attempted assassination was reported in the newspapers. It could only mean one of two things; Marwa was dead or Marwa was captured. He hoped it was the former. She would become a martyr like her brother. If it was the latter he knew she would be tortured until she either told the French what they wanted to know or she died. Her intended target, Aussaresses, would see that she suffered greatly. The thought saddened Saadi.

In a way he had fallen in love with each of the sirens he had trained and transformed. They had bravely carried out his orders and won great victories for Allah.

Only Ludmila was left. She was the smartest of the three and the most ruthless. She was the ideal jihadist. A true warrior of God. Now she was more valuable than ever to the cause. She alone would need to carry on the campaign of terror he had so intricately planned. He had to be more cautious. He would not waste her life. He regretted that he had not trained more girls. He knew there would probably be casualties but he honestly thought the girls would last longer. He had not expected fate to intervene so quickly.

He wondered how Ludmila would respond to Marwa's fate once he knew what had become of her. Ludmila had not shed a tear when he told her about Nihad's death. He wondered if it was because of her faith in an afterlife or if she saw Nihad as competition for his attention. She simply volunteered to deliver the bombs and carry out the assassinations that had been assigned to Nihad for the glory of Allah. Saadi considered her reaction and decided it really didn't matter why she felt the way she felt as long as she advanced their mission. He was not her judge. Only Allah could judge one's heart.

Saadi knew that his bombings and assassinations were having an effect. The MNA leadership had been decimated and many of their members had already joined the FLN just as Bella had planned. He liked Bella and thought he was a good leader, especially when it came to strategy. He also felt that Bella would reward loyalty and that he was assured of a position in the new government once the war was over and Algeria was finally free of the French.

SEVENTEEN

A French coast guard boat approached an Algerian fishing boat. The boat's crew pulled in their nets and sorted their catch. Brigitte sat with her back against the boat's wheelhouse holding an Algerian baby. The child was crying from hunger. Brigitte's skin was dark and her face covered with a head scarf. She tried rocking the child in her arms hoping it would stop crying and bringing attention to her as the French patrol boat drew closer. Nothing seemed to work and time was short. She pulled out her breast and placed her nipple in the baby's mouth. She was surprised by how strongly the child sucked. She looked down and saw how white her breast was compared to the child's face. She tried not to look too obvious as she covered the child's face and her breast with the end of her head scarf.

Damien had asked one of his Algerian freelance photographers to help Brigitte find survivors of the Philippeville massacre that she could interview for her story. He told the photographer that he would buy all his photos of the victims. The photographer was diligent in his quest.

Brigitte was worried that nobody would come forward for fear of reprisal from their pied-noir neighbors or the French intelligence units. She could not have been more wrong. The photographer found dozens of survivors willing to be interviewed and have their photo taken. They wanted the story of Philippeville told. The survivors of Philippeville knew the French would try and cover up what happened. The Algerians saw it as their duty to Allah and the dead to reveal the truth.

Brigitte decided it would be best if the interviews were conducted one at a time and in secret. She didn't like the idea of dozens of survivors gathering at the same place, especially with martial law in affect and French paratroopers still patrolling the streets.

Damien was concerned that it could be a trap and that Brigitte could be kidnapped – or worse. The photographer arranged for two Moroccan bodyguards to protect Brigitte while in Philippeville. The bodyguards were both former Foreign Legionnaires and knew how to fight. They were heavily armed and insisted that Brigitte wear a flak vest with steel plates in the front and back while traveling.

Brigitte believed in what she was doing, but she also realized that she was entering the belly of the beast. She was French and that made her the enemy. She hoped that the Algerians in Philippeville would recognize that she was there to reveal the truth and would not harm her. She was relying on her fame and reputation as a fair journalist. She wondered if the people of Philippeville had read any of her articles.

She wondered how many of them even knew how to read.

The Philippeville airport had been closed since the massacre and all the roads leading into the city had French Army or pied-noir checkpoints. She knew she would be recognized. Her reporting of the siege at Dien Bien Phu was very popular among the French soldiers and her photo had accompanied each article. Any French Intelligence officer would know her purpose and place her under arrest.

The photographer arranged for her to enter the city by fishing boat and hopefully avoid the French coast guard. She would dress as an Arab and wear the traditional head scarf that all Muslim women wore. She would darken her skin with makeup and avoid eye contact whenever possible. The fisherman that owned the boat brought his six-month-old son aboard and suggested Brigitte pretend like she was breastfeeding if they encountered the French patrol boats. Brigitte was not good with children and was especially uncomfortable with babies. She hoped the French patrols would stay away but kept the child at arm's length in case they boarded the boat. Her photographer and the two bodyguards would meet her once the boat docked. It was a good plan. It just didn't work the way she thought it would.

The captain of the French Coast Guard boat ordered the fishing vessel to heave to and prepare to be boarded. The fishermen continued their work as if this was a regular occurrence and nothing to worry about. The fishing boat captain slowed his boat to a stop as the French vessel pulled alongside. Four French soldiers jumped onto the fishing boat's deck and inspected the boat. Two of the soldiers searched the cabin and engine room below while the other two inspected the crew and the deck. They were searching for weapons and contraband more than stowaways. Things were bad enough in Philippeville without giving the Muslims more arms.

One of the soldiers moved toward Brigitte. She kept her head down and pretended to fuss with the baby in her arms. Brigitte hoped the soldier approaching her didn't try to speak to her in Arabic. She won't understand what he was saying and wouldn't be able to answer his questions. She only knew one phrase in Arabic which a friend had taught how to pronounce with the correct accent and told her it could be used whenever a Arab man got too close.

The soldier used the barrel of his submachine gun to brush away the end of her head scarf so he could see what she was holding. He exposed the sucking baby and Brigitte's tit. Brigitte snapped, "aya nik kawed alya" with as much fury as she could muster in her voice. She hoped her attitude would sell it. It did. The soldier backed away and left her and the baby alone.

The French were satisfied. They re-boarded their boat and sped off. As they left, the baby bit down hard trying to coax milk from the barren breast. Brigitte gasped. Strangely, she wasn't mad and didn't pull the child's mouth away. It kept him quiet and was a new feeling for her.

The sun hung low on the horizon as the fishing boat pulled into port at Philippeville. It was quiet. The people of Philippeville were still stunned by what had happened and nobody was in the mood to visit or make jokes. Almost everyone in the city knew someone that had died or been raped. It was not something easily forgotten.

Brigitte thanked the captain and gave him an envelope holding the money he had been promised. She took one last look at the baby in the captain's arms before stepping onto the dock.

She was met by the photographer and the two Moroccan bodyguards. They escorted her into a nearby car. One of the bodyguards sat in the passenger seat and the other in back with Brigitte. The photographer climbed in behind the wheel and drove off.

The two bodyguards kept watch out the front windows of a house where Brigitte sat at a table across from a Muslim woman. Brigitte watched as the woman's husband made tea for the visitors. It was unusual for an Algerian husband to make refreshments when his wife was in the home. The wife sat quietly and waited with her head down. Brigitte could see the cuts and bruises on her face.

The tea was served as was the custom before the conversation began. Brigitte sipped from the glass and smiled. "It's delicious. Thank you," she said, as the photographer translated for her.

Neither the husband nor wife spoke French. A toddler cried for his mother and the father picked him up and comforted him. "Can you tell me what happened?" said Brigitte.

The woman began to cry. Brigitte was an experienced journalist and knew that it was best to give the woman time. Let her express her emotions. Don't rush her. She would talk when she was ready. It took five minutes before she spoke in Arabic. "I was in the market when they took me. We had run out of food and my children were hungry," said the photographer as he translated.

Brigitte knew that most Algerian families could not afford refrigeration and shopping was a daily necessity. "Who took you?" said Brigitte and the photographer translated.

"There were two of them. They were French soldiers," translated the photographer.

"French soldiers did this to you?"

"No. The soldiers took me to a coffee house owned by a pied-noir family. There was a man there. I think he was Spanish. There was dried blood on the floor and the walls had been burned. The soldiers told me that the Muslims had killed this man's family while he was away. The soldiers put me on a table and held me down. The man took his revenge."

"The soldiers held you down as the man raped you?"

"She says 'no'," said the photographer.

"What did he do?" said Brigitte almost afraid to ask.

The woman sat silently as she considered. She looked over at her husband. He nodded his consent and ushered the toddler into the next room. The woman moved her head scarf to one side. She slid her robe off her shoulders and let it drop to her waist. There were bandages around the woman's chest. "Oh my God," said Brigitte.

The woman gingerly unwrapped the bandages. The photographer stopped her and spoke to her in Arabic. "What did you say to her?" said Brigitte.

"It is not necessary. We understand," said the photographer.

Brigitte looked in the woman's eyes as they teared up. She seemed to be pleading as if she wanted Brigitte to see what had been done to her. It was her testament. "It is necessary. And make damn sure your camera is in focus," said Brigitte.

Brigitte nodded to the woman and the woman continued until her wounds were revealed. Brigitte struggled not to show emotion but couldn't hold back the tears. A surgeon's sutures bound together the skin where the woman's breasts had once been. "I am so sorry," said Brigitte crying openly. "This is not who we are. This is not France."

But it was.

Brigitte interviewed twenty-one women and girls over the next two days. There was only one male survivor but he could not speak. His tongue, eyes and ears had been removed. His photo would be his testimony. While many of the atrocities in Philippeville were committed by the pied-noir, many had been committed directly by the French soldiers, especially the paratroopers. Brigitte was thankful that nobody implicated Bruno in the massacre. She knew he had participated in the battle on the hillside but had been ordered away before the massacre in the city began.

It was the night of her last interview when the French Intelligence unit raided the house and arrested Brigitte, the photographer and the two bodyguards. The French officer claimed they had all broken curfew by traveling after sundown. Brigitte questioned how the officer knew they had traveled after dark and hadn't just stayed over after a late lunch with their Muslim friends. The officer didn't respond.

Her notes and the film from the photographer's camera were confiscated. Brigitte was separated from the others and whisked away in a jeep. She thought it laughable that two paratroopers were assigned to guard her as she rode in the jeep. Did they really think she was dangerous enough to warrant two of France's elite?

Brigitte was taken to a building near the port and placed in a windowless room. Even through the thick walls she could hear the heavy horns of ships as they made their way out to sea. She was more concerned about her photographer than she was about herself. She was pretty sure the two bodyguards would be deported back to Morocco as punishment for breaking curfew.

The photographer was a different story. He was Algerian. He could be accused of collaborating with the enemy or of being an FLN agent. The French did not need much of a reason to lock him up for an extended period of time. Algerians were treated as second class citizens in their own country and had few rights.

Brigitte waited three hours in the windowless room before being removed and escorted to Trinquier's office. Trinquier stood as she entered and was placed in chair. "Mademoiselle Friang, so good to see you again," said Trinquier as he waved the guards out of the room.

"I wish I could say the same, Colonel," said Brigitte.

"I wish you would have told me you were coming. We could have avoided all of this unpleasantness."

"Where is my photographer?"

"Your photographer? I was under the understanding that he was freelance."

"Either way. Where is he?"

"I believe he is being questioned at another facility."

"Questioned?"

"Yes. It seems there was a problem with some of his identification papers. I am sure they will get to the bottom of it... in time."

"And the two bodyguards that were with me?"

"On a truck bound for Morocco. The Algerian governor elected to revoke their visas. They will be dropped unharmed at the border."

"Have you informed my editor that I am in custody?"

"No. I don't believe so. I just found out myself a few hours ago. These things take time. The bureaucratic wheels grind slowly."

"I demand to be released immediately. You have no right to hold me."

"Oh, but I do. Philippeville is under martial law and I am currently the authority in charge. That gives me quite a lot of leeway to do what I deem necessary to keep the peace. Including holding those that plan to stir up trouble."

"Like me?"

"Your reputation precedes you. Why are you here, Brigitte? May I call you Brigitte?"

"It's none of damn business and no you may not, Colonel," said Brigitte.

"Everything is my business in Philippeville."

"I have seen your business, Colonel. And frankly, I am appalled."

"I am not surprised. War is a messy affair. I am often appalled myself at the things that are necessary."

"Necessary?"

"You didn't think the Algerians would just snap to after our loss in Vietnam, did you? Dien Bien Phu made all things possible. We must show them otherwise. We must show them that France is still powerful and determined."

"And massacring twelve thousand civilians is how we are going to show them?"

"Where do you get these numbers? You have been grossly misinformed."

"Pardon me. Would you care to set the record straight? I'm sure you've counted the bodies by now, haven't you?"

Trinquier did not respond and chose to change the subject. "I've read many of your articles, especially those on the jumps you made with the paratroopers. Very well written. You should be commended."

"Save your flattery, Colonel."

"Very well. I have been told you are a patriot."

"I am."

"Then why do you insist on focusing your attention on France's most guarded secrets?"

"Guarded secrets? When has France considered torture and murder of civilians a guarded secret?"

"Since Philippeville."

"This was not France's doing. You are not France, Colonel."

"Oh but I am. Do you honestly believe that I would embark on such a mission without express permission or that my commander would give such an order without the support of Paris?"

"You are saying the government ordered you to massacre civilians?"

"I am not saying anything. It is merely a supposition."

"Stop playing games, Colonel. Who ordered the massacre?"

"Which one?"

"Which one? What are you talking about?"

"Ask your friend Colonel Bigeard. Ask Bruno about El-Halia."

"What happened at El-Halia?" said Brigitte.

"You are free to go, Mademoiselle Friang," said Trinquier buzzing his receptionist on the phone. "See that Mademoiselle Friang is driven to the closest airport and placed on a plane back to Paris. Her time in Philippeville as at an end."

"What about my photographer?" said Brigitte.

"He is no longer your concern," said Trinquier.

"I want the film your men took," said Brigitte.

"I am afraid it has been misplaced in all the commotion," said Trinquier. "I would see that the men that lost it reimburse your photographer for the cost of the film if you wish."

"The people will know what you have done here. This will not stand," said Brigitte.

"Of course," said Trinquier considering her choice of words. He watched with amusement as Brigitte was escorted out of his office by the two paratroopers.

Brigitte stayed silent on her trip in the jeep to the airport at Constantine. She boarded the plane to Paris without putting up an argument with the two paratroopers escorting her.

It was a connecting flight through Nice. When the plane landed in Nice, Brigitte exited the plane with some of the other passengers. She entered the terminal and bought a ticket for the earliest flight to Algiers. She refused to go back to Paris without answers to her questions. It was too important.

It was early morning when the helicopter carrying Bruno and his command staff approached at the French Army airfield. He was surprised to see Brigitte standing on the edge of the field. She looked cold, like she had been waiting there all night.

When the helicopter landed he jumped out and trotted over to greet Brigitte with a smile on his face. "This is a nice surprise. What are you doing here?" he said.

"What happened at El-Halia, Bruno?" said Brigitte.

Bruno was taken aback by the seriousness of Brigitte's tone and even more by the mention of El-Halia. "Let's go inside and get some coffee. You look cold," said Bruno.

"I'm fine. Tell me what happened, Bruno."

"Coffee first. Then we'll talk. I promise."

Bruno and Brigitte sat for a long time without talking. Brigitte knew this would be tough for Bruno and she waited patiently as he composed his explanation. This was a courtesy for a friend. Normally she would not wait and press her interviewee until her questions were answered. But this was Bruno. A man that had saved her life more than once. A man who was once her lover. She felt she owed him time to think. She had to admit that she hoped what Trinquier had alluded to wasn't true but Bruno's silence suggested otherwise. Bruno took at long sip of coffee before he started, "It was after Philippeville. Trinquier asked me to take a platoon up to investigate a fire at the mines of El-Halia. To be honest I knew he was planning something at Philippeville and I wanted to get as far away as possible before it happened."

"You knew he was going to massacre all those people?"

"No. I had no idea he would go that far but Trinquier had a reputation for being harsh with the Vietnamese villagers and I had no reason to believe this would be any different. You must understand, Brigitte. I was there as an observer. I had no power over Trinquier and his men."

"So why did he ask you to accompany the platoon?"

"I imagine he wanted me out of the way. He didn't want any high-ranking witnesses. But I didn't come to that understanding until later after the affair was over."

"Affair?"

"You know what I mean, Brigitte. I am not good with words like you."

Brigitte nodded, "Go on."

"When we arrived in El-Halia the streets were empty. It was like a ghost town. The Muslims were hiding in the hills. They had good reason to suspect the French Army would retaliate. They had killed dozens of pied-noir families. Men, women, children… even babies. Anyone they could find they killed in a most vicious manner. Over one hundred and twenty in all."

"Why would they do that? They must have had a reason."

"They did. There was a fire at the mine. Eighteen pied-noir miners were killed. The pied-noir believed the Muslims had set the fire. They rioted and attacked the Muslim community near the mine. Over thirty Muslims died. The pied-noir were also very vicious. The Muslims retaliated. They outnumbered the pied-noir and their vengeance was swift."

"So what happened when you got there?"

"I suggested to the officer in charge of the platoon that military trials were in order. He and his men rounded up one hundred and fifty Muslim men. Each was given a trial and…"

"And what, Bruno?"

"And hanged… in the village square where all could see."

"You murdered one and fifty Muslims?"

"No. We murdered no one. They were tried and found guilty. They were punished according to the law."

"French law?"

"Military law."

"They were civilians."

"They were terrorists and mass murderers."

"So were the pied-noir."

"I was not sent to judge the colonists."

"Then you agree. You were given orders to single out the Muslims."

"Not orders per se. There was an understanding. I knew what needed to be done and I did it. That's what being in command means. Doing the hard things."

"Except you weren't in command."

"I will not hide behind a technicality."

"I didn't imagine you would. Those men listened to the great Bruno Bigeard, hero of Dien Bien Phu."

Bruno stayed silent. The point had been made.

"Did Massu know?"

"I will not blame my commander for my decisions."

"Of course not. You'll just fall on your sword because that's the honorable thing to do."

"And what is wrong with honor?"

"One hundred and fifty civilians dead. That's what's wrong with honor."

"They had to be shown that France will fight for what is hers."

"Tell me. When does it stop, Bruno? When does an eye for an eye stop?"

"When everyone is blind, I suppose."

"I used to think you were the bravest man alive. Turns out you're just a bully with a reputation."

Bruno remained silent but she knew her words stung. She knew Bruno better than he knew himself. She rose and left the building.

Brigitte sat in Damien's office as they finished the last

of the brandy. "So, what are you going to do?" said Damien.

"I don't know," said Brigitte. "If I write the truth the reputation of a man I once loved will be in ruins. Even if the generals don't court martial him, his military career will be over. He'll never recover."

"I could get someone else to write the story."

"Thanks, but no. If it's going to be written it should be me that writes it."

"You don't think you are too close to it?"

"I'm a professional. I'll do my job."

"You could wait."

"What do you mean?"

"You said yourself that you're not sure who is really behind it or how far up the ladder it goes. So… find out."

"Bit of cop out, isn't it?"

"Maybe not. I don't want to put the magazine's reputation on the line for a half-baked story."

"Really?"

"Yeah. Really. Quit whining and do your job, Friang. Find the truth. All of it."

Brigitte smiled. She got up from her chair, walked over and kissed Damien on his bald spot. "Tell your wife she's a lucky woman," said Brigitte. "And if she don't want you, I'll take you."

"Perish the thought," said Damien.

Brigitte laughed and walked out.

EIGHTEEN

Brigitte had her arms full of groceries when she returned to her apartment. Bottles of wine were cheap at the grocery store and she had decided to stock up on her favorites – the dry style of Semillon from the Bordeaux region, the deep Pinot Noirs grown in the Burgundy region and the Grenache from Southern France. She would save the best for when Coyle was with her and they spent the evening together. He didn't know too much about wine but she enjoyed teaching him. They needed hobbies together. It was strange to love someone so much but to have so little in common with them.

The elevator was out of service again and she had to hike up the flight of stairs carrying the two heavy bags. She pushed the bags against the door and used the weight of her body to hold them in place while she fished for keys in her purse. She noticed someone at the end of the hallway. The hallway bulb was out, making it darker than usual and she couldn't see the person's face. She supposed it was a man by the size and the bulky overcoat. The person stared a moment as if considering what to do. *Is he wondering if he should help me or is it something else,* she thought. Brigitte didn't like the feeling it gave her. She found her keys, shoved the apartment key in the lock and turned it without thinking what would happened next. She just wanted to get inside.

When the door swung open the bags of groceries came crashing down. One of the bottles of Pinot Noir shattered and soaked the vegetables she had purchased with red wine. "Fuck," she said.

She heard footsteps approaching from the direction of the end of the hallway. Instinct told her not to turn and look but to get her ass inside and close the door. She followed her instinct. She kicked the groceries on the hallway floor inside, slammed the door shut and threw the deadbolt. She stepped back and watched the door knob. It was motionless and she sighed with relief. She was being foolish and it had cost her a bottle of wine. Even though she was laughing at herself, something kept her eyes transfixed on the door knob… and she watched it move. She held her breath. It occurred to her that it might be Coyle. He could have forgotten his key and was waiting at the end of the hallway. Why he hadn't waited in the lobby below she wasn't sure. But it was a possibility. "Tom?" she said.

The door knob snapped back into its previous position and stopped moving. She listened for foot falls but heard none. Whoever was outside her door was still there. She wasn't sure what to do but figured she had better arm herself. She picked up the neck of the shattered wine bottle and waited. It was a wooden door and could be easily kicked in by a large man. *You've faced worse*, she thought. *Keep your head and don't stop fighting if it comes to that. And scream. Screaming is good. Screaming gets attention. Rape is a good scream word. Fire is better. Everyone will come at the sound of the word fire.*

She waited by the door for seven minutes and nothing happened. She moved into the kitchen and retrieved a better weapon – a carving knife. She grabbed a dish towel and moved back out to the door. She sopped up the wine that had now stained the white grout in her tile floor. "Double fuck," she said starring at the red stained grout.

Brigitte called the airbase in Algeria were Coyle was stationed. She wasn't sure what she would say to him. If she told him the truth and that she was frightened he would drop everything and come home to her. That's what she wanted but didn't want to admit it to herself. She would figure this one out on her own. The officer on duty informed her that Coyle was unavailable at the moment and that perhaps she should call back tomorrow. That meant he was on a mission. He was doing what he did best and she wanted him to continue doing it. She asked the officer to leave Coyle a note and tell him that there was a gas leak in the apartment. She was going to spend the night in a hotel and call him in the morning. The officer agreed. She hung up.

The man still could be waiting outside the door, she thought. *I need to get past him.* She considered the situation for a moment. She picked up the phone and called a taxi. She asked the driver to come up and help her with her luggage. She said her suitcase was heavy so it should be a driver that was big and strong. She hung up.

She grabbed her biggest suitcase from the bedroom and brought it into the living room. She filled the suitcase with the unbroken wine bottles weighing it down. She grabbed a change of clothes and her toiletries. She placed them in the suitcase and closed it. She thought for a moment. She reopened the suitcase and placed the carving knife inside. She retrieved a smaller knife from the kitchen and waited by the door.

A few minutes later there was a knock. She placed her foot sideways several inches back from the door and opened it so that her foot only allowed the door to open a couple of inches. A large man was standing in the hallway. "You called for a cab?" he said.

"Yes. Can you help me with my suitcase?" she said.

"Of course," said the man. "You'll need to let me in."

"Oh, sorry," she said, opening the door.

She stayed near the open door as the man entered and picked up the suitcase. She wasn't sure about him. He wasn't wearing a uniform and he could have heard her conversation while listening through the door. She kept the small knife hidden against her wrist in case she needed it. He exited the apartment. She grabbed her purse and locked the door behind her. "I'm sorry. The elevator is out. You will have to use the stairs," she said glancing back down the opposite direction to ensure they were not being followed or attacked from behind. The hallway was empty and someone had repaired the light.

"Yes. Yes. I noticed when I came in," he said. "It is fine. It's not so heavy. I used to operate a beer delivery truck. Two kegs of beer on the shoulders. Now those are heavy."

They moved down the stairs and out the front door. Brigitte kept watch the entire time. The driver loaded her suitcase in the trunk of his taxi and heard the bottles inside clank. Brigitte climbed in the backseat, closed the door and locked it. The driver climbed in and said, "The airport or train station?"

"Oh. Ah… neither. I want to go to a hotel," she said.

"Which hotel?"

"I don't know. Can you recommend one?"

"The Hotel Champ Ceramic is small but nice. Tourists like it because it's by the Arc de Triumph."

Brigitte liked the idea of being near a lot of tourists and said, "I'm sure that will be fine."

The drive pulled out into traffic and drove away. Brigitte watched out the back window. She saw nothing suspicious in front of the apartment building and wondered if she was imagining things.

Brigitte sat on the edge the bed in her hotel room. She felt emotionally exhausted but her mind was still racing. She needed to relax. She looked over at their suitcase and thought for a moment. She walked over, opened it and pulled out a bottle of white wine – the Semillon. She picked up the phone and it connected to the front desk. She asked the receptionist to send up a bucket of ice, a corkscrew and a wine glass to her room.

Behind the front desk in the hotel lobby, the receptionist, a man in his late forties, agreed to Brigitte's request and hung up the phone. He repeated

Brigitte's request to Saadi standing next to him holding a Webley top-break revolver leveled at the man's chest. "Take off your jacket," said Saadi.

The man removed his jacket and handed it to Saadi. Saadi laid the jacket on the counter and removed a stiletto-style switchblade from his pant pocket. He whipped around opening the knife as he turned and cut the receptionist across the throat. Blood flowed and the man collapsed to the floor behind the desk. Saadi plunged the knife into the man's heart to end his suffering. Saadi was not without compassion and had no desire to see people suffer if it served no purpose. Stopping the man's heart also stopped the bleeding. Saadi did not relish the idea of standing in a pool of blood. He put on the receptionist's jacket.

Ludmila appeared through a back room doorway. She was holding a housekeepers uniform. Saadi told her to put the uniform on and retrieve the items that Brigitte had requested from the hotel kitchen along with a serving cart covered with a table cloth. Ludmila nodded in obedience.

Ludmila wheeled a cart down the hallway and stopped in front of Brigitte's room. She looked down both sides of the hallway to ensure that nobody was watching. She knelt and lifted up the table cloth to reveal a stack of three towels on the second shelf of the cart. She opened the middle towel to reveal a bomb. She pulled out her pair of pliers and crimped the pencil detonator. She noted the time on her watch. It was a 5-minute detonator which should give her and Saadi plenty of time to escape before the bomb went off. She closed the towel and let the edge of the table cloth drop back over the shelf.

She knocked on the door and waited. Ludmila had questioned why she was not allowed to just shoot Brigitte when she came to the door as Saadi had done with the receptionist. Saadi reminded her that a bomb had much more social impact than a bullet. Brigitte's assassination would draw international headlines and the fact that a bomb was used would achieve the desired effect on the public. Ludmila didn't understand nuances of propaganda but she was obedient and did as Saadi instructed.

Brigitte opened the door two inches and looked out through the crack. "The ice and glass you ordered, Mademoiselle," said Ludmila.

"Great. Come in," said Brigitte.

Ludmila wheeled in the cart and set it in the middle of the room as she had been instructed by Saadi. She turned to leave and Brigitte said, "Would you mind putting the bottle of wine on the bed in the ice?"

"Of course not, Mademoiselle," said Ludmila turning back around, picking up the wine bottle and placing it in the bucket.

Again Ludmila turned to leave and Brigitte said, "Go ahead and uncork the bottle. I'd like it to breathe a few minutes before drinking it."

"Yes, Mademoiselle," said Ludmila again turning back and opening the bottle with the corkscrew. "Will there be anything else?"

"No, I think that's it. Thank you," said Brigitte.

Ludmila moved toward the door. "Oh, wait. I almost forgot," said Brigitte moving to the bedside table.

Ludmila glanced at her wristwatch. Saadi had explained that while the pencil detonators were very reliable their mechanism was chemical and therefore not exact. Ludmila knew she was cutting it close. Brigitte opened her purse and handed Ludmila a tip. Ludmila curtsied and left the room, closing the door behind her.

Coyle entered the hotel lobby and approached the front desk. Saadi considered just shooting him in the face but Ludmila had not returned yet and Saadi did not know how long Coyle's body would be lying in the middle of the lobby. Even if he moved Coyle's body there would surely be a large blood stain on the carpet. He was also concerned that the gunshot might alert Brigitte and ruin the mission. He decided to buy himself some time and see what the approaching man wanted. "How may I help you, Monsieur?" said Saadi.

"I am here to see Mademoiselle Brigitte Friang," said Coyle.

"You are American?" said Saadi.

"Yeah. Accent gives me away every time."

"Your name, Monsieur?" said Saadi picking up the phone.

"Tom Coyle. But don't call her. I want it to be a surprise."

"I see," said Saadi placing the phone back in its cradle and sliding his hand over the pistol.

"Her message service didn't know her room number, just the hotel name," said Coyle.

As Saadi raised the pistol, Ludmila appeared at the top of the stairs on the first floor. Saadi stopped and reconsidered. *An American will die in the blast and cause an international incident. An embarrassment for France,* thought Saadi. *That is better.* "Room 306, Monsieur Coyle," said Saadi with a smile.

"Thanks," said Coyle as he moved to the elevator. He entered the elevator, closed the iron fence and pressed the third floor. The elevator shaft was enclosed in decorative wrought iron painted black.

Ludmila walked down the stairs to the lobby and approached Saadi. "Is everything as expected?" said Saadi.

Ludmila nodded.

"Good. Wait for me outside," said Saadi.

Ludmila exited the hotel through the front door. Saadi placed a newspaper over his pistol and walked across the lobby to the front door. He waited. He knew the blast would not enter the lobby and that he was safe. He wanted to ensure that the journalist's and now the American's assassination was successful.

There was a knock at the door. Brigitte moved to answer it. She opened the door two inches and peered out to see Coyle. She flung the door open and hugged him. "Well I'm glad to see you too," said Coyle with Brigitte's arms wrapped around his neck.

"Where have you been? I tried calling."

"I got your message after I landed. I tried to call you. Your message service told me you were here. I thought I'd surprise you."

"Well, it worked."

"I can see that."

"Come in. I just opened a bottle of wine."

"I am starving. Let's go grab something to eat."

"We French do not grab something to eat."

"Okay, fine. I will take you to dinner."

"I can't, Tom. I'm a mess. I was just going to take a bath."

"Come on. You look great and smell better."

"All right. At least let me fix my hair."

"Put it up in a bun. That's faster."

"You're impossible."

"No. I'm hungry. Like lion hungry if you know what I mean."

"Okay. I get it. Two shakes and I'll be ready," said Brigitte shaking her hips as she disappeared into the bathroom.

"Oh, I like that two shakes part."

Ludmila stood outside the hotel and kept watch. She looked at her wristwatch, nervous. It was time. She moved back inside to warn Saadi. He waved her off and stared at the third floor landing. Ludmila went back outside. Saadi heard the faint sound of door closing, laughter and two voices a man's and a woman's.

Coyle and Brigitte walked down the hallway from her room toward the elevator. Coyle pulled open the iron fence and they entered. He pressed the button for the ground floor. The elevator moved downward.

Saadi watched the elevator from the lobby. He could not see who was inside. Not yet. As the elevator moved past the second floor the angle changed and the occupants became more visible. He saw the faces of Coyle and Brigitte. His expression sharpened and he dropped the newspaper covering his pistol. The

Webley was a large caliber revolver that kicked like a mule. He took aim at Brigitte and fired three times.

The bullets hit the wrought iron that surrounded the elevator shaft and sent sparks into the elevator. Coyle knew immediately what was happening and pulled Brigitte to the floor. He lay next to her, putting his body between her and the gunman.

The bomb in Brigitte's room detonated and the building shook violently. The explosion ripped the front door to her room off its hinges and hurled it into the hallway. A ball of fire traveled down both directions of the hallway. The fire burst through the wrought iron surrounding the elevator shaft. The oil that lubricated the elevator cables caught fire and raced upward until it engulfed both cables inside the shaft.

The elevator continued downward. Coyle realized that they were headed for the ground floor and would be at the mercy of the gunman when they arrived. He reached up and hit the emergency stop button. The elevator jolted to a stop as it approached the first floor landing.

Saadi moved toward the stairway. If he could climb higher he could get a better angle and kill the journalist and the American. His mission could still succeed. Ludmila ran through the front door and said, "The police are coming. We have to go now."

Saadi was not afraid of the police. He was prepared to die for his cause but he also knew that if he survived he would be able to kill many more

French men and women. He fired at the elevator until his pistol clicked empty. He turned and ran out the front door with Ludmila.

Coyle did not see the gunman disappear but he could see the cables holding the elevator were on fire. He wasn't sure what would happen. They were made of steel but even steel behaved strangely when super-heated. He could hear the cables groan.

At the top of the elevator shaft one of the cables was anchored with an eye-hook attached to a steel girder. The eye-hook was a loop at the end of cable secured by several U-bolt vises. The fire heated the U-bolts and the vises expanded, loosening their grip on the cable. The cable slipped inside the vises but caught before slipping all the way out.

Coyle and Brigitte felt the elevator drop and stop. "That can't be good," said Coyle.

Coyle kicked at the iron gate blocking the elevator's doorway. It didn't budge. He kept kicking. Brigitte looked out over the edge of the elevator into the lobby below and saw that it was empty. "I think he's gone," said Brigitte.

"Let's hope so," said Coyle giving the gate an extra hard kick.

The gate flung open. Coyle grabbed Brigitte.

The cable slipped through the U-bolts and off the girder. It dropped down the shaft like a snake coiling back to strike.

The elevator was in free fall. Coyle and Brigitte leapt out of the doorway onto the first floor landing as the elevator sped downward. Any part of their bodies still in the elevator would have been sheared off by the sheer weight of the elevator as the top of the doorway passed the first floor.

The elevator did not stop in the lobby but continue to fall, crashing into the bottom of the shaft in the basement of the hotel.

The hotel's hallway and stairway filled up with guests confused and panicked. Smoke billowed upward. Fireman rushed into the lobby. Coyle and Brigitte pushed past them and out into the street. They could hear more sirens approaching.

Outside the hotel Coyle and Brigitte looked around. They didn't know what the gunman looked like. They didn't know whom they could trust. "It could have been the woman that brought the ice that planted the bomb," said Brigitte.

"Do you remember what she looked like?" said Coyle.

"Yes. I think so."

"You should give the police a description. It may help."

"Yes. Of course. Right after I write my story."

"You really think that's a smart idea?"

"Are you kidding? It's a brilliant idea. I'm featured in my own exclusive. It will sell a hundred thousand magazines."

At the end of the corner, Saadi and Ludmila watched Coyle and Brigitte. Saadi cursed as he broke open his revolver and reloaded. Ludmila could see that he was frustrated. "Shoot them," said Ludmila.

"No. There are too many witnesses and the police are already on their way," said Saadi as he slipped his pistol under his belt in the back of his pants.

"Shoot them now. It is Allah's will."

"I said no. We should go."

Ludmila grabbed Saadi and kissed him deeply. He was surprised. Algerians did not usually display affection in public. Ludmila released him and turned away. She marched down the street toward Brigitte and Coyle. Saadi saw his pistol in Ludmila's hand. "Ludmila, no," said Saadi.

It was too late. Ludmila had made up her mind. She would carry out Allah's will. As she closed the distance between herself and her prey she raised the revolver. It was heavier than the pistol Saadi had used to teach the sirens how to shoot. It was difficult to aim. She focused on Brigitte. She was the real prize and would be the first to be killed. Ludmila fired. The revolver kicked hard almost knocking itself free from her hand.

The bullet whizzed by Brigitte's head. Coyle turned around to see Ludmila advancing with the pistol. Coyle grabbed Brigitte and pulled her off the street where there was no cover. The terrified hotel guests scattered every which way, creating confusion.

Ludmila decided to use two hands to steady her aim. She fired two more rounds as she moved forward.

Both rounds missed Brigitte and Coyle but one hit a woman wearing a hotel bathrobe, killing her. Saadi had taught her the importance of counting the rounds fired. *Three out of six,* she thought.

Coyle pulled Brigitte behind a newsstand to one side of the hotel. He had no weapon. Nothing to defend Brigitte from the approaching assassin. He felt helpless.

Ludmila was frustrated and decided she needed to get close so she would not miss again. She moved toward to the newsstand. Under the elevated legs of the newsstand she could see a glimpse of the legs of two people hiding. She moved around the edge of the stand and leveled her pistol.

Coyle was there holding a bundle of newspapers. He threw them at Ludmila. She fired. The bullet buried itself into the newspapers. The bundle hit Ludmila, knocking her backwards. "Run," said Coyle to Brigitte.

Ludmila landed on the asphalt and the gun bounced from her hand and skidded across the street.

Coyle saw the gun and ran for it.

Ludmila saw Coyle. The gun was on the street behind her but Coyle had the momentum and would reach it before her. She flung her leg out, tripping him. He fell to the street. She scrambled to her feet and ran for the pistol. Coyle regained his feet and ran after her.

Ludmila reached the pistol first and picked it up with one hand. She swung it around toward Coyle and fired a shot wildly without aiming. The bullet sailed between Coyle's arm and chest. He grabbed her hand holding the pistol before she could fire again. She raked her fingernails across his face. He screamed in pain but held on. She kneed him in the groin with everything she had. He recoiled to grab his crotch, releasing her hand. Coyle bend over in pain. Ludmila kicked him in the head knocking him unconscious.

Ludmila swung the gun around using both her hands and took aim at Brigitte still standing by the newsstand. "Drop your weapon," said a man's voice from behind her.

Ludmila turned to see a police officer standing by his motorcycle aiming his pistol at her. She swung the pistol toward him and fired. He fired at the same time. The officer was hit in the face by her bullet and fell backward. He would survive but would have a terrible scar on his cheek.

Ludmila was hit in the shoulder. The bullet's impact swung her around but she held on to the pistol. Blood poured out of the wound. She raised the pistol with her good arm and took aim at Brigitte. She didn't fire. Instead she walked forward until the barrel of the gun was just a foot from Brigitte's face. Brigitte spit at Ludmila and said, "Terrorist bitch." Ludmila smiled and wiped the spit from her face and said, "Imperialist whore."

Coyle regained consciousness and struggled to his feet. He turned to see Ludmila and Brigitte. He ran wildly toward them but it was too far and too late.

Ludmila squeezed the trigger and released the hammer. The revolver clicked empty as the hammer struck an already used cartridge. Ludmila had lost count in the excitement.

Coyle tackled her from behind and they fell to the sidewalk. Ludmila released the pistol from her hand. She twisted and turned against Coyle lying on top of her with his full body weight. She refused to give up and continued to fight like a wildcat.

Brigitte picked up the pistol and swung the steel butt of the weapon into the side of Ludmila's head, knocking her unconscious.

It was over. Ludmila would be arrested and turned over to French Army intelligence. Aussaresses would cut off all her hair before the interrogation began. There was no escape for Ludmila.

Saadi watched from a distance. He considered running to Ludmila's aid and saving her from the pain of what he knew would be her fate. But Saadi knew that Allah had weightier matters that would need tending to and he was an obedient soldier. He turned and walked away, disappearing into the crowd of onlookers. The last of his three sirens was gone.

NINETEEN

Bella, flanked by four FLN bodyguards, walked through the stadium tunnel. Both the French and the MNA had raised the bounty on Bella's head and there had been multiple attempts to collect it. All had failed. The tunnel was swarming with futbol fans like bees going in and out of their hive. It was hard to tell between friend and foe even though he considered this friendly territory.

Bella and his bodyguards entered the stadium. The crowd cheered. The home team goalie had deflected a shot at the net. Futbol was the one thing in Algiers that seemed to have no politics behind it. Appearances were deceiving. He studied his ticket and looked for his seat. He spotted Saadi and Si Larbi sitting together about halfway up in the pied-noir section. The seats around them were occupied by more FLN bodyguards. Bella wondered why the seats were in the pied-noir area of the stadium but decided now was not the time to scold Saadi. It was a simple mistake and Saadi had a lot on his mind.

Bella climbed the stair and took his seat between the two soldiers. They watched for several minutes in silence. *It's nice,* thought Bella. *Getting together like this and watching a game.* It had been a long time since he had done anything that remotely resembled fun. He imagined it was the same for Saadi and Si Larbi. He took a moment to consider his words and said, "I am sorry for your loss."

"Our loss," said Saadi.

"They were very brave."

"Yes, but impatient. They did not listen. Too young, I think," said Saadi.

"Too pretty, I think," said Si Larbi. "The pretty ones are overconfident. Find some ugly ones next time. They'll do fine."

Saadi turned and grabbed Si Larbi by the shirt and said, "Shut the fuck up, boy. Nobody asked you."

"Remove your hands or lose them, Baker," said Si Larbi.

"Knock it off, both of you," said Bella. "You're drawing attention."

Saadi released Si Larbi and smiled as he straightened Si Larbi's shirt.

"How long will it take you before you are ready again?" said Bella.

"I'm ready now," said Saadi.

"No. I don't want you delivering packages. It's too risky."

"As you say then. It will take weeks, maybe a month to find and train new girls."

"All right. One month. Si Larbi, what about you and your men?"

"The French have taken their toll. I have more wounded and missing than soldiers available to fight.

Their helicopters are maddening. They drop troops wherever they want whenever they want. We're lucky to escape."

"I though the idea was to fight, not escape," said Saadi.

"Like you said, Baker... shut the fuck up."

"Neither of you is being productive," said Bella growing angry. "I would just let you kill one another but I don't have the time to find your replacements. Now, answer my question, Si Larbi. How long before you and your men are ready to strike again?"

"It depends on the French. If we can get some time to reorganize without being attacked... maybe three weeks."

"You will have your time."

"How?"

"A distraction."

"By whom? You?"

"No. Not me. A friend."

Si Larbi and Saadi exchanged a look. Why was Bella being so mysterious with them? Had they lost his trust? "Have faith. Help is on the way," said Bella. "Si Larbi, I want your forces ready to move at a moment's notice once you've reorganized."

"Move where?"

"Just have them ready. The council has decided a change in strategy is in order."

Si Larbi nodded.

"We must go. There is much to do," said Bella.

"Wait just a moment," said Saadi pulling an English-style picnic basket from under his seat.

"What's that?" said Si Larbi.

"A message from the fallen," said Saadi pulling a pair pliers from his shirt pocket.

Saadi opened the bag. Inside were three metal tea biscuit boxes stacked one on top another. He opened the lid on the top box and crimped the English pencil detonator with the pliers until he felt the glass acetone vial inside crack. He closed the lid and pushed the bag back under the seat. "Can we go now?" said Bella.

"That would be a good idea," said Saadi.

They and their bodyguards left the stadium just as the referee blew his whistle to signal the end of the match. The home team had won. The fans stood and cheered.

The explosion killed fifty-two and seriously wounded over two hundred more. Most of the fallen were pied-noir. Some were Algerian. One of the home team forwards that was signing autographs would lose his leg to shrapnel wounds. The FLN considered it a victory.

It was a cloudless morning in Paris. Brigitte and Coyle sat enjoying their coffee and croissants on the patio of a café near her apartment. It had been three weeks and no bombings anywhere in Paris. There had been a bombing in an Algerian futbol stadium but that seemed a world away. Coyle was happy to see Brigitte smile and even laugh at one of his jokes. She seemed relaxed which was unusual for Brigitte. "I'm taking the day off," said Brigitte.

"Really?"

"Why not? I deserve it."

"You're not going to get any argument from me."

"Besides, things have calmed down. There's not as much to write about."

"You could take another shot at your book?"

"Did you need to remind me?"

"Sorry. I was just trying to be helpful."

"Yes. And that is why I love you. You're always looking out for me."

"I do my best."

They sat quietly for a moment. "I wonder how Bruno is doing? I was pretty harsh the last time we met."

"I think it'll take more than harsh words to take down Bruno," said Coyle. "Do you think it's over? The war?"

"I doubt it," said Brigitte. "More like a lull."

"The calm before the storm?"

"Let's hope not. I'm not sure how much more storm France can take."

"She's a pretty tough broad from what I've seen."

Brigitte cringed at Coyle's metaphor and shook her head in mock disgust. "Americans," she said.

Bruno finished his raw onion breakfast in a seaside park along the Mediterranean. Even he had to admit it was disgusting and he had to force down the last two bites. He thought about stopping by his favorite Algerian bakery and picking up some bread and a coffee after his run. He used a bench to stretch his legs. As he aged he noticed he was more prone to cramps. *Not enough salt,* he thought.

He took it easy the first two kilometers. He let his muscles warm up and stretch out before pushing them to their limit as he always did. He noticed a woman kneeling next to her bicycle repairing a flat tire on the side of the path. She was young and attractive. It was hard to tell her nationality but she dressed like a European. He thought about stopping and offering to help her until he tested his breath in the cup of his hand. He decided he would be doing her a favor not to stop.

He ran past her without saying a word or even looking down. She rose, pulled out a pistol and shot him three inches to the left of the center of the back, right where his heart would be. Bruno fell forward and slid across the gravel. He couldn't believe it. He was angry that he had been so careless to get shot again. He wanted to get up and fight. He willed his body but nothing moved. He found it hard to breath and even harder to focus. He heard the woman walking toward him, the gravel on the path crunching beneath her shoes. She stopped next to him. He could not see her but he could feel her. *A coup de grace,* he thought. *It is what I would do. A thorough job.* He heard a police whistle and heard footsteps running away from him and another set of heavier footsteps running toward him. *The policeman has chased off the assassin before she can finish the job,* he thought. *I am saved.*

It was getting even harder to breath and it felt like the air around him was getting colder. His lips were dry. He felt a shiver ripple through his body. "Brigitte," he whispered as everything went black.

Five thousand civilians died in the Café Wars.

Almost one million Algerians died during the War for Independence.

Dear Reader,

Thank you for giving Café Wars a try. I hope you enjoyed reading it. If you are interested, the next book in the Airmen Series is called *Sèvres Protocol*. It is available in paperback and eBook formats on Amazon.

To view Sèvres Protocol click here.

As always, your review on Amazon or Goodreads is most appreciated. I read each one and they help my writing.

Sincerely,

David Lee Corley

DEDICATION

I dedicate this novel to my daughter Danielle Jessica Belfatto. She reminds me of Brigitte Friang, the French war correspondent that wrote about Dien Bien Phu and is in my stories. Danielle has no problem jumping out of a plane and has done so before. She doesn't have the fear that most people hold in their hearts and charges ahead when in doubt. She is bold, smart and beautiful. She is her father's child and I love her deeply.

ACKNOWLEDGMENTS

I want to acknowledge and thank Antoneta Wotringer for her wonderful book cover designs. She is a true artist and has an excellent sense of style.

I also want to acknowledge and thank JJ Toner for proofreading my books. He makes it appear that I can actually spell which most of my family and friends know... I cannot.

I would also like to acknowledge all of the men and women that fought and died on both sides of the conflict during the Algerian War of Independence. I am humbled by the thought that most of the victims and combatants believed in a cause and were willing to lay down their lives. We can dispute their ideals and methods but their bravery and dedication to their beliefs should not be in dispute but honored by all.

NOTE FROM AUTHOR

This is a work of fiction based on historical events. It is not history. To create a coherent story and to satisfy the need for brevity I found it necessary to combine characters and create fictional events. In such cases I did my best to remain as genuine as possible to the events and true to the nature of the characters as I saw them. Many of the character names in this story belong to real people. This was done to allow the reader to research the true stories behind these people if they wish.

Made in the USA
Columbia, SC
08 March 2021

34056425R00166